War for the Waking World

Other Books by Wayne Thomas Batson

Dreamtreader Series

Dreamtreaders

Search for the Shadow Key

The Door Within Trilogy

The Door Within

The Rise of the Wyrm Lord

The Final Storm

Pirate Adventures

Isle of Swords

Isle of Fire

The Berinfell Prophecies

Curse of the Spider King (with Christopher Hopper)

Venom and Song (with Christopher Hopper)

The Tide of Unmaking (with Christopher Hopper)

The Dark Sea Annals

Sword in the Stars

The Errant King

Mirror of Souls

Imagination Station

#8: *Battle for Cannibal Island*

#11: *Hunt for the Devil's Dragon*

Other Endeavors

Ghost

War for the Waking World

Wayne Thomas Batson

Thomas Nelson
Since 1798

War for the Waking World

Published in Nashville, Tennessee, by Tommy Nelson. Tommy Nelson is an imprint of Thomas Nelson. Thomas Nelson is a registered trademark of HarperCollins Christian Publishing, Inc.

Tommy Nelson titles may be purchased in bulk for educational, business, fund-raising, or sales promotional use. For information, please e-mail SpecialMarkets@ThomasNelson.com.

ISBN-13: 9781400323685

Library of Congress Cataloging-in-Publication Data on file

Printed in US

15 16 17 18 19 RRD 6 5 4 3 2 1

Mfr: RRD / Crawfordsville, Indiana /October 2015 / PO #9362109

Dedication:

Per Gratia Dei

Contents

The Laws Nine

Law One: Anchor first. Anchor deep. This means constructing an anchor image that is a rooted and deeply powerful emotion. It must be dear to you.

Law Two: Anchor somewhere you can find with casc, but no one else can. If your anchor is destroyed or otherwise kept from you, your time may run out.

Law Three: Never remain in the Dream for more than your Eleven Hours. Your Personal Midnight is the end. Depart for the Temporal . . . or perish.

Law Four: Depart for the Temporal at Sixtolls or find some bastion to defend against the storm. For the Nightmare Lord will open wide his kennels, chaos will rule, and the Dreamtreader could be lost.

Law Five: While in the Dream, consume nothing made with gort, the soul harvest berry. It is black as pitch and enslaves your body to those of dark powers.

Law Six: Defend against sudden and final death within the Dream. Prepare your mind for calamities that may come or be shut out from the Dream forever.

Law Seven: Never accept an invitation from the Nightmare Lord. Not even to parley. He is a living snare to the Dreamtreader. There is no good faith bargain. With him, the only profit will be death.

Law Eight: By the light of a Violet Torch, search yourself for Tendrils, the Nightmare Lord's silent assassins.

Law Nine: Dreamtread with all the strength you can muster, but never more than two days in a row. To linger in the Dream too often will invite madness. The Temporal and the Dream will be fused and shatter your mind.

ONE
CHANNELS

"DAD, LOOK OUT!" ARCHER SHOUTED. FROM THE BACK-seat, Kaylie shrieked.

Mr. Keaton swerved, but it was too late. The SUV clipped *something*, and it sent the vehicle spinning on the icy road.

"Archer, help!" Kaylie cried.

"I'm on it!"

Archer threw out a buffer of his will, a spongy cushion of blue light that adhered to the SUV and gently fought the wild rotation. As the vehicle's spin began to slow, Archer increased the tread on the tires. They caught, and Mr. Keaton regained control of the steering.

"Whew!" Kaylie gasped, huddling in a pile of blankets all restrained by the shoulder harness and lap belt. "Good one, Archer."

"You . . . you saved us," Mr. Keaton said, the emphasis of his words so vague Archer couldn't tell if it was a question or a statement. His father white-knuckled the steering wheel as he slowly increased speed once more. His eyes were riveted to the street. "What . . . what was it? What did we hit?"

"I don't know," Archer said. "All I saw was a blur of white."

Kaylie's hand appeared over the armrest and pointed. "I think it was one of those."

Archer turned his head. Ten feet away lumbered a twelve-foot mountain of white. It was bulbous and thick, moving at impossible speed. Kaylie screamed.

Mr. Keaton turned the wheel, but the SUV didn't respond. It careened sideways into the snowman . . . and a snowman it was, but not any lovable Frosty or Olaf. This snowman wore a gaping, toothy scowl. Its branchy appendages moved as if hinged in a dozen places. A blurry green fire blazed in its eyes as the thing put its leering face right up against Archer's window.

Archer jumped back, yanking at his seat belt. He didn't think, didn't plan. He just reacted, calling up his will and unleashing a flaming fist right through the window. But the glass didn't shatter or crumble. It flash-melted, as did the snowman's face when Archer's will-infused flame struck it. The creature howled through what was left of its mouth. Its brambly hands flew up to its misshapen head . . . and knocked it right off the torso.

"Snot rockets!" Archer yelled. "Go, Dad, go!"

Mr. Keaton hit the gas and pulled away. Archer watched the snow creature; he saw a new head rise up out of its body, turn, and scream. There were others, more demented snow beings, emerging from the woods and lumbering toward the interstate.

"Better stay in the left lane, Dad," Archer said.

"Uh . . . yeah," Mr. Keaton replied. "Left lane. Good idea."

Archer launched out of the SUV, cut across the front lawn, and was on the steps in a heartbeat. "C'mon, Dad! We need to get inside."

Mr. Keaton scooped up Kaylie and loped across the yard. When they were safely inside, Archer shut the door hard and turned the lock.

"Don't," Mr. Keaton warned. "Don't lock it. Mrs. Pitsitakas, Amy, and Buster will be here any minute."

Archer stared at the door as if it might bite him. "Okay, right. I forgot. But only until they get here. Then we lock up like Fort Knox, okay?"

"Archer," Mr. Keaton whispered as he lowered his daughter to stand on the foyer floor. "What . . . what is this?"

"It's the Rift, Dad," Kaylie said, as if that fact were such an elementary concept.

Mr. Keaton hung up his jacket and scarf. "I don't know what that means," he said. "One minute, I'm all chained up in the dark, thinking I'm having the worst nightmare of my life. Then, Kaylie and that Australian guy show up, and the sky—it just ripped apart. Next thing I know, I'm at the hospital—but if I've been dreaming, I still haven't woken up. Creatures in the snow? You . . . making things out of thin air—it's all impossible."

Kaylie frowned. "It's a Dream-Temporal fusion," she explained. "Brought about by the fragmentation of the dividing fabric."

Mr. Keaton stared. "I . . . *still* don't know what that means."

Archer blew out a sigh. Kaylie was correct, but in her eight-year-old genius explanation, she hadn't gotten to the heart of what their father was asking. The events of the previous forty-eight hours raced through Archer's mind in ragged visual strips . . .

The bizarre dinner meeting with Rigby, Kara, and the Lurker in the Dream . . .

The showdown between him and Rigby, each holding the life of a loved one against the other . . .

And then the Rift.

It had all been a part of Kara's ultimate power play. Every bit of it, every moment. Archer shook his head. He could hardly believe it all himself. How could he explain it all to his father?

Maybe that's it, he thought. *Maybe I don't explain it all. Stick to the basics. Keep it simple. I'm a Dreamtreader. I help control the Dream, but even I can't describe it most of the time.*

A muted *whump* sounded in the distance outside. Archer looked up. "I can't explain right now," he said, scrambling to look through each of the living room windows. He did the kitchen next, and then ran toward the den. "I will, Dad, I promise. But I need to check something first."

"C'mon," Kaylie said. She took her father's hand and led him toward the kitchen. "Let's get a glass of chocolate milk."

Just before she disappeared around the corner, she nodded at Archer, whispering, "There ya go. Do what you need to do."

Dang, she's smart. Archer laughed to himself at the understatement. He hesitated at the bottom of the stairs but only for a moment. The Creeds would have to wait. He had to make sure. He raced to the TV and flipped on the digital receiver. A sports network came up first, but there was no live action. Just a still image of a pro basketball player pulling up for a jump shot.

Archer flipped through the channels, searching for one of the overseas news programs. He had to know . . . had to be certain it was worldwide. He stopped on channel 278B, the International News Network.

"This is Cassandra Weems for the INN," the tall reporter said, her breath visible in the cold. "What you see behind me is the wreckage of Kyiv Central High School in northern Ukraine. First thought to be a terrorist attack, and then a massive petroleum explosion, we have now learned this tragic destruction was caused by something that . . . well . . . something that has to be seen to be believed."

Archer held his breath as the screen cut away to shaky, handheld footage of the school. It looked like any large high school in the US: blocky structures and several levels of glassed-in stairs. The only difference was, instead of the Stars and Stripes, the blue and yellow Ukrainian flag flew on the tall pole outside. The footage flickered, and the overcast sky behind the school began to churn. From the depths of the murky clouds, a massive, ten-story pillar of darkness had begun to form. It undulated as if something were trapped inside and struggled to get free. Then, there it was:

A creature. No, a monster.

It looked like a badly drawn tyrannosaur, but with horns jutting back behind its ears and a single prong upon its snout. It was a skyscraper-tall, lanky thing, all muscle, sinews, and scales. And it was angry. That much was clear in its oddly small, slanted eyes.

The camera jiggled, and the view seemed to go in and out as if the photographer were so terrified that he couldn't control the zoom properly. No wonder. The beast trudged forward, instantly demolishing the front of the high school. Power lines fell, and electrical sparks flew into the air. A burst of flame erupted almost as high as the creature. It roared and, with one punch of its clawed fist, the school's central structure collapsed. In moments, the lumbering swings of the monster's great tail, its heavy stomps, and its unrelenting jaws reduced the school to rubble.

The clip ended, and the reporter reappeared. She was joined by several police officers and a young man who sported a purple-frosted Mohawk. He should have looked tough. Instead, he was weeping.

"Among the survivors, sixteen-year-old Petro Goryvman," the reporter said, gesturing toward the youth. "Apparently traumatized by the attack, Petro claims the incident was his—"

Petro suddenly lurched forward and grabbed the reporter's microphone. He spoke in a language Archer couldn't understand. Ukrainian, most likely. The expression on the teenager's face chilled Archer. He noticed the small subtitles scrolling along the bottom of the screen. It was a translation.

It's my fault, he cried. *That teacher, that class—I could not afford to fail this test. I was so angry. I imagined it just for a second, but I didn't mean it. They're all dead now. All dead. It's all my fault!*

Click.

Archer changed the channel and fell backward into an easy chair. This channel showed a family huddled in a blanket and standing in front of a fire truck. A reporter, this time in Chicago, held the microphone out to a teenage girl, *Sarah, age 15,* according to the caption. She was tall and thin, with somewhat pointed ears sticking through her long, brown hair. She was shaking and in clear distress, but her large, speckled eyes darted intelligently, reminding Archer of his genius little sister.

"He whispered to me," the girl named Sarah said.

The reporter moved the microphone back and forth and asked, "Who did?"

"The shadow man," she replied, her eyes looking far away. "He whispered that he was going to take me away . . ."

"Then what happened?"

"I told him he wasn't real, that he was a figment of my imagination."

"That was brave," the reporter said. She seemed impatient. "Then what?"

"He touched me," she said. "It felt so cold."

"And? What did you do then?"

Sarah looked back and forth sheepishly. A little blush colored her cheeks.

"It's okay," the reporter urged, "just tell what you told me."

"Well," Sarah said. "I . . . uh . . . kicked him in the shins and ran. The next thing I knew the house was on fire. I'm just glad my family is safe."

Click.

Archer switched to a new channel. It was some kind of daily top-ten View Tube video show. The smarmy host had just finished introducing the number-one clip. A young woman, a university student in London, appeared on screen. Streaks of mascara dripped down her cheeks. Her eyes were bloodshot and glistening wet with tears. The picture wobbled and jittered—another handheld camera—and the woman mumbled so much Archer could barely understand her.

She wiped the back of her arm across her face as she said, "I woke up . . . thought . . . I . . . did, and it . . . so cool, at first. The student union . . . voted me Festival Queen. But then they locked me in a closet . . . so dark . . . so cold. I kept trying to wake . . . wake up. Lights came on, and there . . . a mirror. I . . . saw myself. And my . . . teeth . . . started falling out."

Archer watched in horror as the young woman opened her mouth to reveal toothless, angry-red gums. "But . . . it was . . . all real," she shrieked.

Click. Archer switched off the TV.

It was happening all over the world. The Rift was real. The Dream and the Waking World had merged, and now no one knew reality from dream. No one knew their imaginations, their very own thoughts, could now turn deadly.

The world has gone mad.

Head clutched in his hands, fifteen-year-old Archer Keaton stared through his fingers and the sweat-soaked curtain of red hair that hung over his forehead at the blank television screen.

The Rift.

He and his fellow Dreamtreaders had tried so hard to keep it from happening, but too many breaches had been torn into the Dream fabric. The boundary between the Dream and the Waking World had been ripped wide open, and now the world was paying for it.

Archer balled his fists and muttered, "Looks like our job description has changed." He was still a Dreamtreader, but there would be no more passing from the Waking World into the Dream. No more scurions and no more stitching up breaches. Now, there was only one goal: to save the world from destroying itself.

Determination simmering in his eyes and locked into the set of his jaws, Archer turned to join his father and Kaylie in the kitchen when . . .

Bang! The front door crashed open.

TWO

INTO THE CALAMITOUS NIGHT

ARCHER LEAPED UP, CAUSING THE EASY CHAIR TO ROCK violently, and raced toward the front door. In walked a motley crew. First? A young man with a mop of blonde hair and skin way too tan for winter, followed by a girl Archer's age, appropriately pale with owlish glasses and white blonde hair tied back in a light blue band. The woman who came in last looked like the girl aged thirty years but had her hair dyed a bit darker.

"Buster!" Archer exclaimed, flying to hug his brother. "Amy, Mrs. Pitsitakas—I am *so* glad to see you."

"Glad to be off the road," Mrs. Pitsitakas said.

Amy nodded emphatically. "Yep."

"Dude!" Buster said, squirming out of the embrace. "I saw a flying elephant—I kid you not."

"I believe you," Archer said. "Now, move so I can lock the door!"

"I've already done it," Mrs. Pitsitakas said. "We don't want what's out there . . . getting in here."

Pigtails jiggling, Kaylie peered around the corner. "Hurry, hurry!" she said. "We've got chocolate milk and cookies!"

"Rock on," Buster said, charging toward the kitchen. Amy and her mom followed.

A splintering crack of thunder shook the house. Only, it wasn't thunder. A blue-green flash flooded through all the windows. Archer charged back into the den and peered through the picture window. Far beyond the roofs and trees of his neighborhood, a brightly pulsing mushroom cloud rose into the night sky. The color seemed supernatural, like something from the Dream. Whatever it was, Archer was glad it was miles away.

Something shattered in the kitchen, followed by a frightened chorus of screams. Archer raced from the den and tumbled into the kitchen to find his father, his little brother, Buster, and his friends Amy and her mother, their faces twisted in horror. Their backs were pressed hard to the sink and counters, trying vainly to back up farther. A gibbering snarl turned Archer's attention to the other side of the kitchen.

There, a three-headed wolf crouched. It had eyes like red-hot coals, jaws full of tusk-like teeth, and fur-lined bat wings. It seemed ready to spring, but one person stood in the creature's path and defied it.

"Bad dog!" Kaylie yelled. Archer couldn't have been gladder his little sister was far from the typical eight-year-old. Kaylie was a fellow Dreamtreader, and one of the most powerful ever. She held up her hand, and a ball of pink lightning swirled in her palm.

"Sit, doggie!" she commanded. "Heel!"

The wolf heads snarled. Suddenly, all three heads began to speak at once. "Stupid girl," it chorused in a wet slur, "you think we are some mortal pup? We will eat you!" The creature pawed at the ground, shredding the tile with its talons. It flared out its wings, gave a tremendous flap, and rose into the air.

"Kaylie, look out!" Archer cried. He readied his will, the massive reserve of mental energy that allowed Dreamtreaders to create from imagination. But he needn't have bothered.

Kaylie stood her ground, pajamas and all, held up her hand, and the ball of lightning became a long staff made of pink driftwood. She took the staff in both hands, stared up at the hovering creature, and yelled, "You . . . shall not . . . pass!"

She slammed the staff to the floor, creating a rippling wave of white flame that rolled along the kitchen floor, and then rose in the shape of a hand of white fire. It snatched the wolf creature from the air and slammed the beast to the floor. The thing arose unsteadily, all three heads wobbling loosely, but the burning coal eyes all still gleamed. Gnashing its teeth and snarling, it leaped.

Mrs. Pitsitakas darted protectively in front of her daughter as did Mr. Keaton with Buster. Kaylie had it covered, though. She swung her pink staff and sent a white wave of power crashing into the creature. With the sound of a thousand shattering glasses and a faint howl, the creature burst into a swarm of darting sparks, and then vanished. There was nothing left behind but a cascade of falling ash.

"No giant newspaper this time?" Archer asked, snatching Kaylie off her feet. "Had to go stealing Gandalf's line?"

"It just felt right," Kaylie said, snuggling close. Archer reluctantly put her down and turned to his frantic family and friends.

Buster joined their embrace and gave his surfer-lingo stamp of approval by saying, "Sis, you just dropped the hammer on that thing. Gnarly!"

"W-what was that?" Amy's mother cried out, her mouth half-twisted as if she might scream. "That . . . thing, it's not possible. And K-Kaylie . . . what did you . . . how did you do that?"

Amy didn't give Archer the chance to answer. Her owlish green eyes wide with fear and fury, she grabbed him by his coat and demanded, "You know, don't you? You know what's happening?"

Archer mumbled, "I—"

"All this time!" she interrupted. "You were doing that Dream stuff, the top-secret stuff, right?"

"Dream stuff?" Amy's mom blurted. "What dream stuff?"

"I . . . it . . ."

"Why couldn't you stop it, Archer?" Amy asked, her voice sad and plaintive. "Why couldn't you?"

The question felt like a sledgehammer to the gut. Archer had asked the same question of himself over and over again in the hours since the Rift occurred. There were answers, but all in a tangled web: the Nightmare Lord, the Lurker, Bezeal, Rigby—they'd each played a role. Even the Wind Maiden, Archer's best friend Kara . . . well . . . former best friend. In the end, she had turned out to be at the center of it. In all their many schemes and plots, they'd managed to rip and tear and gouge the Dream fabric until the Dreamtreaders finally couldn't mend it fast enough.

Archer's father spoke, his voice quiet but braced with iron, "Son, if you know what's happening, I think you'd better tell us."

Archer faced his father, the others, endured their accusing and frightened eyes, and said, "You won't believe me."

"We just saw a three-headed, flying wolf-thing!" Mrs. Pitsitakas practically spat. "Try us!"

Archer's father grasped his son's shoulder and gave a reassuring squeeze. "A week ago," he said, "none of us would have believed any of this crazy stuff. Those shadowy things that took me, the sky splitting open, all that happened at the hospital, and then . . . this." He gestured at the pile of ash, the remnants of the creature. "But now, we've seen too much to doubt. Just tell us what you know."

THREE
NO SAFE PLACE

ARCHER TOOK A DEEP BREATH, LOCKED EYES FOR A FEW moments with Kaylie, and thought of Master Gabriel, the leader and trainer of all Dreamtreaders. Before the Rift occurred, it would have been against the rules to tell people about Dreamtreading, to reveal age-old secrets, and to expose the hidden world. *But now?* Archer wondered. The Rift had changed things. The hidden world had been exposed. Everybody was a part of this now. *Master Gabriel may not like this,* he thought, *but my family and friends' sanity—maybe their survival—depends on their understanding. Survival . . .*

Archer knew just how he'd do it. He gave a glance to Kaylie. She nodded back. "Okay," Archer said. "I'll show you what I know—what Kaylie and I know. But to do it, we need to go downstairs."

"To the basement?" his father asked. "I don't see—"

"To your workshop, Dad," Archer said. He didn't give them time to argue, but instead strode away and bounded down the steps. He heard them following behind but waited until his family and friends were all inside the basement workshop. Archer shut the door . . . and locked it. This wasn't going to be easy.

Archer stood by his father's workbench and gestured to an intricately built, ornamental wishing well his father had been working on lately. It was one of many such pieces in the room. Archer's mother had so loved the family wishing well in the backyard that Archer's father began building beautiful models of it to buoy her spirits as she battled the cancer that eventually took her life.

"You've been crafting again, Dad," Archer said.

His father swallowed deeply and set his jaw. "She wouldn't want me to give up," he whispered.

"No, Mom would never want you to give up," Archer said. "These wells are incredible. I think maybe Kaylie and I got the creative ability from you."

"You got the brains from your mom," Mr. Keaton said with a quiet laugh.

"Could be," Archer said. "It's the creativity and the brains together, I think, that make Kaylie and me Dreamtreaders."

His father echoed, "Dreamtreaders?"

Archer explained the basics of Dreamtreading as best as he could. The Nine Laws, the moral and physical rules that governed life in the Dream; the Creeds, a kind of anthology of Dreamtreader wisdom and lore; the Three Realms of the Dream, Forms, Pattern, and Verse; Breaches, the small tears in the Dream fabric; and the Rift, the cataclysmic collapse of the barrier between the Dream and the Waking Worlds—everything from Master Gabriel's summoning to the Nightmare Lord's downfall to the present day. More than that, Archer showed them what Dreamtreaders could do. Calling up just a small measure of his mental will, Archer went to work.

The well's original cinder blocks and mortar melted away by Archer's command, revealing the wall of half-frozen earth behind it. A glob of silver-gray appeared. It spun in the air like metallic taffy and began to form long cylinders. An interlocking grid of carbon-steel struts formed next, and then something like molten granite flowed over it all . . . and hardened. Before the astonished audience could take three breaths, Archer replaced the basement walls, floor, and ceiling with ten-foot-thick, carbon steel, blast-proof shields.

Amy and her mother gasped. Archer's father made no sound but gaped. Only Buster said anything, and that was a whispered "Whoa."

"Pretty impressive, Archer," Kaylie said.

"You feel it, don't you?" Archer asked. "Since the Rift? We're—"

"Stronger," she said. "Much stronger. And we can do it in this world."

"I don't understand," Amy said. "What's with the bomb shelter?"

"He's keeping us safe," Mrs. Pitsitakas said.

"Safe? What?" Amy exclaimed, her owlish eyes wide with confusion. "But, Archer, we can help you."

"Maybe," Archer said. "But for right now, until we can figure out how to fix this, you're better off here."

"Dude," Buster blurted out, "you're gonna leave us here?"

"What about Kaylie?" Mr. Keaton asked, his voice pleading. "She's just eight. She'll be in danger. She can't—"

"Dad," Archer intervened. "Did you see what Kaylie did to that wolf monster?"

Mr. Keaton's mouth closed with a snap.

Archer nodded. "Kaylie is the strongest Dreamtreader ever. She'll do okay, I think."

"Better than okay," Kaylie said, smiling smugly and crossing her arms.

Archer grinned, but his expression became serious as he strode toward the newly created blast door. "Listen to me. Mrs. Pitsitakas, Dad, please keep everyone down here. You saw it. There's crazy stuff—deadly stuff—going on outside."

Archer's father paused. Then, he laughed. "Never thought I'd see the day when *you'd* be telling *me* I'm grounded."

Archer smiled. It felt like his father was finally coming out of his grief-stricken depression. "Well, you're not grounded," he said. "Not really. You can open this door from the inside. You can get out. I just don't want you to. It's not safe."

"We'll bunker down here, son," Mr. Keaton said. He held up his cell phone. "Looks like we've still got service, so we can call you, right?"

"We still have service?" Archer echoed. "Really?"

"See," Mr. Keaton said. "Five bars."

"That's surprising in all this chaos," Archer mumbled. "So, yeah, I guess call us if you need us."

"Will do. And be careful."

"Razz?" Archer called out, staring at the ceiling. "Razz, come here. I need you."

There was a melon-sized puff of blue smoke, a streak of purple sparks, and a shrill voice from the midst of it all, saying, "Here I am!"

Razzlestia Celeste Moonsonnet—Razz to her friends—hovered just above Archer's shoulders. The Dreamtreader breathed a deep sigh of relief. "Glad to see you," he said. "I wasn't sure what would happen to you . . . with the Rift."

"Dude," Buster said, "you've got a flying rat with two tails!"

"Awwww!" Amy cooed. "It's so cute."

"I am not a *rat,*" Razz said, her words fringed with feistiness. "Nor am I an *it.* I am a flying squirrel of dreamy proportions with an unrivaled fashion sense." She struck a pose in midair, pushing her acorn-top beret to one side of her fuzzy head and twisting her body to emphasize the shimmer of her sparkly boutique tunic dress.

"Oooh, pretty!" Kaylie exclaimed. "You look like a thousand facets of blue corundum!"

Archer looked sideways at his precocious little sister. "Blue corundum?"

"Oh, sorry," she said, her grin revealing a distinct lack of sorrow. "Sapphire, silly."

"Anyway, Razz," Archer said, holding out his hand so she could perch, "you're coming with us, but on the way out, make sure you get your bearings. I want you to know how to get back here."

"Why, boss?" Razz asked.

"So I can send you back from time to time to make sure they're all safe."

"Right, Archer," Amy quipped. "You mean, to make sure we aren't sneaking out. Yep?"

Archer smiled thinly. "C'mon, Kaylie, we have some Dreamtreading to do." He gave the huge spindle wheel on the blast door a spin. After a pressurized hiss, he pulled the massive door open. "Close this behind us," he said. "And don't open for anyone but us."

Archer turned to leave, but Kaylie yanked on his shirt. He stopped and turned. "What?"

"There's one more thing," she said, her eyes widening. She turned to her father, her brother Buster, and Amy and her mother. "You need to keep control of your imaginations."

"What do you mean, sweetie?" her father asked.

Archer went very rigid and whispered, "Of course."

Kaylie frowned, and Archer could see the familiar dilemma forming on her brow: how do you explain something extraordinarily complex to non-hyper-geniuses?

"We Dreamtreaders have always been able to create things out of thin air," she began at last, "but only in the Dream. The Rift has mixed everything up, mixed the Dream and Waking together, allowing the free exchange of Dream matter and the Waking World. People can create like Dreamtreaders now—that's why everything's gone so crazy. That's why monsters like that wolf-thing can appear. You have to be careful what you let yourself imagine because . . ."

Archer's father nodded and said, "Because we might summon up something else? Something terrible?"

"That's right," Archer said. "It's kind of like what Dreamtreaders are trained to do, but it could happen randomly. One minute, you think everything's normal, the next minute a weird thought enters your mind and—"

"Whoa!"

All eyes turned to Buster who had both hands wrapped around a gigantic cheeseburger.

"Dude!" Buster said. "All I did was think of it and, shazam!" He took a monstrous bite. "Mmm, so good."

"Cool!" Amy exclaimed, holding a tall strawberry shake in her left hand.

"Okay!" Archer growled. "Great, so you see how it works, but don't mess with it. One wrong thought could be a big problem."

"Hey," Buster said. He took a wobbly step and seemed to sway. He dropped the cheeseburger and started to fall, but his father caught him. His eyes flickered and he said, "Like . . . I feel wrecked. So tired now . . . all of a sudden."

"I think I'd better sit down," Amy said. She found a spot on the workbench. "That making stuff. It really takes a lot out of ya. Yep."

"It's your mental energy," Archer explained. "Your brain isn't used to working at this level."

"Archer," his father said, "what happens if you create something really big or really complex?"

"For Dreamtreaders, we get tired," Archer said. "For regular people, I'm not sure. It wouldn't be good."

"Good safety tip," Buster muttered, rubbing his eyes.

"Look, I know how fun the new power can be," Archer warned, "but this isn't something to fool with. Keep your thoughts clean."

"No worries, dude," Buster replied. "We've got Dad's old workshop TV, and we've got our phones to play games on. We'll be fine."

Archer took one last look at his family and his friends, and then pulled the blast door shut. There came a dull clank from inside. They were locked inside.

FOUR
Storm Warning

"Brrr," Razz muttered in the winter air outside Archer's home. The front yard was covered with snow that had begun to melt and then frozen over during the night. "So cold. Time for a new outfit."

In a purple puff of smoke, Razz reappeared, decked out in an arctic pilot's uniform, complete with a thick woolen scarf, goggles, and a leather bomber jacket.

"Good idea," Archer said. "Kaylie, let's gear up."

It required the barest, tiniest amount of will, Archer noticed, to transform his clothing completely. For Kaylie, he thought, it must have been as easy as breathing. But in the end, they were both as warm and protected as they could be, decked out in military issue, cold-weather combat jackets, insulated fatigues, and combat boots.

"What are we doing?" Razz asked. "The Rift's here. There are no more breaches to mend. What's our job now?"

"For starters," Archer said, "we help people."

"There's a lot going on," Kaylie said. "Where do we start?"

"Up," Archer said. "We've got to get a bird's eye view. And then we go where the trouble is."

"Roger that, captain!" Razz said, soaring skyward.

Archer leaped into the air, but Kaylie flew directly toward her bedroom window.

"One second!" Kaylie cried out.

"What? What's wrong?"

"Patches!" she squeaked, tearing the screen from the window and tossing it onto the front yard. "I can't go without Patches!"

Archer watched her disappear into the house and used the time to think. *Patches. She still clings to that old ratty doll. Not as much as she used to, but she hasn't left it behind either. Duh. She's only eight.* The concept seemed surreal . . . impossible. How could she still be just eight years old?

But she was.

Archer shook his head. *She should be making bunnies and unicorns out of Play-Doh, not fighting off three-headed werewolf monsters!*

Sure, Kaylie was mentally way ahead of her peers . . . light years ahead. And with that astounding intellect came off-the-charts Dreamtreading ability. If the Rift could be fixed, if victory over Kara was possible, Kaylie might very well be the key to it all. But at what cost?

Again, Kaylie didn't bother with the door. With Patches tucked under her arm, Kaylie leaped from her bedroom window and climbed into the night sky. "Hey, wait up!" Archer called. He watched her fly for a moment. She and Razz were painted silver in the waning moonlight. It gave Archer a thrill, reminding him of a scene from his favorite book growing up: *Peter Pan*. But instead of Wendy, John, and Michael with his teddy bear, it was Razz, Archer, and Kaylie with her Patches. Archer smiled and soared up to meet them.

"Follow me. We need to go up high to have a look around," he told them.

The ground fell away, the trees and the neighborhood next. In the Dream, flight had been absolutely exhausting. There were so many variables to monitor and manipulate: aerodynamics, drag, weight, lift, and thrust. After even a short flight, Archer's mental will could be sapped. Now, after the Rift, things were different. As he flew, Archer could feel the will draining, but it was replenished almost as quickly as it left. The newfound strength and resilience thrilled him. His imagination thrummed with new possibilities. But he'd give it all back in a heartbeat . . . if only the Rift could be repaired.

The Dreamtreaders reached a suitable altitude and cast about. Fortunately, the greenish mushroom cloud had dissipated. From that sky-high vantage, the surrounding territory looked, for the moment, somewhat peaceful. Archer scanned a complete circle—much of the area was suburban neighborhoods with a ton of forest patches—before the first signs began to appear. Bursts of fire flickered in the deep woods to the west, and then a glowing greenish tornado formed several miles to the east.

"Kaylie, Razz, take out those fires," Archer said. "I'll take the twister, but I might need your help, so meet me when you can."

"Roger that!" Razz said.

Kaylie nodded. "Let's go!"

"Kaylie?" Archer called.

"Yeah?"

"Anchor first," he said.

"Anchor deep," she replied, finishing the Dreamtreader maxim. But the expression she wore was uncertain. "Archer, what are our anchors now?"

Archer saw the fear in her eyes. He felt it too, but conviction overtook it in a heart's beat. "Our anchors are the same as they've always been, Kaylie. Truth doesn't change."

Kaylie smiled, tentatively at first, but then it became a broad, confident grin. "Operation Fire-Quench, activated!" she hollered as she and Razz streaked away into the night.

Archer lowered his flight goggles and floored it, following the undulating contours of the half-frozen western Maryland foothills. He felt his mental will coursing through every movement of his flight, and he exulted in the experience. He swooped low and swiped at the tops of the pines, sending a spray of powdered snow blasting into the air wherever he went. He curled left and right, keeping the funnel cloud in his sights.

It was an eerie thing to behold, a slim tendril of churning air lit in the same phosphorescent green as a child's glow-in-the-dark toy. This was no toy, though. Someone, somewhere, had dreamt this storm up, a violent, twisting serpent of carnage, throwing up massive debris clouds and threatening to obliterate anything in its path. Before the Rift, such a nightmarish storm would have been a danger only to Dreamtreaders doing their duty in the Dream Realm. *This* impossible storm was real.

A streak of ice plunged down Archer's back. The tornado was growing and moving faster, approaching a sprawling expanse of farmland where many homes lay. Archer charged ahead, plotting his moves even before he entered the outermost circulating winds of the storm.

The storm seemed more menacing than any tempest in the Dream. The clamor of the wind was a violent combination of sounds, a phasing of a freight train, a lion's roar, and the ever-present thunder. Lightning crackled close overhead. Archer flinched at the sound. He had to adjust his level of mental energy to fight the strengthening crosswinds that threatened to knock him off course. The Dreamtreader banked a hard left against a fist-like gust, and then blasted through to temporarily calmer air.

Man, this storm is moving fast, Archer thought. *Almost like it's got its own purpose.* The turbulent black mass was getting to the scattered farms. Archer needed to snuff out the storm, and he needed to do it quickly or those homes were history. He summoned up his will and created a bunker buster bomb. It was the sort of thing the military would drop over a terrorist's underground lair, an explosive so powerful it could penetrate concrete and steel.

The oblong device was about as large and aerodynamic as a potato, but Archer clutched it in his will and hurled it into the heart of the storm. He dropped to the ground and willed up a thick shield. Just as he covered his head, Archer decided the shield had not been one of his brighter ideas.

Fire. Light. The deafening explosion sent a shock wave hurtling outward, buffeting Archer's shelter. He tried to hang on, but the force spun him sideways. The blast wave bellowed into his shield like a burst of wind filling a sail. Archer used his mental will, strengthening his grip to keep the shield from being torn out of his grasp. The shock wave yanked the shield, and then propelled it and Archer to the west like a cannon shot. Archer tumbled along the ground. Jarring concussive bounces left Archer disoriented and dizzy even before he hit the trees.

The shield and Archer collided with a thick trunk. He ricocheted with a grunt and then careened off a sturdy white oak. Like a human pinball, Archer bounced from trunk to trunk until finally running out of blast-driven momentum. He collapsed in a heap at the base of a prickly blue spruce. Rolling on the carpet of needles, Archer groaned and coughed. Finally, he blinked back to reason and consciousness.

"Why am I not dead?" he whispered. There were sharp pains and throbs as he stumbled back to his feet, but nothing too serious. He brushed the muddy slush, dead leaves, pine needles, and other branches off of his jacket and fatigues.

Then, at last, he dropped the shield. In fact, he hurled it, and that's when he figured it out. If he had tried to toss the shield prior to the Rift, using just human power, he might have managed to launch it a few feet, maybe a couple of yards. But as Archer watched the shield spin away over the treetops, he realized his post-Rift will had infused his physiology with new strength—and durability. *Bouncing off tree trunks should have pulverized me,* he thought. But it hadn't. He'd survived with nothing more than scrapes and bruises, and even those felt like they were healing.

Archer took to the air, dodging branches until he was clear of the forest. By then it was nearly too late. The tornado had ripped up and scattered the fields surrounding the farms and was currently tossing farm equipment into the air like toys. The storm bore down on the farmhouses, and Archer had no idea what he could do to save them. He poured a new infusion of will into his speed and rocketed toward the storm. In moments, he entered the storm's debris field. Timber and sheet metal came careening at him. Something struck him in the knee, but he didn't see what it was. There'd surely be a welt left behind, but at the moment it was a tiny concern.

"How do I stop a force of nature?" he growled, tearing free once more from the storm's grasp. As he hovered in the turbulent air between the approaching storm and the nearest farmhouse, the truth became very clear. This was no force of nature. It was worse, a supernatural amplification of someone's greatest fears that had been given life by the collision of worlds in the Rift.

A piercing cry from below and behind forced Archer to spin around to face the farmhouse. He saw a man racing across the farm's front porch. He was carrying two little blond children, one in each arm, clinging to his neck and shrieking. A woman and a girl of maybe seven or eight crouched low and followed an erratic path behind him. They clambered off the front porch and fought the wind to get around the backside of their farmhouse, where a pair of large metal doors lay recessed into the ground.

Storm doors, Archer thought, *and just in time.* Glowing tendrils of cyclonic wind churned closer as the man handed off the toddlers to his wife and struggled to open the way down to the cellar.

"No," Archer whispered.

The farmer bent over the doors, straining and pulling, but they didn't budge. But the tornado had shifted its track, lurching forward, cutting Archer off from the farm and eating up the ground. Rows of crops were stripped and shredded, sucked up into the glowing storm. A scarecrow vanished, then a hundred yards of fences.

The storm was upon the farmer and his family, and there was no way Archer could fly to them in time.

FIVE
AGAINST THE WIND

ARCHER DID NOT HOVER THERE, STUCK LIKE A DEER IN the headlights. The misbegotten monster tornado would not have this family. Archer would see to that. There was no time to fight the winds and cover that distance, but he didn't need to. His will traveled at the speed of thought.

First, Archer thought up a stone barrier. He built the forty-foot wall much like the blast vault and placed it between the oncoming windstorm and the farmer's home. But this tornado was infused with something supernatural. It tore into the wall, its invisible fingers prying open the smallest seams in the wall. The wall began to fall apart, and that would turn each lifesaving chunk of the barrier into a deadly, bludgeoning projectile.

Archer wrenched the strength of his concentration to unmake the wall. "C'mon, Archer!" he berated himself. "You can do better than that! Think!"

Archer threw his arms forward and created giant hands of blue light, much like the ones Kaylie had created to deal with the wolf beast. But Archer used his to lift the farmer and his family up from the ground. "No!" Archer cried out. The flaw in this attempt became painfully clear. The farmer, his wife, and children . . . they were terrified. They'd never seen giant, magical hands. To them, they were sinister things . . . ghostly even. They fled from the palms faster than Archer was able to scoop them up. It was maddening, and the tornado closed in.

Finally, Archer let them down and removed the hands. The farmer huddled his family at the storm doors and once more tried in vain to yank them open. "Stupid!" Archer yelled, but he wasn't referring to the farmer and his family. He was thinking of himself. He'd panicked and, once again, his solution had been too complicated. This time, he'd keep it simple.

The Dreamtreader willed a crowbar to appear in the man's hands. The farmer stood very still for a moment, looked skyward, and then went to work. With Archer applying a little will to assist, the man got the doors open. He hustled his family down below, and then slammed the doors shut. Archer added a few layers of reinforcing steel before turning back to the approaching nightmare.

Ducking debris and shielding his eyes, Archer rose well above the farmhouse and faced the twister. Thunder sent deep, vibrating shock waves rolling over Archer. He steadied himself and fought down the panic rising within. He had a hundred storm-stopping ideas careening through his mind—putting up a massive shield, building a box around the storm, or creating some gargantuan vacuum cleaner—but none of them made any sense. They were all stupid, panic-driven absurdities like the bunker buster. The storm was so close now it cast an eerie pale green aura on the entire farm. Intensifying crosswinds threatened to yank Archer from the air, but each time he readjusted some facet of flight to hold . . .

His . . .

Position . . .

An idea burst into Archer's mind. He went into a power dive. For the plan to work, he needed his feet firmly on the ground. He had no idea if he could stay conscious, much less maintain flight, with the amount of mental will he was about to attempt. He had his limits, even with the Rift supercharging them.

The roar of the storm seemed to become a physical thing. The glowing funnel itself grew right before Archer's wide eyes. It became a massive wedge of churning debris, blotting out the horizon on either side and even the sky overhead. The roar intensified to a constant thunderous explosion. The winds tore the fence line and its concrete footings out of the ground. So powerful and voracious was the wind that it began to gouge out huge strips of earth, carving hundred-yard trenches with each advance. It might have been an F5 storm before. Now, no F-scale could measure its wind speed. Archer's ears popped as the air pressure dropped. Phantom gusts raked at his coat, relentlessly trying to pull him into the churning vortex.

"I don't know if I can pull this off!" he yelled. "But . . . I need to!" Archer narrowed his thoughts and thrust both arms forward. Slowly, deliberately, he began crafting his own tornado.

It was small at first, just a ropey thing, but it was growing, and, more importantly, it was rotating in the opposite direction of the nightmare twister. As if his mental energy were sand in an hourglass, Archer could feel it draining quickly as he willed his tornado to grow. His funnel spun faster and faster, sucking up more soil and debris. The wind speed of his anti-nado picked up. F2 then F3—the thing was getting harder and harder to control. He had to keep it churning, keep it spinning in the right direction, so he filtered in a little blue light. Now he couldn't just feel the wind's movement; he could see it. Yet the nightmare twister was still so much bigger, so much stronger. It was like a ghostly silhouette looming behind Archer's baby storm.

But Archer was far from finished. His roar joined the thunder-train sound of the other two storms, and he spent a chunk of his will all at once. It was so large he swayed where he stood and almost toppled. His storm tripled in size. Still not quite there, it was more like a light-heavyweight boxer against a heavyweight, but at least now, it was a fight.

It wasn't a moment too soon. The nightmare twister lurched forward, and the two storms collided. In that moment, there was a flash of green light and the sound of a thousand high-speed car crashes. The funnels of the two storms became enmeshed. Clockwise blue strove against counterclockwise green. The strain took its toll on Archer, depleting his mental will at an alarming rate.

But he fought. He fought with everything he had. That nightmare tornado could not win. Archer's storm grew again. Now it was close to equaling the rival twister.

As if in protest, the raging storm began spitting lightning. A luminous bolt scorched the earth right at Archer's feet. He flinched but that was all. One lapse in concentration, and people would die. He poured his will into controlling the winds of his storm. He could feel the tension of their striving, the grating, clutching winds ripping at each other. Still he poured more will into the clockwise wind. He had to counterbalance the luminous green storm's power, had to tear the funnel apart.

Archer felt a jarring catch within himself. It was like his heart skipping a beat; only this halting sensation was in his mind. For a moment, he couldn't think at all. There was a dull blankness and a ringing in his ears. An ounce of awareness came back and he knew . . . he knew he had released all the mental energy he could afford to spend. The storms went oddly silent, and then there was a black shadow in the corner of his vision.

Something struck him, and a curtain of darkness fell.

Archer awoke with a start. Sweat trickled cold down his back, his heart jackhammered, and he gasped for breath.

"Easy, Archer," came a soft voice. "Lay your head back."

Archer obeyed. He felt a firm pillow placed beneath the back of his head, and turned toward the voice. It was too dark, just enough moonlight spilling in through his bedroom window to silhouette the woman sitting next to his bed. Her outline . . . and her voice were somehow familiar.

She moved, and Archer felt a warm comforter tug gently to rest beneath his chin. "I had a terrible dream," he said. His speech felt dry, like the first words spoken in years. "There was . . . a storm. Something hit me."

"That wasn't a dream, Archer," the woman said. "Worst storm since the derecho last year."

Archer started to sit up but felt the gentle pressure of the woman's hands pressing him back to lying horizontally. "You need to rest," she said.

"But I'm confused. There . . . was a storm?"

"You took quite a rap on the head," she explained. "Piece of flying debris, most likely."

"Wait," he muttered, snippets of images stirring in his imagination. "I was helping . . . trying to stop the storm."

"You were helping all right," she said, her tone amused. "Kaylie had gotten caught out in the storm. It came up so quickly she just had time to duck down by the well. She was so scared, but you went out and brought her back inside. That's when the board hit you."

"She okay?"

"Kaylie's fine, thanks to you," she said. "She's in bed, sound asleep. You got the worst of it, you know. Well, you and the porch. Screens are all shredded. Guess your father will need somewhere else to smoke now."

Archer closed his eyes. A dull ache throbbed at the base of his skull. "I was supposed to be doing something," he said. "Supposed to be fighting."

"You're fighting sleep, that's all," she said. "Rest now. Just rest. We'll get it all figured out in the morning."

Archer tried, but his mind kept spinning. Something bad had happened, right? They'd been at a hospital for some reason. Then, they were home, but Amy and her mom were there. And then the storm. Archer turned his head to look at the woman's silhouette. That's why she seemed so familiar. Amy's mom. Archer's dad had a great many skills, but he was no good at being a nurse.

"There's nothing I have to do?" Archer asked.

"No, just rest."

"You sure?"

She laughed quietly. "Yes, I'm sure. Sleep now."

Archer felt a rolling tide of lethargy ready to envelop him. He felt slow . . . and warm. But there was something off, something he felt he should be able to get to. It was like an itch that he couldn't scratch no matter how he twisted. A moment or two later, he felt the heaviness on his eyes winning out. He turned over on his side, toward the closet, and closed his eyes. "Good night, Mrs. Pitsitakas," he mumbled.

There was a long pause, and Archer thought she might have already left. But then, she replied, "Good night, Archer. And don't worry . . . things will all become clear tomorrow."

SIX

GHOSTS

ARCHER'S BOWL OF FRUITY FLAKES TASTED NORMAL. THE January air at the bus stop was its usual frigid. Amy chattered away on the bus just as she always did. Everything seemed . . . normal.

Except it wasn't.

The same impossible-to-reach mental itch he'd felt the previous night was still with him all morning. And now, as he sat through third period English class, the feeling was almost unbearable.

Snot buckets, Archer thought. *Can't focus. Especially not on this.* He looked down at his worn copy of Aldous Huxley's *Brave New World* and shook his head.

The other students in the room seemed to be doing fine. Even Rigby, who had already read most of the classics a dozen times, seemed to be deeply engrossed in the book. Mrs. Mangum sat at her desk and pecked away at a keyboard. Feeling restless, Archer left his desk and signed out the bathroom pass.

He didn't need to go. He just wanted out. Wanted to take a walk, get a drink of water, clear his mind . . . if he could. He walked along rows of lockers and absently tapped the padlocks that hung from each locker. It was a long hallway, mostly dim and shadowy where Archer was, but far up ahead near the main office, the windows of the front entrance were aglow with nearly unbearable bright light. Archer squinted as he bent to the fountain for a drink. A man and a woman, both dressed very professionally, stood outside the main office. From their silhouettes, Archer thought it was two of the school's guidance counselors: Mr. Raymond and Mrs. Coonts.

As he slurped from the fountain, he wondered what the counselors might be talking about. Probably about the storm. Everyone was talking about the storm. Such a strange thing: high winds but little precipitation. It had gone out to sea, sucked up a bunch of moisture, and became a nor'easter, dumping a ton of snow in New England. *Too bad,* Archer thought. *It could have . . . been . . . what?*

Startled, Archer pressed the fountain latch too hard. Ice cold water went right into his nose. "Snot rockets!" Archer exclaimed, wiping his nose frantically. He stood up and stared. The two counselors were still there, talking, gesturing. But for a moment, one of them . . . flickered.

Archer blinked and kept staring. Maybe *flickered* wasn't quite the right word. Mr. Raymond's silhouette—just for a few seconds—seemed to become semitransparent and flake away . . . like a pile of ashes stirred by air currents. Then, he was there again: still a dark silhouette . . . but all the way there.

"Hey!" came a voice from behind. "Keaton, ya gonna drink or what?"

"Guzzy?" Archer mumbled, spinning around. "But . . . I thought you . . ."

"You thought what?" The notorious school bully was pale as ever. A thin curtain of black hair partially concealed the smoldering *just-give-me-a-reason* look in his dark eyes. "Just get outta the way so I can get a drink, man. I'm parched."

Archer hastened from the fountain, backing away from Guzzy.

"What's wrong with you, Keaton?" Guzzy asked, looking at Archer sideways. That's when it happened. Guzzy's face went from lack-of-sunshine pale to ashen gray. For just a few seconds, his face disintegrated in a whirl of gossamer flakes. Then, Guzzy was all there again, sneering as always.

Heart racing, Archer backpedaled away from Guzzy, jogged back to the English classroom, and ducked inside. His back now to the door, Archer found the entire class staring at him.

"Everything okay, Archer?" Mrs. Mangum asked. "You look like you've seen a ghost."

"Fine," Archer muttered, quickly sidling to his chair. Just not quickly enough.

"Hey, Keaton," Rigby called. "Couldn't get away from the scene of the crime fast enough, eh?"

Red-faced and mortified, Archer plopped into his chair and glared at Rigby. His nemesis in the classroom, however, didn't meet his gaze. He'd gone back to reading. Archer stared at Rigby. Long sideburns, uber-cool flop of hair, and that ever-present sideways smirk. Archer mentally dared him to look up, but he never did. Instead, Rigby Thames became ashen gray, withered in a split second, and then was back to normal before Archer could blink.

There, in the midst of the quiet classroom, was a distressing thing to behold. It wasn't gruesome, not like some time-lapsed footage of a dead thing rotting away. But seeing a tangible, flesh-and-blood person reduced to layers of ash right in front of you—it was a rattling experience. *It's the head injury,* he thought. *Gotta be. I've got a concussion, and it's messing with my perceptions.*

Archer scanned the room. If anyone else had seen Rigby's disintegration, there should have been some reaction. But the class, even Mrs. Mangum, continued to work as if nothing had ever happened.

The rest of the school day left Archer questioning his sanity. There'd been no more dissolving people, but that irresistible, unreachable itch was still there. Only the bus ride home gave a welcome bit of monotony, a time to think.

C'mon, Archer, he told himself. *You can figure this out. Just think it through.*

But the answers eluded him. It just all felt wrong. It felt like he was supposed to be doing something, like he'd forgotten a very important task or mission. The answer was getting closer. It was there, hovering at the edge of his consciousness, just as the bus hit a bump.

Archer had been staring at the tall, dark green seat in front of him. The bus seemed to bounce and shake all at once, as if the driver had gone much too fast over a speed bump. But, in that moment, Archer looked up.

It happened again.

Two seats up on the left: Emy Crawford. The seat directly across the aisle to Archer's right: Jay Stephago. Another three seats up on the right: Kara Windchil. Two more sitting side by side near the front of the bus: Bree Lassiter and Gil Messchek. The moment the bus jolted, they became disturbed blotches of whirling ash. A moment later, everything was normal.

When the bus came to Elvis Lane, the next stop on its normal route, Archer was the first to get off. It wasn't his stop, but he didn't care. He just wanted off that bus, away from . . . well . . . whatever was happening. Archer raced down Elvis Lane, cut the corner by leaping chain-link fences and racing across snowy backyards, and then finally crossed into his neighborhood.

All the while, his thoughts continued to clash. He was half-prepared to ask his dad to arrange a doctor's appointment for him—maybe with a concussion specialist—but the other symptoms just weren't there. No dizziness. No vomiting. No sensitivity to light.

No, he thought dismally, *I'm just seeing people dissolve.*

Archer tried to reach back into his memories. Maybe he could piece things together, find out what was causing all this, the visions and that interminable mental itch. He'd awakened in the middle of the night to find Amy's mom sitting by his bedside. There'd been a terrible windstorm, and he'd been knocked unconscious. But what had come before? His previous memories were a blur, a mix of achingly beautiful and nightmarishly terrifying images: a massive tree with a castle nestled in its boughs, crimson tornados, beastly red-eyed hounds, and a small hooded figure with a sinister glowing grin. And then there was that big tower clock—what was up with that? It was like a ghost of Big Ben. It seemed to be everywhere—

Archer stopped right there in the middle of the road, just fifty yards from his house. The answer was there, bobbing at the edge of his consciousness like a piece of treasure floating just offshore. Archer flailed at it mentally. He had some kind of job . . . a specialty, something he was very good at, something that helped people. But what?

Archer sat at his dining room table and munched absently on a big sourdough pretzel. His father stood at the sink and stared out of the window to the backyard.

"Good day at school?" Mr. Keaton asked, his face lit white from the sunlight reflected off the snow outside.

"Decent day," Archer said. "Strange day."

"Really? How so?"

Archer hesitated. "Well, I had trouble focusing," he said, omitting the most troubling details. "It was like I just couldn't think straight."

"I suppose that's to be expected," Mr. Keaton replied, grabbing a tall coffeepot from the counter and beginning to fill it at the faucet.

Archer nodded. He heard a series of car doors shut somewhere outside. *Guess Kaylie and Buster are home from school,* he thought as he took another bite of pretzel.

"If it's still bothering you after today," Mr. Keaton said, "we should get you to the doc's for a look-see."

Archer heard the front door open and the giggle-ruckus of snow boots being taken off. Buster said, "Dude, you got snow on my socks."

"Did not," Kaylie argued.

Yep, Archer thought. *Just like normal.*

"Full pot?" Archer's father asked without turning from the sink. "Or half pot?"

Archer blinked and took a bite of pretzel.

"Full pot," came a voice from the foyer.

Archer chewed thoughtfully and said, "It was nice of Amy's mom to stick around so late last night. Y'know? To make sure I was okay."

His father shut off the kitchen faucet. "Amy and her mom went home at eight last night."

Archer felt the terrible itch in the back of his mind again. "Then . . . who was sitting by my bedside?"

"Good to see you up and around, Archer," a woman said, just a blur in his peripheral vision, entering the kitchen from the foyer. "I was afraid school would be too much for you today. How are you feeling?"

Archer knew the voice before he turned around. The chill vanished, overwhelmed by a complicated mixture of feelings. Almost involuntarily, he sprang up from the table. Tears already streaking his cheeks, he ran to the woman. He embraced her and wept on her shoulder, holding on as if she might at any moment be pulled from his grasp, pulled from his life once more.

SEVEN
ARRESTING DEVELOPMENTS

"MOM," ARCHER SAID. "MOM, I'VE MISSED YOU SO MUCH."

"Group hug!" Kaylie announced. She and Buster latched onto their mother, enthusiastically joining the embrace.

"Awww, Archer. Thank you," she said, "but you missed me that much from a day at school?"

The sweetness of that embrace . . . soured a little. Archer pulled back a pace. "But, Mom, you have been gone . . . gone for so long." It wasn't so much a memory filling his mind as it was a sense of certainty, like a cold piece of iron hammered into the ground. Archer found himself saying, "You died, Mom. The cancer took you away."

"Archer!" his father cut in. "Don't say that!"

"Mommy?" Kaylie squealed. "You have cancer?"

Archer's mother dropped down to look Kaylie in the eyes. "No, sweetie," she told her daughter. "Not anymore." She tweaked Kaylie's chin, stood, and took a firm grasp of Archer's shoulders. "Archer, I've been in remission for years. No sign of the cancer. I still think it was the well water." She giggled lightly. "Maybe we should get you a sip of well water—if it's not frozen solid that is."

The well.

His mother's favorite well.

Archer felt dizzy now. He swayed where he stood and might have fallen if his mother's arms hadn't held him steady. He stared hard at her.

"Archer," she said, "what's wrong, sweetie? You look pale. Maybe you should sit—"

"No!" Archer exclaimed, pulling away from her. "Something's wrong."

"It's the injury," she replied, glancing over her shoulder at her husband. "I told you it was too soon for Archer to go back to school."

Mr. Keaton shrugged. "He seemed fine to me this morning."

Archer resisted his mother's attempts to hold him, but part of him didn't want to resist. Something at his core, something raw and needy, urged him to just fall into her embrace and soak up the feel of her warmth, the scent of her perfume, the melodic sound of her voice. He almost did.

But he suddenly found himself careening out of the kitchen, past Kaylie's and Buster's wide-eyed attempts to slow him down, past his shell-shocked father's haunted expression. Archer stumbled around the corner, banged into the basement door, and bounded into the laundry room. In a tear-streaked blur, he pounded out of the side door, charged for the backyard gate, and . . . without a jacket, without a hat, without even his shoes, he ran out into the snow.

He slip-slid down the hill through the slush, crusty snow, and ice until he collapsed hard at the base of the wishing well. Ignoring the shooting pain of the bitter cold on his bare feet, Archer crouched by the well and clung to its stone. He didn't wish. He prayed. "Oh, God, please . . ." he cried. "I want her to be real. I want her back . . . please let this be . . . true."

Tears burned at the corners of his eyes and streaked down his cheeks. Memories flashed: bare feet cushioned on the warming summer grass and well water sloshing as he carried a cool bucket up the hill; the delicious tang of his mother's lemonade, made from fresh-squeezed lemons, cane sugar, and well water; and the grateful look in his mother's eyes when he delivered a glass of water . . . a look that communicated the simple but powerful message: *You matter to me.*

With all five senses firing, Archer could see, smell, taste, hear, and feel all of it. And it was all connected to her.

"Archer?" Her voice was there now, right beside him. "Archer, please come back inside."

"Dude, get some shoes on!" Buster advised. "It's cold out here, man!"

He felt a tugging at his elbow. "C'mon, Archer," Kaylie said. "Let's go back inside."

Archer reluctantly pulled away from the well and let himself be led back up the hill, back inside. His father was waiting for him in the den. "Son, I'm sorry," he said. "I know your head injury has taken its toll on you. I know things don't seem right to you . . . but you've got to take control of your emotions. You're hurting. I get that. But you can't lash out like that. Now, please, don't mention your mother's cancer ever again."

Archer looked from face to face. Buster looked confused, Kaylie looked afraid, and his father seemed determined but somehow fragile too. Archer turned to his mother. He so dearly wanted just to get lost in her welcoming, understanding, loving eyes. "I'm sorry, Mom," he said. "I'm so sorry. I don't know what's wrong . . . what's wrong with me. I—"

He'd seen it in her face, an ashen ripple. So small, just a tiny feathery distortion, but it was enough. "No, this isn't real!" He backed away, backed into his father.

"Archer, settle down," he said. "You're getting all worked up. You need—"

"Get off of me!" Archer demanded. "All of you. This isn't right. None of it."

He turned from them, and as he rocketed from the den the whole scene whirled with ash, and he saw, just for a moment, the dreary darkness of a cold, winter night. He saw the emptiness of the home. And, through the hallway, he saw the damage to the kitchen cabinets the three-headed wolf creature had caused, back when . . .

It all came flooding back into his mind: Dreamtreading, the Rift, the world gone mad. That's what had been lingering just outside of his consciousness. Archer tore up the stairs, flexing his mental will, constricting the tiny muscles around his eyes to see, to *really* see. It was spectris, a skill only experienced Dreamtreaders could master, and it allowed Archer to see beyond the norm.

Like a curtain of undulating ashes, the daylight world parted, revealing night once more. He heard his father at the bottom of the stairs yelling, "Archer, wait! Come back!" But when Archer turned, he saw nothing but the night-darkened stairs.

"Archer, please!" his mother called, just a faint echo.

But Archer knew what he needed to do. He ran into his room, threw open the closet doors, and took out his copy of the Dreamtreader's Creed. He needed Master Gabriel, and he needed him now.

He snatched the gossamer-white Summoning Feather and tossed it into the air. As the frame around his room door became sealed in luminous blue light, Archer felt a presence in the room behind him. He spun around.

There, dressed fully in his Incandescent Armor was the leader of all Dreamtreaders, Master Gabriel. He wasn't alone. Two figures Archer had never seen before accompanied him on either side. They looked so similar that they might have been male and female fraternal twins. And they wore armor like Master Gabriel's.

Archer didn't waste another moment. He let it all out in a rush. "The Rift!" Archer cried out. "It's worse than I thought! It's hidden. There's a spell over everyone, a spell of make-believe . . . like nothing bad ever happened."

"I am sorry, Archer," Master Gabriel said.

"Don't you see?" Archer demanded. He whipped his forearm across his face and swiped the tears from his eyes. "The Rift has put people in a living dream—they don't know what's happening to them. They can't see reality!"

"I truly am sorry," Master Gabriel said. "Now, please hold out your hands."

"What?" Archer tilted his head. He held out his hands but had no idea why. "Master Gabriel, we need to wake up the world!"

"Archer Percival Keaton," Master Gabriel said. "By the power vested in me—"

"We don't have time for this," Archer cried out. "What . . . what are you doing? People are dying out there . . . and they don't even see it!"

"Archer!" Master Gabriel thundered. His armor lit up the room like the flash of a lightning bolt. "I am well aware of the plight of this world. Now, be silent."

Archer had never seen Master Gabriel in so severe a mood. What was he talking about? Archer's mind reeled. That's when Master Gabriel turned to one of the strangers and grabbed a pair of dull metal shackles joined by a thick chain. In one swift motion, he placed them on Archer's wrists. The shackles clicked and turned fiery white.

"Aaah!" Archer cried out. "Aaah, that hurts! What is this? Master Gabriel? What are you doing to me?"

"It is not what I am doing to you," the master Dreamtreader snapped. "It is what you have done to yourself. I say once more, be silent, Archer! You stand accused of violating Dreamtreader law. Though it grieves me to do so, I hereby place you under arrest."

Dreamtreader Creed, Conceptus 11

Anchor first. Anchor deep.

The Dreamtreader must secure himself to truth at all costs. You must remain grounded and perform your duties, not just to the best of your abilities, but beyond simple effort to . . . ultimate success. For yours is not a mundane occupation. Yours is no routine in which from time to time you might just go through the motions or simply . . . get by.

For you, success is the only acceptable outcome. For to fail would mean the destruction of lives . . . and worlds.

EIGHT
CORPORATE TAKEOVER

KARA WINDCHIL FINISHED WRITING, PUT DOWN HER pen, and gazed at her flourished signature.

"That," Frederick said, "makes it official."

Kara smiled and gazed at the Baltimore city skyline. The Dream Inc. Building, often called the Dream Tower, was the tallest in Baltimore, of course. She had based the design on several skyscrapers she'd seen in her research. It had been months in the planning, and then, the moment the Rift became a reality, Kara had spent a tremendous amount of will to build the Dream Tower from the ground up . . . in a matter of a few hours. The view of the surrounding world from just more than 660 feet suited Kara perfectly.

It's my world now, she thought, not gloating but rather a pondering of fact.

Frederick adjusted his ever-present dark glasses, and then made the knot on his black tie a little bit tighter. "It's a shame about Mr. Thames," he said.

Kara stood and waltzed to the window. "A loss for all of us," she whispered, staring at the dual image in the glass: the city and her own reflection. She wore a smart business suit, custom tailored so the suit sleeves stretched beyond their usual length into decorative cuffs that reached her knuckles. She raised a hand to her frozen-plum lips and continued to ruin a perfect manicure by nibbling at her pinky nail.

"A greater loss for some," Frederick said dryly. "Doctor Scoville won't be easy to pacify."

"Just make sure the restraining orders keep Scoville a hundred miles away from me at all times."

"Of course," Frederick replied. "But the man has assets."

"Not like ours," Kara said.

The room went utterly quiet until Frederick popped the clasps on his briefcase and said, "There's one more form to sign."

"Oh?" Kara asked without turning around. She flung back a silky black curtain of hair and tilted her head so the setting sunlight reflected in her pale blue—almost turquoise—eyes. "And what's that? I thought you just said my sole ownership is official."

"I did, and it is," Frederick replied curtly. "This form has nothing to do with your ownership of Dream Inc. and everything to do with your self-ownership. You still wish to be an emancipated minor, I trust?"

Kara broke eye contact with her reflection and said, "Oh, that. Yes, of course." Kara spun on a high heel and returned to the table. She snatched up the pen and signed her name once more. "I'm due every privilege of adulthood without fear that my mother would meddle in my affairs. She's not of sound mind, you know."

"So I've come to understand," Frederick replied, tucking the newly signed document into his briefcase. "And, if I may say so, it is quite kind of you to create a fund for her. She'll never want for another thing in her life."

"It's the least I can do," Kara said, turning to leave the conference room. She paused at the door. "And, Frederick?"

"Yes, Ms. Windchil?"

"Once the ownership portfolio has been ratified by the board of directors, please send me a few copies."

"I'll have them delivered within the hour," he said. "Where will you be?"

"I have . . . a few errands to run," she replied cryptically. "Send the digital files to my tablet; put the master copies in my personal vault."

Kara didn't wait for his answer but waltzed to the lobby and slapped the fleet elevator's down button. If she'd stayed, Frederick might have given her an earful about taking orders. They'd had a business relationship for some time, longer than most suspected, but that didn't mean he liked being bossed around.

Tapping her feet impatiently, Kara glared at the floor symbols and willed the fleet elevator to get to her floor faster. She looked at her watch, and then nibbled on her bottom lip. The meeting with Frederick had gone overlong, and time was running short for her *errands*.

The doors opened at last. Kara stepped in, sighed, and decided she needn't be worried about the time. After all, Dream Inc. operated according to her schedule—not the other way around. Moments later, the fleet elevator came to a stop at the medical clinic. She didn't smile or wave at any of the employees. She quickly bypassed the public section, stopped to punch in a door code at her private suite, and then rushed inside.

The pressure-sealed door closed behind her, and she was talking before she was halfway down the corridor. "I'm sorry I'm late," she said, "but it couldn't be helped. And, no, I don't want to reschedule. I'm worn-out. And I need a recharge."

Something flashed from around the corner as a being transported itself into the room. It was followed by a gleam of chrome . . . and a voice. "Things do not always go as we have planned," it said. "For the queen of the world has many demands, but fortunately for you, Kara, your wish is my command."

An hour later, feeling completely refreshed and energized, Kara left the medical clinic. She checked her tablet computer, saw the message waiting, and read that her ownership documents had been approved, of course. As per her instructions, Frederick had attached the digital files and put the master documents in her private vault. He'd even had the presence of mind to make a copy and sent it via—

"Courier for Ms. Windchil," said the young man who'd just appeared at her side. He wore the gray Dream Inc. uniform and held out a translucent plastic mailing tube.

"Thank you," Kara said, taking the mailing tube. She eyed the courier for a moment. He must have been in his mid-twenties. How happy he looked. How content. Not to mention efficient. She glanced at his name tag. "Hartsfield, is it?"

"Yes, ma'am."

"Well, Hartsfield," she said, "you didn't disturb me with this delivery but made sure I received it the moment I left the clinic. Consider your salary doubled."

The courier's eyes lit up. "Thank you, Ms. Windchil. Thank you. And if I may say, you're a joy to work for. I mean, it doesn't feel like a job at all but—"

Kara held up a hand. "Duly noted," she said, turning her back on the courier and heading for the fleet elevator. She stepped inside and hurriedly typed a code into the keypad.

"Floor please?" an automated voice demanded.

"Beneath," Kara said, tearing open the mailing tube.

"Floor restriction," the voice replied, "initiate recognition protocol or choose another floor."

Kara put her palm to the screen. "Protocol Wind Maiden One," she said. The screen flashed several colors, and the elevator began its long descent. Beneath was the code name of the lowest subterranean floor. The Dream Inc. Building went slightly deeper below the surface than its 660-foot height above. The Research and Development labs were on the bottom floor, but Kara's private section was even farther down and completely unknown to all but her—hence the name.

As the high-speed elevator hummed along, Kara found her reflection again, this time in the chrome doors. She loved the way the fluorescent light danced in her eyes. She gave a thought, spending just the tiniest measure of will, and her eyes began to glow, phasing blue, green, and purple. She gazed down at her fingernails and watched the now-scrolling colors for the most attractive hue, settling at last on opalescent plum. With barely a thought, she highlighted her silky, black hair with streaks of white blonde.

She took in the new look and muttered, "So easy."

"Nearing Research and Development," the digital voice announced. "Do you wish to notify?"

"Do not notify," Kara commanded. She'd meant to fix that feature. If she were getting off at R&D, fine, but if she were heading Beneath, she didn't want anyone to know she was even in the area.

As the elevator slowed, Kara removed the ownership documents from the tube and skimmed them for a few moments. It was all there. Frederick had been very thorough.

Kara watched the monitor and readied herself. Sublevel after sublevel went by, then Research and Development, and then . . . it happened. She willed her new appearance customizations not to change in the least, but she felt the boundary.

As soon as the elevator slipped below R&D's floor and over the threshold of Beneath, the air itself changed. It felt to Kara like the peeling away of a fuzzy layer. Not fuzzy like cute stuffed animals and cuddly kittens, but rather like the feel of static electricity. She felt it crawl up her body, her neck, her chin. She closed her eyes. It always stung the eyes a little.

And, then, it was done. Kara breathed out relief.

Her personal floor, Beneath, was the only place left on earth where her will-driven, dream-vision of reality—what she called the Harlequin Veil—did not penetrate. The elevator doors opened. Kara stepped out into the world as it really was and breathed the fresh air. It was cold air, barely regulated by the machines she'd installed, but its crisp, clean nature was superior to veiled air.

Kara stepped off the elevator into a long cavern carved from slabs of blue-gray granite. At the far end of the cavern was a throne. It had once belonged to the Nightmare Lord. And, for a brief time, another had occupied the chair.

"But it's mine now," Kara whispered. Summoning a little will, her feet left the ground. She hovered across the long floor until dropping lightly into the seat. She crossed her legs, placed her arms upon the rests and, with a glance, lit the torches all around the cavern.

Then, pouring as much smugness into her smile as possible, she decided it was time to visit with an old friend. She nodded, and a sixty-foot section of the floor began to rise. There had been no visible crease or mark to show this hidden chamber, but it rose smoothly and came to rest as if it had been there an eternity. Kara flexed her will. A place in the air right before her eyes went pitch-black, and a very old key emerged from the darkness. Made of bronze, now weathered, pitted, and streaked with patina, the Shadow Key hovered for a moment, and then streaked off to the waiting keyhole in the massive chamber that had risen from the floor.

With her mind, Kara turned the key in the lock, and a huge slab door slid open. And there, wrists manacled, top hat dangling limply from one hand, stood Rigby Thames. But he was not alone. Shadows swirled around him.

NINE
BENEATH

"YESSS, MY QUEEEEEN?" ONE OF THE SHADOWS HISSED.

"Need us for mischief?" rasped another. There was a glimmer of furtive, darting eyes. The Scath were humanoid, possessing a head, torso, limbs, but they were also fluid: pouring, spilling, and swirling like liquid darkness. They could move like cats or spiders or bats, whatever type of locomotion suited the moment, and their voices slithered with a raspy, stumbling cadence.

"Growing weary of taunting this one."

"Little left of the fleshling but a shell."

"We've done as you asked."

"Might we go free?"

Kara leered at the Scath. "Be patient," she said. "I'll have errands for you soon. Now, hide yourselves away for now. I wish to speak to Rigby . . . alone."

The Scath hissed but obeyed. They whirled between Rigby's legs, around his torso, his neck . . . and then departed. Rigby stood in the threshold of the chamber. He smiled, but his shoulders drooped, and very dark circles hung beneath his bloodshot eyes. Slowly, with chains jangling, Rigby lifted his top hat and placed it upon his head.

"Why don't you just get rid of me?" Rigby said, his English accent not so charming with such a weak, raspy voice. "Those beastly Scath won't let me sleep."

"Awww," Kara said. "Poor Rigby. Maybe you'd sleep better with some reading material." She reached into her coat and removed the courier's mailing tube. "Here." She tossed it in the air, and then willed it to Rigby's hands.

"What's this, then?" he asked, popping the cap off of the tube and shaking it until the document slid out. "Your last will and testament, I 'ope?"

"Last will?" Kara laughed. "No, Rigby, I've only just begun to will things into being."

"What is it then?"

"Open it."

Rigby sighed. He tore open the envelope and removed the document within. With a flaming glance at Kara, he began to read. His grip on the document tightened, and tiny streaks of red lightning flickered around his eyes. "You revolting, backstabbing letch! You've stolen the company!"

"Stolen is hardly the appropriate word, Rigby," she said. "This is business. Call it a hostile takeover."

"You can't do this," Rigby growled. "I founded Dream Inc. Without me, there is no company. Frederick will—"

"Frederick helped me put this document together," Kara replied curtly. "And it's a done deal, I'm afraid. You're out. I'm in."

Rigby let the documents fall from his hands and, for a moment, Kara thought he might try once more to use his mental will. After all, he had been a formidable Dream Walker once upon a time. But Rigby tried no such thing. Pain from the cobalt manacles made for a pretty intense teacher. He'd learned, apparently. *A shame,* she thought.

When Rigby spoke, his words were quiet, reserved. "Why'd you do it?" he asked. "Why, Kara? We 'ad a good thing going. We 'ad plans."

Kara shot up from the throne, her eyes ablaze. "*We* had a good thing going?" she spat. "You wouldn't even let me sit in your chair! You were always about yourself . . . you and your beloved Uncle Scovy. And, after the Rift was complete, I suppose you and your uncle wouldn't have just cut me right out?"

"Of course not," Rigby shot back. "I knew I needed you. I knew we'd need each other to 'elp the world adjust . . . to a new reality."

"You were always an awful liar, Rigby Thames," Kara said dismissively. "Turns out, helping the world adjust isn't so terribly hard. I've already done it."

"What exactly 'ave you done?"

"The Harlequin Veil."

Rigby straightened so abruptly that his top hat fell off. "The . . . the Veil?" he scoffed. "It never worked. That's why we dubbed it the *'arlequin* Veil—a fool's veil, right? It was a nice theory, but a broken one."

"Not so broken," she said, once more taking her seat. "The Harlequin Veil works. It's working right now as a matter of fact. The entire world believes it has awakened from the worst nightmare, awakened to find life far better than they ever dreamed it could be."

Rigby shook his head. "I don't for a minute believe you've pulled it off, Kara," he said. "But even if by some miracle you did manage to get the Veil up and running, it wouldn't last. People would see through it eventually. The intelligent ones would, anyway. Our species is far too analytical. They won't accept it. It—it'll be like the body rejecting a transplanted organ."

"I've already got that covered," Kara said, nibbling on her pinky nail. "As we speak, under Frederick's supervision, Dream Inc. clinics will be opening all over the world. Five thousand clinics so far, and then double that in three months."

"Clinics?" Rigby chuckled. "Clinics for what?"

"Reorientation," she replied. "For people who don't accept the new reality. Dream Inc. will help them adjust."

"Impossible," Rigby replied. "That's why Uncle Scovy and I gave up on the Veil concept."

"You gave up on it because you lacked the resources to see it through," she said. "But I've learned from the Masters Bindings. You forget; I spent quite a bit of time with the Nightmare Lord. He taught me a thing or two as well."

Rigby bent down to retrieve his top hat. He didn't put it on, but stared inside.

"Thinking you'll pull a rabbit out of your hat?" Kara jeered. "It won't work. Those manacles won't let you use your will."

If Kara's dig had stricken a nerve, Rigby didn't show it by his expression. He shook his head, and when he looked up, he wore a hint of a smile. "What 'ave you done with the Masters Bindings?" he asked. "They used to be 'ere in the chamber with the Scath."

"Wouldn't you like to know?" she mused. "I can only imagine how much you must be longing to get another peek at them. Pity you didn't think to make yourself copies."

"I did think of it, Kara," he growled. "I'm not an idiot. The Masters Bindings cannot be copied. No amount of mental will can do it."

"You're certain?" she asked coyly. "Even a superior mental will?"

"There's no world in which you 'ave an intellect superior to mine," Rigby hissed.

"And yet how easily I caught you," she said, absently examining her fingernails once more. "It was foolish of you to go after Kaylie in that way. No good could come from extinguishing her extraordinary power."

"Well, she's got to be accounted for," he replied. "You'll see. And if you mess with 'er, you'll 'ave to deal with Keaton—"

"Archer is out of the picture," Kara said. "By the time he's back in, it'll be too late."

"What do you mean by that?"

"Archer's past has caught up with him. A terrible shame, really." Kara began to laugh quietly. "In many ways, you and Archer have taken a similar path . . . and share a similar fate."

"Enjoy your miserable riddles." Rigby sneered, shaking his top hat at her and jangling his chains. "Enjoy it while you can. It's all going to come down, Kara. It's going to burn down and take you with it."

"Oh, Rigby, don't be so bleak." Kara waved her hand dismissively. She stood from the throne and approached her captive, stopping just out of Rigby's reach. She crossed her arms and studied him for a few moments.

"You might beat Keaton," Rigby said. "Might." His expression showed that outcome to be very much in doubt. He smirked and continued, "If 'e doesn't get to you in time, you might even manage to fool most of the world. But you'll never fool my uncle for long. Scovy has research you know nothing about. Don't you think the inventor of the Veil concept will figure out the Veil . . . and your schemes? And when 'e does, 'e'll come for me."

"I'll deal with your uncle when the time comes," Kara said. "But he'd better come soon."

"Or what? You'll sic the Scath on me? You've already done that. What else can you do, kill me?"

"No, I'm not going to kill you, Rigby," she quipped. "If I did, where would I get my entertainment? You're like my own private puppet show."

Rigby strained against his chains. "You—"

"Good-bye for now, Rigby," she said, reaching for the Shadow Key. She gave it a twist, and the slab doors began to close.

"Wait, what did you mean?" Rigby demanded. "What did you mean by 'e 'ad better come soon? What's the time component?"

Kara grinned as the doors slid slowly, like some giant arachnid's mouth. "Isn't it obvious, Rigby?" she quipped. "No? Put it this way. If your uncle takes too long, I'll release you into his custody and wish you both well. In a matter of days, neither of you will care anymore."

TEN
THE CHARGES

MASTER GABRIEL'S ARMOR FLARED, THE RUNE-LIKE tracings in each articulated plate burning brightly with white fire and lighting up Archer's bedroom. The other two soldiers wearing Incandescent Armor similar to Master Gabriel's stepped to either side of Archer and took hold of him at the elbows and shoulders. Gabriel drew his sword, Murkbane the Nightcleaver. For a surreal and terrifying moment, Archer thought the blade might be meant for him, a rather quick sentence for his crimes.

But Master Gabriel turned to Archer's closet, and slashed the glowing blade up, across, back down, and across once more, carving a ribbon of light in a gate-sized rectangle that reached from the ceiling to the floor. Master Gabriel sheathed the blade and waited. Archer was about to ask, but snapped his mouth shut.

The glowing frame began to fill in. Silver tendrils of light cascaded down, spreading to the edge. An image was forming. For Archer, it was like watching a thousand invisible hands painting; only, their brushstrokes left not paint but streaks of lightning. He blinked and squinted, watching with open-mouthed astonishment as a rolling stairway of light came into being. It was not a spiral stair, nor was it a staircase. It was an undulating staircase that climbed, disappeared over a wide ethereal hill, only to reappear beyond with more inclines and hills as far as the eye could see.

"Come, Archer," Master Gabriel said quietly, and he stepped through Archer's closet onto the stair. The soldiers led Archer forward, following their leader. A few steps forward made all the difference. Archer's closet seemed less real, while the stair became more.

It was a long journey up and down, but it was not arduous, not taxing. Instead, Archer felt energized. His will pulsed within him, surging and tingling. Each step seemed more effortless than the one before. There was an occasion when he just happened to glance at the horizon to his right. He blinked. He thought he'd seen the faintest hint of an image . . . Old Jack, the Dreamtreaders' timekeeper. Its clock face seemed strange, though, at the time, Archer couldn't decide why. What time did it say? Six o'clock? But in light of the Rift, what did that even mean? Archer had little time to consider it. In a blink, it was gone, hidden by a whorl of stardust.

In the midst of the journey, Archer made the mistake of looking down. Through the shimmering light, the veil-like corona emitted by the stair, he saw down to the world he'd always known. His heart fell, for he saw the toll of the Rift. Archer saw little but fire . . . and destruction.

At the end of the rolling stairway in the sky, Master Gabriel and his soldiers led Archer through a dense bank of mist, destroying all sense of direction. In fact, all of Archer's senses seemed muffled. He knew the soldiers still marched on either side, and the shadow ahead must have been Master Gabriel, but it was disorienting. Once, he thought he heard faint music, but it was gone in an instant.

When they at last emerged from the mists, there was a blue sky and snow-covered terrain, all brilliantly lit but with the sun nowhere to be seen. They picked up the pace now and followed a winding path down into a valley thick with pines. At its heart stood a stone fortress guarded on all sides by towering pines and monstrous snowdrifts. Where he was on earth—or even if he were still on earth—Archer could not tell.

Inside the fortress, Master Gabriel led Archer down a narrow hall. They stopped for a moment at a pedestal upon which lay a large open book. Master Gabriel took up a quill pen that looked remarkably like the Summoning Feather, and then scrawled a few lines into the book. The soldiers led Archer too quickly past to see what the Master Dreamtreader had written. Archer itched to ask, but the place was so eerily silent that he wondered if it might be an additional crime to speak in such a sacred place.

They turned left ninety degrees, and Archer winced, thinking they were going to walk straight into a plain white stone wall. But they continued on as if it were nothing but air. Each time they approached dead ends, they neither slowed nor turned but somehow passed directly through. When they at last came to a stop, Archer walked straight into Master Gabriel's back.

A door opened, and Master Gabriel cleared his throat audibly. "This cell is yours, Archer."

Archer hadn't seen any other cells, but this one was real enough. A bunk, a desk, a restroom—all white as snow, but that was it. As the soldiers led Archer inside, Master Gabriel said, "Thank you for your service. You are dismissed."

"But, sir," one of the soldiers said, hesitating, "we're supposed to remain with the accused."

"We have orders," the other soldier added.

"Given to you by your commander," Master Gabriel replied curtly. "Yes, I know. This commander is my subordinate. Have I made myself clear?"

The two guards nodded repeatedly as they hastily disappeared around the corner. Then, the Master Dreamtreader turned his scowl to Archer.

Gabriel's ferocity drained away, leaving upon his features something closer to sadness. "You must know I would have avoided this if there were any way I could have, Archer," he said. "Even at my level, there is an order to things, and order must strictly be adhered to."

That first glimpse of sympathy was enough to release Archer to speak his mind. "What's going on?" he asked. "Master Gabriel, everything has gone haywire. The Waking World is dying."

"Indeed. It is killing itself," Master Gabriel replied. "People no longer know what is real and what a dream is. They cannot find their anchors."

Archer dropped to his bunk. He ran his hands feverishly through his hair, and said, "Look, I don't know what I've done—whatever it is, I'll answer for it. I'll take whatever punishment I'm due, but can't you suspend sentence or something—just temporarily—so I can help the Waking World?"

If not for the gravity of the situation, Archer would have laughed at Master Gabriel's slack-jawed expression. The Master Dreamtreader's gaping mouth closed, and then turned into a broad grin.

Archer frowned. "What?"

"It's nothing," Master Gabriel replied. "Pride, a touch of admiration. How much you've grown in so short a time."

Archer wasn't entirely sure what Master Gabriel meant, but he didn't allow himself time to ponder it. "So, what about it? Is there some way I can get out of here? Can't we post bail or something like that?"

Master Gabriel's fist constricted around the pommel of Murkbane. "Our system of justice has no provision for that sort of thing. You will remain in custody until your fate is determined by trial."

"When will that be? A day? A week?"

"We do not reckon time in the same way here as you do in your realm," Master Gabriel explained. "No hours, no minutes. Just order. Your trial will begin once the evidence has been collected and documented."

Archer shook his head, stood, and paced the room. "I guess I should know the charge against me."

Master Gabriel clasped his hands behind his back. He seemed to hesitate before saying, "I am afraid there are many charges, Archer."

"This . . . that makes no sense," Archer replied. "Just tell me."

Master Gabriel sighed. "The first charge is insubordination, for repeatedly disobeying the commands of a Senior Dreamtreader."

"When did I—oh. Right . . . when I went after the Nightmare Lord and cut the horn off his helmet."

"That and entering the Lurker's lair in Archaia," Master Gabriel explained. "But those charges will be easily enough dismissed. You were young and stupid, not defiant."

"Thanks. I guess. What else?"

"The second charge is that of incompetence," Master Gabriel said gently. "For failing in your Dreamtreading duties, failing to prevent a Rift."

"That . . . well . . . ultimately, that's true."

"Well," Master Gabriel said, "not entirely. Given the circumstances—Rigby's and Kara's betrayals, the Lurker's secret breach-tunnels—I believe we can beat those as well."

"Okay," Archer replied, mentally running back through the events that had led to the Rift. He wondered what he could have done differently, wishing he could go back and fix things.

"The third charge is much more serious," Master Gabriel said, "but, fortunately, the easiest of the lot to defend. You are accused of high treason for the murder of fellow Dreamtreaders, Duncan and Mesmeera."

Archer felt like he'd just taken two punches to the gut. "When I burned the Nightmare Lord's trees," he said, "I didn't know they were there. I couldn't have known . . ."

"Precisely your defense," Master Gabriel said. "This charge in particular is utterly preposterous. Duncan and Mesmeera are lost, and for that we most heartily grieve. But they made their own decisions, the choices that ultimately led to their capture by the Nightmare Lord's trickery. It was a tragedy, but you are not to blame."

"Thank you," Archer said. "So that's it, then? Tough charges, but beatable?"

Master Gabriel turned his back on Archer and stared through the cell's bars. "There is one charge that troubles me," he said quietly. "And I do not know how it will play out in the trial."

"Wh—what is it?"

"Attempted murder," Master Gabriel explained. "In your efforts to prevent the Rift, you went to Rigby's home, down to the basement, and threatened to kill a helpless human being."

"Doctor Scoville?" Archer whispered. "But Rigby was threatening Kaylie. I didn't . . . I couldn't figure out a way—"

"I know, Archer, but the facts there are dangerous." Master Gabriel turned to face Archer. "With premeditation, you went to Doctor Scoville when he was helpless, and you were willing to kill him."

"But I didn't," Archer said. "I didn't kill him."

"I understand, Archer, I do. But that is the charge against you. And these are the charges we must defeat if you are ever to leave this place."

"This is crazy," Archer muttered.

"Nonetheless, we must prepare your defense," Master Gabriel said. "Of course, I will be your defender. I have . . . some experience with this sort of thing. I am confident of—"

"No," Archer said, his voice quiet, but the word weighted.

Hands on his hips, eyebrows and mustache bristling, Master Gabriel demanded, "What do you mean, no?"

"You can't defend me," Archer explained. "The Waking World, my family and friends, they're all running blind. It was bad enough right after the Rift occurred. People were accidentally dreaming up all sorts of terrors. At least then, when a monster appeared, people could see it. But now everyone's been somehow brainwashed. They don't even see the tragedies occurring all around them."

"What do you believe has caused this?" Master Gabriel asked.

"I don't know," Archer admitted. "It might just be an unexpected result of the Rift, but I think Kara's behind it somehow. All along, Kara's always had a new trick up her sleeve. What better way to rule the world than to brainwash everyone into believing everything is just perfect?"

"Hmm. I suspect you are right," Master Gabriel replied. "The Wind Maiden rules without opposition so long as the world continues to drink her sweet-tasting poison."

Archer nodded. "Kaylie's lost in it too. She thinks my mom is still alive. She needs to wake up. And . . . I have no idea where Nick is." Archer thought about the newest Dreamtreader, Nick Bushman. The Australian had done well for having such a steep learning curve: playing his part at the dinner with Kara, Rigby, and Doc Scoville . . . and fighting valiantly. "My father told me Nick helped save him just before the Rift occurred, but I've lost him since. For all I know, Nick might be under the same spell I was under. He might be too inexperienced to wake himself up. He'll need help—the Waking World needs help, needs someone to fight for it. It can't be me; I can't leave here. So you'll have to."

"Me?"

"Yes, you," Archer replied, trying to be firm but treading lightly at the same time. "Kaylie and Nick, well, they're your team. You trained them to be Dreamtreaders, but they can't do the job unless you help them now."

Master Gabriel thought on this. He tapped his lips for a time. "I . . ."

Archer waited.

"Yes, you're right," Master Gabriel explained. "I must see to Kaylie and Nick; I must see to the Waking World. But what of your defense?"

"I'll defend myself," Archer said. "If I can't do it with my will, I can do it with my mind."

"Very well," Master Gabriel said, putting a hand on Archer's shoulder. "This is our plan, and we will see it through."

"One thing still bugs me though," Archer said. "Who's bringing these charges against me? Kara? Rigby? Doc Scoville? I don't even know who could know all these things well enough to accuse me."

"There is one," Master Gabriel explained, "who has been a behind-the-curtain party to all of this. One who, for devious reasons of his own, would like to see your downfall."

"But who?"

There came a soft shuffling from the hall outside the cell. And then, on the other side of the bars, a shadow appeared.

ELEVEN
THE SIXTH DOOR SINISTER

WHEN KARA HAD AT LAST LEFT RIGBY ALONE AND THE door to the Karakurian Chamber shut, Rigby spun on his heels and practically leaped down into his prison. He hoped his act of pitifulness had convinced Kara he was done. He'd laid it on thick, projecting a wimpy, broken will that was sure to please *her highness.*

Truth was, Rigby Thames was far from done.

Rigby raced around the chamber's great stone pillars and ducked under arches. He blew by the massive—but now virtually empty—bookshelves, and darted down the hall of many doors. At the sixth door on the left—the *Sixth Door Sinister* he called it—he entered and found a grand desk strewn with parchments, quill pens, and a few squat bottles of ink.

Chains jangling like mad, Rigby flew to the desk. He crashed into the chair, grabbed up a quill, and stabbed it into a bottle of ink. "Okay, Scath!" he cried out. "Come to me!"

There came from behind a slithering and a whispering. The torch-light flickered. "We need not follow its command!" one Scath rasped.

"Disappointed us."

"Weaker than she."

"I am not weaker than Kara," Rigby fired back. "Now, cut your nonsense. If you ever want to be set free . . . I mean, really free, get over 'ere."

"Promised us once, you did."

One of the Scath suddenly appeared at Rigby's shoulder. "Liar!" it hissed.

In one swift motion, Rigby dropped the quill pen and threw his arms up and over the Scath's shadowy head. He drew his fists together, tightening the chain around the creature's neck like a noose.

"Whatever Kara did to these shackles to cripple me," Rigby growled, "might just be enough to unmake you, Scath."

The chamber exploded into a swarm of shrieking, spitting-mad Scath, streaking around Rigby like they were hornets and he had just hit their hive with a bat. Their scowling faces passed within inches of Rigby's, but he did not yet relent.

"Let us go!"

"It betrays us!"

"Now it kills us!"

"We will tear the Walker apart!"

Rigby tightened his chains. "No," he said bluntly. "No, you won't. If I feel so much as a pinprick from you, I'll pull these chains so tight his little Scath noggin will pop off."

"It mustn't!"

"The Walker wouldn't dare!"

"I would," Rigby said. "But I don't want to. I mean for us to work together to the betterment of us both. Now, stop flitting about and be civil. We have a plan to discuss."

Slowly, the storm of Scath decelerated. When at last they formed a huddle around him, Rigby uncrossed his wrists and released his captive.

"Why should we listen to you?" the Scath asked.

"The Walker is not master."

"No," Rigby said, picking up the quill pen. "I'm not, but I plan to be again soon."

"How does it?"

"It is trapped like we are."

"*Trapped* is the key word," Rigby said, beginning to sketch on the parchment. "You will recall that when I took the Shadow Key, I kept my end of the bargain. I set you free, and I wanted it to be permanent. I tossed the key into Xander's Fortune."

"The cauldron of undoing?" a Scath asked.

"Impossible!"

"Nothing survives within that volcano. The Walker lies again!"

"Enough!" Rigby pounded his fist, splattering black ink across the parchment. "I did not lie to you, and I am not lying now. I threw the blasted key into Xander's Fortune and meant for it to be gone forever. 'ow was I to know it landed on a ledge, saving it from ultimate destruction by mere inches? It is a long story, but remember, when I 'ad the Shadow Key, my goal was to set you free. It's still my goal, but now that Kara 'as the key, I can't 'elp you. And if I'm stuck 'ere, I can't do anything for you. Do you see?"

"We sees. We sees."

"So we need to 'elp each other," Rigby said.

"But we cannot," a Scath said.

"She holds the key now."

"She is master."

"We cannot defy her."

"No," Rigby agreed, "no, you can't. Not directly." Rigby began to sketch once more on the parchment. He stopped and pointed. "Can you find this place?"

"Yes, yes, we knows it."

"We have been there before."

"Excellent," Rigby said. "I thought as much. Now, to the plan."

"What does it want?"

Rigby wondered if his expression managed to convey accurately the mischievousness he felt. With a knowing smirk, he said, "I want you to kill me."

There was a hissing of Scath laughter. They said, as one, "Gladly."

TWELVE
SCATHING LOYALTY

LATER THAT EVENING, KARA FLOUNCED ACROSS THE BED in her penthouse suite. Even the grand twinkling view of Baltimore at night couldn't assuage the feelings that nagged her. Her plan—her meticulously orchestrated plan—had gone off without a hitch. She'd won. She'd beaten them all at their own game, forced the Rift, and figured out how to make the Harlequin Veil work.

But that night at the hospital, the look on Archer's face . . . haunted her. When she'd revealed that she was the Wind Maiden, he'd looked so utterly betrayed, so completely undone. And then, if that weren't bad enough, she'd even taunted him with her success.

"I gave the Shadow Key to the Wind Maiden," Archer had said. "You . . . you're the Wind Maiden?"

"Poor Archer," she'd replied cruelly. "You never had a clue, did you? Not even from my last name? Really? No? Well, now you know. It has been a good ride, Archer. A brilliant game of chess. But this is checkmate."

Back in the present, Kara flopped over on her side and stared at the mirrored closet doors. Though she fought hard against the feeling, she couldn't shake the reality that she wasn't completely satisfied by her reflection. She couldn't fathom why she needed, not just to win, but to rub everyone else's faces in it. The Nightmare Lord used to taunt people like that. Rigby had made an art form of ridicule. But it wasn't like her.

Then, she thought about the vault behind those mirrored closet doors. She thought about the Masters Bindings within. Perhaps the answer was there. Maybe she'd already found the answer in the Bindings, but it just hadn't yet fallen into context. Hadn't the Bindings spoken of the unique position granted the possessor of ultimate power? Was that it? Could it be that by her cunning and power—the Rift and the Veil—could grant everyone in the world a sense of ultimate peace and satisfaction . . . but not do the same for her? It was a maddening question.

Kara rolled off her bed and calmly opened her closet to reveal her massive vault: six feet tall, four feet wide, and eight feet deep. "Kara Windchil," she said, activating the voice recognition on the display.

"Place palm here," the automated voice told her. She did.

"Key combination." Kara did. From top to bottom, the stainless steel bolts slid back, and the ten-inch-thick door swung open. When the fluorescent lights blinked to life overhead, she stepped inside and went straight to the set of shelves in the back. She selected volume four of the Masters Bindings, noted only by the crimson Roman numeral *IV* emblazoned upon its thick spine.

She didn't even bother to leave the vault. She knelt right there, found the place where she had left off last time, and began to read. Her eyes bulged. Tendrils of crimson lightning flickered on her fingertips.

Sometime later, Kara became aware of a bell ringing . . . and it was ringing rather incessantly. The bell seemed familiar. It was something she should know, but it was also absolutely irritating. "Please, shut up!" she cried from the vault.

Then, she heard voices, but there was something odd about them. They had a tinny sound, a kind of mechanical quality. Kara's mind cleared a little. There was no one in her penthouse apartment. She was certain of that. That meant the intercom, but who would dare interrupt her in the middle of the night?

At last, she recognized one of the voices. It was Frederick, and he sounded upset. Swiftly, but with great care, Kara replaced the fourth volume on the shelf, exited the vault, eased the heavy door until it closed and locked, and then shut the mirrored closet doors.

"Open front door!" she called out, rounding the corner from her bedroom to the study. Near the kitchen archway, she nearly ran into Frederick and two technicians wearing white lab coats and frowns. "What on earth?" she asked.

"Ms. Windchil, what took you so long?" Frederick asked. "With all due respect, we've been waiting outside for several minutes."

Kara frowned. "It is the middle of the night," she said, holding her temper. "What's going on? It's not Doc Scoville, is it?"

"No," Frederick said. "We may have a larger problem than Doc Scoville."

"Go on," she said. "Speak plainly."

Frederick gestured to the two technicians. "Smith and Harvey here are from R&D. They've discovered a potential flaw in the Harlequin Veil. Gentlemen, please explain."

Kara heard them out. It wasn't the all-fired disaster Frederick seemed to think it was, but it certainly warranted research. And, unfortunately, that research involved Rigby Thames.

Kara stepped out of her private elevator and planned her approach. She wished she hadn't been so harsh with Rigby the previous day. After all, she needed information, but she mustn't let Rigby know how badly she needed it. And, no matter what, she mustn't let him learn precisely *why* she wanted it. *Easy enough,* she thought. *Rigby can be manipulated.*

Kara settled into her throne and willed up the Shadow Key. She held it in her hands for a few moments, pondering the power that it gave her. This key gave her access to the Karakurian Chamber. It allowed her access to the Masters Bindings and the utterly groundbreaking wisdom within. Most importantly, for now, it gave her control of the Scath.

Well, she thought, *as much control of those little devils as possible.* The Scath were, after all, notoriously mischievous. When she gave them a task to do, it would get done, but there was always collateral damage. She could almost hear their favorite raspy chorus now: *We must play . . .*

Kara made up her mind. She couldn't just sit in her throne. In fact, she thought it might be best to hide the great chair for now. It was likely a very sore reminder to Rigby of all he had lost. With a twitch of her will, the throne, as if it had been sitting on hydraulic risers all along, began to drop down into the floor. In a moment, it was gone from view.

Then, Kara flexed her will to lift the Karakurian Chamber up from its recessed place in the floor. She inserted the Shadow Key, twisted, and watched the slab doors slide open. She put on a stern face. She expected Rigby to be standing there, top hat in hand, and she didn't want him to think she needed him.

But Rigby was nowhere to be seen.

Usually, the movement of the chamber rising was a clue to Rigby that he was expected to be front and center. *Come when I call, Rigby,* she'd told him. *Always come when I call.*

Yet he was not there. *Fantastic,* Kara thought. *He's going to try my patience today of all days.*

"Rigby!" she called. "Come out, come out, wherever you are."

But there was no sign. For a fleeting moment, Kara feared Rigby might somehow have escaped. But no, that was impossible. The cobalt shackles negated his ability to create with his mental will. *Rigby is stuck here so long as I choose to keep him.*

Then, she heard it: a cacophony of whispering. The Scath.

"Ssssss."

"What is it?"

"Not moves. Not moves again."

"Fleshling has done this . . . to us?"

"Don't tell; don't tell!"

"No, the master mustn't know!"

Kara rolled her eyes. What were the Scath up to now? What was all this nonsense?

She stepped over the threshold of the Karakurian Chamber. The torches were guttering, the amber light burned low. It was shadowy and difficult to see beyond a few feet ahead of her footsteps. But Kara was not afraid. There was no threat she couldn't handle. She had all the power she needed. All the power in the world.

Still, she wasn't about to get cocky. That was Rigby's greatest flaw, something she'd exploited many times. She would proceed cautiously, eyes wide open, all senses on alert. The doors on either side of the long hall were unevenly spaced and every door was closed. Seeing no sign of Rigby or the Scath, Kara delved deeper into the chamber.

Of course, Kara thought. In spite of her power and resolve, memories of every horror movie warned her of impending doom. *Maybe this is Rigby's game,* she thought. *Lure me into the chamber, catch me by surprise when I open one of these doors, and knock me out. But then what?* Kara's thoughts darkened. *Then Rigby will leave me in the chamber to rot, or worse.* Kara felt certain that if it came to it Rigby will have no problem taking care of her in a much more permanent way.

Kara involuntarily swallowed as she reached for the first door. The knob turned, and the door swung soundlessly inward, and all the while, Kara readied her will for an explosive attack. But none came.

There was no menace in this room. Wall-to-wall books, a desk with an already burning oil lamp, and a sturdy chair of dark wood. Door after door, chamber after chamber, it was all the same décor, but no signs of Rigby nor of the Scath.

"We hears her!"

"Shhh!"

"Coming!"

"What do we do?"

"Shhh!"

Kara felt her blood begin to boil. She didn't like whatever the Scath were playing. Did it have to do with Rigby? Of course. "Scath," she commanded, "present yourselves. Now."

"Told you, told you!"

"Shhh!"

"We are done now!"

"Quiet!"

Kara waited at the end of the hall and stared down into the somewhat sunken chamber. Slowly, among the stone pillars and the ancient war chests, shadows began to waver. The darkness became a living thing as serpentine shades sluiced into the center of the chamber. The Scath were useful, to be sure, so Kara held her temper . . . to a degree. "What took you so long?" she demanded.

"Busy . . ."

"Yes, loads of activities."

"Nothing wrong, of course."

The lot of them laughed, sounding like trash bags full of dead leaves that were being crushed under giant feet. "Shut it!" Kara ordered. "I'm not playing games with you. What have you been doing? Where is Rigby?"

"The fleshling?"

"The other fleshling?"

"Yes, the only human who's been locked up with you," Kara growled. "Duh. What have you done with him?"

"Done? Done?"

"Nothing at all!"

"We're not to blame!"

"Shhh!"

"What do you mean?" Kara asked. "Not to blame for what?"

"Better tell her."

"We didn't do it."

"It's not our fault."

"Don't tell her!"

"Silence! She is master!"

Kara flexed a little of her will and hurled an invisible, Volkswagen-sized bowling ball through the center of the Scath.

"Eee!"

"Look out!"

"Hurts are coming!"

The shadows fled. Some scattered in all directions, some—not so lucky—were knocked silly and sent cartwheeling away.

Kara strode forward, flicking aside any Scath who were stupid enough to venture near. The torches flickered wildly as she came to the narrow aisle dividing the rear of the chamber's tallest bookshelves. In the dim light, she tripped, taking a clumsy step but catching herself before falling. She spun around, looked down to see what had caused her stumble, and screamed.

Between two of the tall shelves, Rigby lay sprawled. His still-manacled wrists were thrown up over his head as if he had been trying to shield himself from something. His body was twisted such that his legs seemed to have been frozen mid-stride but going the opposite direction of his torso. Worse than all the other details was Rigby's face. His eyes were open, but they were motionless, staring fixedly up at the chamber's ceiling.

Rigby Thames was dead.

THIRTEEN
At Whim

Archer recognized the shadow standing just outside the bars of his cell. He knew the hooded silhouette all too well.

"Surprised to see me, Dreamtreader in a cage? How easily you act your age. Relax, for soon we will all turn the page."

"Bezeal!" Archer growled. He flew to his cell door, thrust his arms through the bars, and tried to grab the new visitor. But the diminutive robed figure had quickly backed out of reach. "It was you? You're the one who accused me of all this . . . garbage?"

From the corner of his eye, Archer saw Master Gabriel step forward.

"No," Archer said, stepping back from the bars, "it's okay. I'm not going to kill him."

Bezeal's face was invisible beneath the dark hood, but his eyes glimmered with cold light like a pair of distant stars. "Little boy, with grown-up pride, be glad your insolence I abide, you couldn't kill me if you tried."

And then, Master Gabriel did step in. "Careful, Bezeal. You know quite well where you are, and there are empty cells yet. What are you doing here? Visiting with the accused is strictly off-limits for a prosecutor."

Bezeal's eyes flashed and, for just the briefest of moments, his Cheshire cat grin appeared. "In the interests of a fair and interesting trial," he said, "I've come with news that will be worth your while. Behold the motion I felt compelled to file." Bezeal reached inside his robe, withdrew a rolled parchment, and passed it through the bars.

Archer opened the scroll. With Master Gabriel hovering over his shoulder, he began to read. Seconds later, Archer looked up. "What does this mean . . . *the trial shall proceed at whim*?"

"Let me see that," Master Gabriel said, grasping the left side of the parchment to get a better look. A moment later, he began to shake his head slowly. "This is craven," he muttered, "even for you, Bezeal."

The hooded figure said nothing in reply, but simply left Archer's cell and waltzed away down the hall.

"What?" Archer asked. "What's craven? What does *at whim* mean?"

"It means, Archer, that Bezeal has taken the initiative. He's collected and documented all his evidence. He can declare the trial whenever he wants. And I imagine it will be very soon."

"I have to have time to prepare my defense," Archer argued. "Bezeal can't do this. Can he?"

"I am afraid he can," Master Gabriel said. "The trial waits only for the prosecutor to collect his evidence. In most cases, that takes quite some time, but Bezeal was all too thorough."

"What about me? What about my defense?"

"That was, of course, Bezeal's plan," Master Gabriel said. "He wants to take you to trial before you are ready. He wants your defense to depend upon Eternal Evidence."

"Eternal Evidence? I don't know what that means."

"It means your life, Archer," Master Gabriel replied. "Everything related to the charges, as you remember them. Eternal Evidence allows the court to review your memories and, unfortunately, your motives."

Archer plopped down to his bunk once more. "Oh," he said. "That might not be so great."

"Archer," Master Gabriel said, "you have convinced me to go to the others . . . to Nick and to Kaylie, but I could still stay to defend you. The trial could be at any moment."

Archer raised his eyebrows. There was a part of him that wanted to take Master Gabriel up on the offer. But the more he thought about it, the more he saw restraining Master Gabriel when Kaylie and Nick needed him . . . that would be utterly selfish.

"No," Archer said. "I need to do this alone."

"In that case, Archer," Master Gabriel said, "anchor first."

"Anchor deep," he replied.

The Master Dreamtreader stepped outside of the cell and slowly slid the door closed. It latched with a very final sounding clank of metal, and Master Gabriel vanished in a swirl of purple, blue, and bright white sparks.

Archer lay back on his bunk. He thought hard about what the Eternal Evidence would reveal. It was disconcerting to think that events of his life—as well as the attitudes of his heart—would be on display for all to see.

"What if I really am guilty?" he whispered, and the question echoed again and again in his mind. After all, there might be moments in time that he'd misremembered, like childhood stories that grew longer and more colorful in the telling over the years. Maybe, in his passion to stop Rigby from harming Kaylie, maybe he'd gone wrong. It was an icy fear.

But then, in that moment, there was another sensation: this one, oddly warming . . . and freeing. *If I'm guilty,* he thought, *then . . . I am. And I deserve whatever sentence the judge sees fit.*

There was really no use in worrying about the past. *What's done is done,* he thought. *I'll just have to defend myself as best I can, and then throw myself on the mercy of the judge.*

He found it peculiar he wasn't really worried about himself, about what would happen to him personally. But he was still worried about his family, his friends, and all who called the Waking World their home. If the judge ruled that Archer was guilty and needed to be put away, that he wouldn't be able to use his Dreamtreading talents to help—that would be hard to take.

Archer prayed that when the time came his anchor would be deep enough.

Dreamtreader Creed, Conceptus 12

There is a hierarchy in the Ethereal. The Masters are superior to Dreamtreaders, much as Man is superior to Boy. Master Gabriel is chief among Masters, but a former Master holds court over all.

Chief Michael the Archelion wields the hammer of justice. If there is reason for dispute, it is Michael to whom you must turn. If warranted, the High Court would hear your case, but know this: Michael's decision is final.

Dreamtreading is a high calling. Only three are chosen at a time out of billions. You bear the responsibility to perform your duties according to the Creeds. You must not succumb to the temptation of abusing your power. And, Dreamtreader, that temptation will come . . . in one form or another. You will be tempted to misuse your power, perhaps for your own gain or even for a noble intention that strays far off course. But you must not give in. You must not betray your calling.

For if you do, Michael's hammer will be waiting.

FOURTEEN
SOMETHING SCARY

KARA COULDN'T STOP STARING AT RIGBY'S BODY. SHE FELT a twinge of guilt, shed a tear of sorrow, and then her eyes flickered with angry red lightning. "Scath!" she raged. "What did you do?"

She was answered by frantic rustling, hisses, and whispers.

"Scath, I am the master of the Shadow Key!" she cried out, the words flash-simmering like water thrown on hot coals. "I am *your* master! I call you to account for this. I call you to come to me and answer for yourselves. And, so help me, if your answer is displeasing, I will use the Shadow Key to end you all!"

"Nooooo!" came a myriad of cries.

"Mercy upon us!"

"It wasn't our fault!"

"He asked us!"

"He invited us!"

"Told us it was a game!"

Kara stepped back over Rigby and confronted a cauldron of suddenly obsequious Scath. "Speak!" she demanded. "Quickly! Or you'll regret the moment you were formed!"

In a storm of mewling, apologetic rasps, shouts, and interruptions, Kara pieced together the story. Rigby had tricked the Scath into killing him. He'd become despondent over his failures and his capture at Kara's hands. He'd come so close to ruling as the next Nightmare Lord only to have it snatched away at the last moment. But because he was cobalt-shackled, he couldn't use his will to end his own life, so he engaged the Scath in what he had called a game.

This was the part that made the fine hair on Kara's arms stand on end. He'd called the game: Something Scary. The rules were simple: it had been Rigby versus the Scath. Rigby began by asking, "Do you want to see something really scary?" He turned his back on the Scath, and then spun around with the most horrific facial expressions he could manage.

When it was the Scath's turn, they would do the same: "Does fleshling want to see something really scary?" The Scath would then whirl and writhe until, at last, becoming some fearsome sight, each more terrifying than the one that came before. According to the Scath's rambling recollection, they had played five rounds, but on the sixth round, the Scath had revealed what they called "their inner black."

"Did Rigby know about your inner black?" Kara demanded.

"Don't know."

"Rigby studied us."

"Learned from the Lurker, maybe."

"Don't show me!" Kara ordered. "Explain to me. What is this inner black?"

The Scath shuffled nervously. "Inner black is what made us."

"Nightmare flesh."

"Pure, rotten evil."

"Mask of death."

Kara swallowed again. The Scath, she reminded herself gravely, still had their secrets. From their origins as Sages in the Garnet Province Libraries to their corruption by an ancient Nightmare Lord to their current subjugation under the possessor of the Shadow Key, the Scath were full of mysteries. Dangerous mysteries.

And, by Rigby's trickery, the Scath had literally frightened Rigby to death.

She looked down on him and felt pity. Yes, the Scath had killed him, but it was no different from cowardly suicide. "Poor Rigby," she whispered. "I thought you were made of stronger stuff than this."

Her eyes blazing once more, she rounded on the Scath and unleashed a violent torrent of will. Like invisible hands made of hurricane winds, Kara corralled the Scath, tossed them headlong into one of the chamber's many rooms, and slammed the door shut. Kara willed the entire room to harden into cobalt and found herself silently exulting at the Scath's screams of agony echoing through the metal.

Kara turned, took a final look at Rigby, and marched all the way out of the Karakurian Chamber. She collapsed onto her throne seat, but she did not weep. Instead, she thought about where current events had left her. She no longer had Rigby as a resource, nor as a source of entertainment. It meant there were more things to figure out on her own, but that wasn't a problem. After all, she'd studied Doctor Scoville's first papers and experiments with lucid dreaming. She'd learned the techniques and even developed more effective methods.

Doctor Scoville.

Kara felt a chill at his name. Doc Scoville or, as he was known in the Dream, the Lurker, was not an opponent to be taken lightly. And Rigby had said that Doc Scoville had completed even more research. *Things I know nothing about,* Kara thought dismally. *He might know things that could interfere.*

And if Doc Scoville found out his cherished nephew had died while imprisoned by Kara, well . . . he wasn't likely to become an ally then, was he? *No,* Kara reasoned with a sad laugh, *no, he'd probably storm Dream Inc. Tower.* Even if he couldn't defeat Kara in her stronghold, he'd likely batter himself to death in the attempt.

No, Doc Scoville could not learn of Rigby's death. And, just like that, all the pieces fell into place for Kara. She suddenly knew, step-by-crafty-step, what she needed to do to pull this off. She'd begin immediately.

"Scath!" Kara flexed her will to open the cobalt-encased room within the Karakurian Chamber. "Come to me!"

And this time, the Scath were more than punctual. They raced from the Karakurian Chamber as if pursued by ghosts even more frightening than themselves.

"What does master want?"

"Thank you, kind master, for releasing us."

"Hurt room hurts us."

"We are sorry for dead fleshling."

"None of that," Kara commanded. "Listen to me. I want you to take Rigby's body. Go beneath the Veil and hide his body someplace where no one will ever find it." The thought struck her pointedly: how quickly a living person—a *he*—could become inanimate matter and be called an *it*.

"We obeys!"

"Hide the fleshling good!"

Kara stood up from her throne and stared down at the Scath. "You listen to me: you hide his body well. Mess this up, and I won't kill you. I'll lock you in a cobalt prison . . . for eternity."

Doc Scoville stood in the kitchen of his home and sipped on a steaming cup of coffee. *It's a beautiful afternoon,* he thought, staring out through the window above the sink. *Much warmer in January than it ought to be.* The snow had mostly melted away. "What's this?" he muttered, slowly setting his coffee cup down on the counter. He craned his neck a bit and smiled. A happy little group of bright red cardinals were playing in the backyard evergreens. They flittered from limb to limb, resting on a swaying branch for only a moment before leaping to a new perch.

Absolutely stunning day, he thought, lifting the almond-flavored coffee to his lips once more. The sun lit the yard in golden hues and caught on the already-budding branches of the ornamental cherry trees. It were as if spring had broken through the gate of winter to capture this day.

It was, Doc Scoville thought, a welcome invasion. He took his coffee to the kitchen table and sat down to ponder important decisions to come. After all, it was clearly a day for a walk.

He put down his coffee cup and began to scroll mentally through the many exotic pets he had in the basement zoo. Which one would he take on the walk?

Then, Doc Scoville heard something entirely unexpected. The front door to the house opened. There were footsteps in the foyer.

Strange, Doc Scoville thought. *I wasn't expecting a visitor today.*

He started to stand, but then plopped into his seat at the sight of a young man coming around the corner into the dining room.

"Rigby?" Doc Scoville whispered. "Is that you?"

Rigby smiled and scratched at one of his long sideburns. "Of course it's me, Uncle," he said. "It's a beautiful day outside. Care for a walk?"

FIFTEEN
OPENING STATEMENTS

"ALL RISE!" THE BAILIFF-WARRIOR'S VOICE WAS A CLARION call to the courtroom. At once, deep, demanding, sacred and solemn—it was a voice no one would ever dream of defying. "The most honorable High Chief Justice, Michael the Archelion, is presiding!"

Archer bounced to his feet, and so powerful was the moment he had to fight the urge to salute.

The rest of the cavernous courtroom, which had been abuzz with conversation, went absolutely still and silent. It seemed somehow impossible: the courtroom was absolutely enormous. Intricately carved and stained wood paneling divided at regular intervals by tall columns of marble—the interior looked worthy of a palace . . . or a museum. The four chandeliers that hung from the vaulted ceiling high above—each one seven feet in diameter and lit with a hundred candles—flared suddenly.

"Be ye warned," the bailiff-warrior continued. "Leave all deceit behind, and darken not this hallowed court with thy vain ambitions, lest . . . ye . . . die."

Archer swallowed. *No lies. Check.*

A pair of magnificent fourteen-foot-high doors stood on either side of the magnificently carved, throne-like judge's bench. Archer wasn't sure which pair of doors to watch, but the doors to the left opened suddenly, and in strode a being very similar to Master Gabriel, only greater in every way imaginable.

The judge, Michael the Archelion, stood more than half as tall as the doors, was broad shouldered, and clad in Incandescent Armor, but the markings and engravings upon the plates seemed somewhat different from Gabriel's. Or maybe the markings were just more numerous upon the judge's armor. Archer wasn't sure, but either way, the designs gave Justice Michael undeniable authority.

The capes didn't hurt either. The judge wore a black cape, a silver cape, a gray cape, and an indigo blue cape, and they were somehow layered and intertwined so that when he ascended a hidden stair to the judge's bench, a hypnotic ripple of color followed behind him.

Unlike Master Gabriel, the chief justice was clean shaven, but his jaw was square and his expression, grave and determined underneath a full head of long, dark hair layered with dignified ribbons of silver. A single cord of black and silver metal encircled his high and regal forehead conveying an air of royalty. Michael's brow was heavy, and both the size and ferocity of his eyes reminded Archer of a bald eagle's glare.

"Be seated!" the bailiff-warrior commanded.

Archer sat, and for the first time was collected enough to notice anybody else in the courtroom. He noted the seating galleries on either side of the courtroom were now full, populated by scores of armor-clad warriors, both male and female. They sat in unison with such precision that Archer sighed. *So much for a jury of my peers,* he thought.

Even without them, the intimidation factor, on a scale of 1–10, was a 13.5. Archer had done class projects where he'd had to speak in front of the whole class. Once, he'd even spoken to an auditorium full of adults for a school fund-raiser. But he'd never spoken on a stage like this one. And the stakes had never been higher.

The only consolation, if there were any, was that Bezeal didn't seem too comfortable, either. The diminutive merchant, now Archer's chief accuser, sat at a desk across the center aisle from Archer's desk that was far too big for him. His feet dangled comically beneath the chair.

It was the very first time Archer had ever noticed Bezeal's feet.

They were predictably strange, just like the rest of Bezeal. He wore black boots, but they were squat things, tapering from the shin to a blockish heel. The strangest bit was the boots had no toes. There was the back heel but that extended forward into a kind of angular wedge. How much odder could he get?

The bailiff-warrior spoke once more. "The court will now hear the capital case of *Dreamtreader Archer Keaton vs. Humanity.*"

The judge looked at a scroll in front of him, and then leaned forward to speak; "Am I to understand, Dreamtreader Keaton, that you will have no counsel other than yourself?"

"Yes, your majesty," Archer mumbled.

Justice Michael blinked. "I am no king," he said. "*Judge, Justice, your honor,* or even a simple *sir* will do here, Archer."

"Yes, your maj—er . . . sir."

"Are you certain you want to do this alone?" the judge asked.

Want to? Archer thought. *Well, no, I don't want to, but what choice do I have?*

"Judge, I will be my only counsel—"

Poof! In a cloud of purple smoke and blue sparks, Razz appeared. She was wearing a slate gray pantsuit, a black tie, and dark heels. She carried a leather briefcase that was just her size and plopped down to the desktop next to Archer's left hand.

"I apologize for my lateness, your high judgeship," she said, toning down the squeak of her voice a little. "As I'm sure you know, things are not going well with the Waking World down there."

"Razz," Archer hiss-whispered, "what are you doing here?"

"Gabriel sent me," she said. "I'm your co-counsel."

SIXTEEN
Glass House Mountain

Nick Bushman stepped onto his porch overlooking the Glass House Mountains and the surrounding Queensland landscape. He sipped a tall, frosty glass of iced tea and sighed. He couldn't remember a better day in his life. From the moment he awoke to the playful yips of the distant coyotes, everything just felt right.

Some sixty miles north of Brisbane, the Glass House Mountain Township offered Nick a sprawling view of the verdant, almost entirely flat coastal plain. *Almost* because eleven mountains rose up abruptly from the otherwise level vista. The highest, the two peaks called Mount Beerwah, wore a hula hoop of mist, but otherwise there wasn't a cloud to be seen. Just cobalt blue as far as the eye could see.

Nick noticed a little trail of dust kicked up to the east. "Ah, there he is," he muttered. Then, he raised his voice a bit more and called, "Oliver! Lunch in an hour!"

"Thanks, heaps!" Nick's mercurial little brother yelled back. He kicked the brakes on his bike and stirred up a fresh whorl of dirt.

"Don't be late, ya little ankle biter!" Nick hollered.

A hand rose in the midst of the dust cloud and gave a mighty thumbs up.

Nick laughed. "Best day ever," he muttered, turning from the view and heading inside. The telly was on Nick's favorite news station. He paused to turn up the volume so he could hear the headlines while he worked in the kitchen.

Oliver liked roast beef piled high with Muenster cheese and extra tomato, so Nick went to work, slicing a bright red heirloom tomato that was bigger than his fist. "Ahh!" he said, breathing in through his nose. "Nothing better than fresh, sliced tomato, fair Dinkum. And these little beauties are the best I've seen."

"At just .02 percent, unemployment is at its lowest in Australia's history," the anchor on the television reported from the other room. "Prime Minister Davids claims it's the renewed spirit of the Australian people—"

"Bonzer!" Nick exclaimed. He loved listening to the news shows these days. There was nothing but good news. The economy was thriving. The weather was dandy. Murder and violent crime were nearly unheard of anymore. Nick was grinning as he cut a few more slices of tomato and tossed them on his sandwich. Life was good.

"G'day," came a voice from behind. "I hope you have enough for three."

Knife in his right hand and reaching for one of his boomerangs with his left, Nick spun around. He dropped them and stared.

There was a very tall, older gentleman in his kitchen. Nick wasn't used to looking up to make eye contact, but he did for this strange fellow. The man wore a bizarre combination of outback clothing (bush hat, oilskin vest, and cargo shorts) and some sort of medieval reenactment costumery (boots laced to the calf, a sturdy leather sheath, and a very realistic looking broadsword).

And sunglasses. Dark sunglasses with black frames. With his mane of gray hair and a gray beard both full and long, he looked like a wizard who moonlighted as a park ranger.

Feeling no menace from the stranger, Nick chuckled and said, "You lost, mate?"

"No," the stranger replied. "But you are. Fearfully and hopelessly lost in a fairyland that really is far too good to be true."

"Well, color me gobsmacked," Nick said. "You delivered those lines, fair Dinkum. You an actor? C'mon, who put you up to this? Was it Charlie Grubbs? Bet it was."

The front screen door banged open and closed. Nick's brother, Oliver, whipped into the kitchen, skidded to an abrupt stop, and asked, "Um . . . why is Merlin in our kitchen?"

"He was just leaving," Nick said, trying to take the stranger's arm.

The man shrugged loose. His dark eyes smoldered. "Unhand me, Nick Bushman," he demanded. "I am no derelict, nor am I some peddler selling buttons at the door. As you should know, I am Master Gabriel, Chief Dreamtreader and your commanding officer."

"Whoa!" Oliver gasped out.

Nick blinked. "I don't know how you know my name, but I think this has gone far enough."

"Unfortunately," Master Gabriel replied, "not nearly far enough."

"C'mon, mate, just leave. You're scarin' me kid brother."

"Oliver is not afraid," Master Gabriel quipped. "He has the uncommonly good sense to think I am cool. But you, on the other hand, are the one battling fear. Now, gird yourself, and prepare for the news I bear you."

"*Gird myself*?" Nick echoed quizzically. "What does that even mean?"

Master Gabriel opened his mouth, shut it, and frowned. "I do not know the correct expression for your generation—wait, yes, something I heard Archer say once. It means *man up* so you can endure the news I bring."

Nick turned his chin up. "All right. Spit it out and go."

Master Gabriel adjusted his sunglasses and replied, "Good and bad. Which will you take first?"

Nick swallowed. "Bad news first, I guess."

"Very well," Master Gabriel said. "The bad news is that this—" he lifted both arms and made a sweeping gesture, "—is a fantasy. It may look, smell, and feel real, but it is an illusion."

"What's the good news?" Oliver asked.

"Yeah, let's get this over with," Nick muttered, rolling his eyes.

"It is clear to me that you do not take this seriously," Master Gabriel replied. "Given the circumstances, I suppose you must be forgiven for that. The good news, then, is that I have come to open your eyes, to show you the world as it actually is. Nick, I am most heartily sorry for what I am about to do."

SEVENTEEN
THE CASE AGAINST

ARCHER GLANCED UP AT CHIEF JUSTICE MICHAEL THE Archelion and smiled nervously. Then, he glared at Razz. "Wh—what are you doing here?"

Razz frowned. "I already explained," she said. "The Waking World is hanging in the balance, so Master Gabriel sent me to help. Sorry I'm late."

"We are all well aware of humanity's plight, Dream creature," the judge said, a bemused tone in his voice. "But I am curious as to why you believe you are late to an event that you've not been invited to join."

Somehow, Archer knew that beneath the fur Razz's cheeks were reddening like mad. Seemingly undaunted, Razz gave a little bow and said, "Actually, your high justice-ness, I am Archer's co-counsel. Or co-defender, if you prefer. Co-protector? No? Co-keep-Archer-out-of-jail-ish, uh, person . . ."

The judge's stern glare closed Razz's mouth, and he turned to Archer. "Dreamtreader Keaton, do you wish Miss Moonsonnet to assist your defense?"

"He knows my name," Razz whispered under her breath. "I'm a rock star."

Oh, brother, Archer thought. And though he thought it was likely a mistake, Archer was so happy not to be in this magnificent courtroom alone that he said, "Yes, your honor, um . . . Razz will help represent me."

Sinusy snickers came from across the aisle. Archer glared at Bezeal, who seemed to think Razz's assistance was quite amusing.

"And, Bezeal," the judge barked, causing the merchant's Cheshire grin to disappear, "it has been some time since we've seen your hooded countenance in this court, though there has been no shortage of your associate prosecutors. This case must be of particular interest for you to come yourself."

If Bezeal had looked uncomfortable before, Archer thought he looked positively beside himself now. He squirmed in his seat, and his glowing eyes shrank to pinpricks. "Your honor," he squawked, "the Dream was my world, my livelihood, and my home. Until the Dreamtreaders came there to search, meddle, and roam. I came to seek justice beneath this court's dome."

The judge tented his fingers, and his armor flashed brilliant light. "You may have a case," he said, "but let's get one thing straight, Bezeal. No rhymes."

"But—"

"Enough!" the chief justice thundered. "You will not make a mockery of my court with your inane singsong banter. Have I made myself clear?"

Bezeal's eyes flashed. "All too clear," he said, "and I fear—"

"Bezeal," the judge warned, "one more rhyme from you, and I'll hold you in contempt of court!"

Bezeal blinked. "But . . . sir—"

Chief Justice Michael leaned forward. "How do ten days cleaning Gloriana Stables sound to you? I understand the unicorns have been particularly well fed of late."

Archer suppressed the laughter he felt bubbling up inside and silently enjoyed watching Bezeal squirm.

"That will not be necessary, your honor," Bezeal muttered.

"Good," the judge said. "Now, do you as prosecutor have an opening statement?"

Bezeal slid off of the chair and waddled out into the open well of the court, a span that stretched between the two galleries. "Yes," Bezeal said, "if it pleases the court, your honor, the prosecution will speak."

"Much better," the judge said. "Go on."

Bezeal strolled along the rail that enclosed the right side gallery. "A perfect balance," he said to the soldiers seated there. "The Dream and the Waking World coexisted in a peaceful balance for many ages, until now. I intend to prove that a Dreamtreader, one sworn to protect that balance, did in fact cause its destruction; that this Dreamtreader, Archer Keaton, through his action and inaction did cause the Rift. I will show the court Archer's willful disobedience for the commands of his superiors. I will show Archer's careless use of excessive power, a traitorous act that led to the deaths of Dreamtreaders Duncan and Mesmeera."

The galleries erupted in gasps and hurried comments.

"Objection!" Razz shouted, spinning in the air above Archer's head and slapping her two tails together.

"It is an opening statement," hissed Bezeal. "You cannot object."

"It is unusual," the judge corrected, "but legal. To what do you object, Ms. Moonsonnet?"

Razz gave a half bow. "I object because Bezeal called Archer a traitor. That's totally not true."

Archer reached up and yanked Razz's tail. "C'mere!" he said. "That's not helping."

"Ms. Moonsonnet," the judge said, "the prosecution has a right to state the nature of the crime he intends to prove. Your objection is overruled."

"Fiddlesticks," Razz mumbled. Archer quickly covered her mouth with his hand.

"I repeat," Bezeal went on, "that Archer Keaton misused his Dreamtreader powers, betraying the other Dreamtreaders to their deaths. Without the considerable experience of Dreamtreaders Duncan and Mesmeera, the Rift became all but inevitable. Finally, I will prove that Archer, in the face of the Rift, took out his anger by plotting to murder a defenseless human being."

Razz squirmed free. "Objection!" she shouted. The judge turned her way. "Archer didn't kill that old Doc Scoville!"

"Objection overruled," the judge replied curtly. "The prosecutor asserts only that Archer plotted to murder."

"Your honor," Bezeal said, "may I continue?"

"Go on."

"Esteemed court, I will prove that Archer Keaton, a once promising Dreamtreading talent, has been derelict in his duties. From his earliest conflicts with the Nightmare Lord to his mishandling of the Shadow Key even to his most recent negligence leading to the Rift, Archer Keaton has failed . . . failed us all. He is guilty of all these charges. And I will show why he should be removed from Dreamtreading permanently and locked away for good."

EIGHTEEN
Behind the Harlequin Veil

Rigby became painfully aware of a throbbing in his head. He couldn't see, he couldn't hear, and he couldn't feel anything in his arms and legs, but oh could he feel the pounding in his mind. It was, in fact, the first thing he became conscious of after a sea of darkness had taken him away. The pulsing, the pressurized strokes of pain, were excruciating, but they were there. And feeling something, *anything* seemed like a good thing to Rigby. *Thump, thump, thump*—the beat went on.

Slowly, he noticed a sensation of cold, a crawling chill suggesting that he did indeed have more than just a head and a skull. There actually was a body attached, and the chill prickled and spread until Rigby felt uncomfortable and began to tremble violently.

A ringing pierced the silence and grew to such an explosive shrill it dwarfed even the headache's crushing agony. He felt something else now too: burning vapors in his throat, and he was suddenly aware that he was screaming. Then, all at once, he was awake, and all his memories were restored.

Rigby found himself on his knees. He'd wrapped his arms around a prong of stone and listened to his own breathing for a few seconds. The Scath had done it, he realized. They had managed to pull off their part of the plan. They'd put him into an unconscious state, dropping his vitals so low that he had appeared to be quite dead. Rigby shivered at the memory. The Scath had triggered the death-like trance by breathing upon him, and it was quite possibly the most terrifying experience he'd ever endured.

Wispy vapors had emerged from their gaping, open-wound-like mouths. Thin, sinewy strands of gray, the vapors had snaked through the air and into Rigby's breath. He had fought every bodily urge to deny them, but drew them into his mouth, throat, and lungs, sucking deeply at the contaminated air. It had felt like inhaling spiderwebs. Just before everything went dark, Rigby had seen things. Blood, darkness, eyes, rot, teeth, claws—a concentrated mix of all the nightmares Rigby had ever had—and he shook the memory away.

"Finally, the fleshling recovers!"

"We thought you might stay dead."

"Now, hold still."

Rigby went as rigid as the stone he clutched. The Scath were all around him, and there was something holding his arms in place. *The cobalt shackles,* he remembered with dread. He could feel the cold metal on his wrists. "What . . . are you doing?" he demanded of the Scath.

They replied with sniggering laughter. Rigby saw one of the larger Scath on the other side of the stone. This one held something that looked like some kind of axe or hammer. The Scath reared back as if readying to swing the weapon.

"No! Don't!" Rigby screamed, but the Scath paid no heed to the command. The creature swung the heavy weapon around and struck with such an earsplitting *ker-rack* that Rigby's headache began again with renewed strength.

But Rigby's arms dropped away from the stone. The Scath had not maimed him, after all. They had freed him from the cobalt shackles. Rigby felt his will coursing through him as he stood.

Beyond the ring of Scath in all directions was a crater-pocked wasteland. "I knew it," he whispered. "I knew she couldn't pull off the Harlequin Veil."

All of the sudden, the weight of all he observed hit home. Rigby swallowed back the hot bile surging up in the back of his throat.

Where he was exactly, he could not tell. Much like a desert or open sea, everything around him looked the same. Among the craters and scarred-gray terrain, blackened trees leaned, some still burning. Here and there, the thin, barely recognizable skeletons of structures stood. "And this," Rigby muttered. "This is what's become of the world?"

"We've done as you asked," the Scath hissed.

"You are free."

"Now, you must free us!"

Rigby flexed the muscle in his neck and cracked the knuckles of both fists. "I will keep my promise," he told the Scath. "Now return to your master—your temporary master—and I will come for you."

"Will come?" the Scath chorused.

"We wants now!"

"Be patient," Rigby commanded. "Kara is too well protected in that fortress of hers. I'm going to need help."

"We cannot help."

"Not anymore."

"That's okay," Rigby replied. "I am going to visit my uncle."

The Scath departed, and Rigby rubbed his wrists. They were cold and tingly, but the cobalt shackles were gone. His will churned as if impatient to be put to use, and Rigby wasn't going to deny it much longer.

"So where am I exactly?" he muttered aloud. Instinctively, his hand flew to his jeans pocket, but, as he suspected, his personal cell phone was long gone. And that wasn't too much of an issue, not now that the cobalt shackles were gone. Rigby held out his hand, flexed his will, and called up a brand-new cell phone. As it powered up, Rigby wondered if the Rift had shorted out the more delicate electronics systems of the world. He thought it likely that most of the cell towers had probably been fried. But the moment his phone's operating system booted up, Rigby saw it had a full five bars. It was, he thought, a little odd, especially being out in this desolate wasteland like he was, but he was grateful for the signal.

He called up his maps app and discovered quickly he was in Cunningham Falls State Park in Thurmont, Maryland. Quite a hike from Kara's Baltimore fortress, but not terribly far from home, he thought. Once again, the Scath had been thorough.

Rigby jogged down the rocky incline, slid, and almost fell, but, with a thought, he gave himself a pair of tough-terrain hiking boots and found surer footing. Then using his will to maneuver like a deer born to the forest, he raced through the trees and brambles. Leaping, dodging, ducking, and spinning, he darted through the pine trunks and boughs. A strange smell stopped him in mid-stride.

It was the scent of something burned . . . or perhaps, still burning. But it wasn't the rich outdoorsy smell from a fireplace or a wood stove. This smoke reeked of acrid chemicals and . . . something else, something pungent. It was altogether wrong, whatever it was. Rigby charged on, noting the darkening of the trees. Their needled foliage thinned until there was nothing but blackened branches and scorched trunks.

It was a chilling vista. Nearly a third of the forest had been razed. Rigby leaped over the still burning park gate and raced ahead, hoping for a change. The scenery only grew worse.

He found himself in a rural neighborhood. Or, at least, it had been once. Farms, homes, and buildings were shattered, and debris sat strewn about as if a massive tornado had plowed through the area. People wandered aimlessly about the wreckage. Some were out in the street, but most were wandering through the wreckage of their homes. There were even a few people sitting in the driver's seats of cars so damaged they would likely never run again.

As Rigby made his way through the wreckage, he called out to people he passed, "Sir, are you okay?"

No reply.

"Miss, you should get out of the car. It doesn't look safe."

Not even so much as a glance in Rigby's direction.

People were moving about in the oddest way. They gestured frequently, and their mouths were moving, as if they were acting out some silent play.

A dull ringing echoed across the area. It grew in intensity and re-triggered the splitting headache Rigby had before. He fell to his knees and clutched his head. The oncoming flood of sensation was too much. He couldn't bear it. He shut his eyes and fell over on his side. It was tearing at his mind . . . impossible to endure much more—

Gone. It was all gone. Feeling a surge of well-being, Rigby opened his eyes. At first, he was surprised. He gasped as he clambered back to his feet. Blinking against the strong sunlight, Rigby wasn't sure why he felt so surprised. He was standing in the middle of a beautiful rural neighborhood. The sky was bright blue, and kids were out, running around or playing with pets.

Wait, Rigby thought, *shouldn't I be getting home? I'm supposed to be home now. I'm supposed to be home with Uncle Scovy.*

He started walking. He wasn't sure how he knew, but he knew it was the way home. In a few blocks, he'd come to a bus stop. He'd need to take the bus to get back to Gatlinburg. Didn't he have a load of homework to finish up before tomorrow? He was pretty sure he did. He picked up the pace a little, but paused as a woman backed her car out of a driveway to Rigby's left.

She smiled at him and waved politely. Rigby didn't wave back. He stared. An image of this woman and this car flickered in and out of Rigby's mind. He gasped. One second, the car had been a burned-out husk, and the woman had blood streaming down her forehead. The next, she was perfectly normal.

Rigby turned in a slow circle and watched with sickening fascination as the entire neighborhood flickered in and out of two different realities. Suddenly, as if he'd been nearly unconscious only to walk through a refreshing mist of cool water, Rigby came to his senses.

"Well, what do you know?" Rigby whispered. "Kara actually did it. The 'arlequin Veil works." He stared at the real-as-life beauty all around him and shook his head. He'd only been awake for a few hours, and yet already the Veil had taken hold. How had Kara gotten the Veil to be so widespread and so . . . immediate?

Rigby scanned the treetops and the sky and muttered, "It's not like she 'as a bunch of broadcast towers placed all over the world, right?"

He rolled his eyes at his own momentary stupidity. "Of course," he muttered, sliding his cell phone out of his pocket and staring at it in his palm. "Very clever, Kara."

NINETEEN

ETERNAL EVIDENCE

HIGH CHIEF JUSTICE MICHAEL THE ARCHELION LEANED forward from his judge's bench and turned his eagle glare to Archer. "Dreamtreader Keaton," he said, "do you wish to make an opening statement?"

"Go, Archer, go!" Razz whispered.

Archer hesitated in his seat for a few moments. He felt as if three hundred spotlights had just been turned on him. "Um, yes, your honor," he said, while thinking, *Here goes nothing.*

The judge nodded. "Proceed."

Archer stood and wandered around the defense table to face the gallery on the left. He'd seen a few courtroom drama movies. He'd even visited a courtroom for a civics class field trip. He thought he knew what to say, but that had been a while ago.

"Ladies and gentlemen of the jury," he said, "esteemed high judge, my accuser has leveled charges against me . . . serious charges. I do not take these lightly, and to be honest, I have to admit the charges are . . . *mostly* true."

The courtroom erupted in chatter. For about five whole seconds.

The judge raised his right arm, and a massive steel gavel appeared in his hand. When he slammed the hammer down to his desktop, there was a flash of dangerous light, followed a split-heartbeat later by the sound of thunder. Actual thunder. It was the kind off sudden thunderclap that rattles the windowpanes, causes the foundation of the house to shake, and generally scares the bejeebers out of anyone nearby.

It certainly scared Archer. Involuntarily, he jumped and ducked at the same time. Abruptly, the courtroom chatter ceased. Archer swallowed and glanced over to Bezeal, whose pinprick eyes had grown to the size of half-dollars.

"I will have order in this court," the judge said quietly. And no one argued nor dared to speak. "You may continue, Dreamtreader Keaton."

When Archer spoke, his words at first came out in some sort of half-strangled, gravelly chicken-squawk. "While the charges are—" He cleared his throat. "While the charges are somewhat true, the motives—suggested by my accuser—are absolutely false. I intend to prove that as a Dreamtreader in the midst of the most difficult circumstances imaginable, I did my job. In fact, I did my job the best way I could, and I intend to prove that each time something tragic happened, it was caused by an opponent seeking to cause the evil that occurred. When we look at the evidence, you will see I am not innocent. I made mistakes. But after you see my motives and my actions, my enemies in action, and the destruction they caused . . . I am content to accept whatever verdict seems right to you as well as whatever sentence seems fair."

Archer took his seat. Silence reigned.

"Prosecution," the judge said, "call your first witness."

"Your honor," Bezeal began. "My first witness comes from the past. She entered the courtroom moments ago so fast. She is—"

The thunder-gavel fell once more, and this time Bezeal jumped.

"I warned you about that singsong, rhyming nonsense," the judge growled. "It gives me a headache. Bailiff, if the prosecution rhymes again—even one time—I want you to take him into custody for contempt of court. And then I'd like you to find the coldest, dankest cell and lock him away."

The bailiff seemed extraordinarily happy with that command. "Yes, your honor," he said, cracking his knuckles. "I will most certainly see to that."

Bezeal's eyes shrank once more to a pair of pale dots, and he made an exaggerated bow. "With all due *respect*, your honor," he said, putting a strange emphasis on the word. "I do my best thinking in rhyme. To take that from me is . . . well . . . a rather unfair handicap."

The judge lifted his gavel. Archer winced, expecting a blast. But it didn't come. Instead, the judge stayed the hammer in his hand and said quite tersely, "That we have allowed you into this court at all, Bezeal, is a courtesy greater than any but you and I can know. Do not fool yourself into thinking you might gain additional courtesies. You will not find them here."

At this point, Archer was feeling pretty good about the way things were going. Chief Justice Michael did not seem to be really on anyone's side, but he was definitely not extending Bezeal any favors.

"My first witness, then," Bezeal said, "shall be Archer's Dream companion, Razz."

"Objection!" Razz shouted.

Archer gave himself a face-palm.

"What now, Ms. Moonsonnet?" the judge asked.

"I object because I am co-counsel. How can I be expected to be a witness against my client?"

The judge's granite expression didn't soften in the least. "Ms. Moonsonnet, we have no exceptions for truth. If your testimony will shed light on your client's innocence or guilt, we will hear it. Now, take the stand."

Razz frowned. She looked at Archer for guidance.

"Just tell the truth," Archer said.

Razz nodded and whooshed to the stand. She hovered a moment over the seat, decided against it, and sat instead on the rail.

"Ms. Moonsonnet," Bezeal said snidely. "Would you please tell the court what Archer whispered to you just now."

"I'd rather not," Razz mumbled. "It was private."

"What was that?" Bezeal asked. "So you're saying you won't share with the court? Could it be that Archer was feeding you things to say?"

Muttering rippled around the court.

"Um, no," Razz replied, "Archer just ordered me to tell the truth."

Bezeal stopped in midstride. "Oh."

The muttering turned to giggling.

"Very well," Bezeal said. "Ms. Moonsonnet, I'd like you to recall a little trip you and Archer made to Archaia."

This, thought Archer, *isn't good.*

"Could you state for the court what you and Archer were doing in that part of the Dream Realm?"

"Stitching up breaches," Razz replied. "The usual Dreamtreader stuff."

"Just the usual," Bezeal repeated. "But there was a point where Archer insisted on doing something else, wasn't there?"

Razz didn't answer right away.

"Wasn't there?"

Razz finally muttered, "Yes."

"And what was that?" Bezeal asked. "What caused you to abandon Archer for the rest of that evening?"

"It was a good idea," Razz muttered. "I was just frightened."

"What was it?" Bezeal demanded. "Tell the court what Archer planned to do."

Razz sighed. "Archer wanted to travel to the Lurker's lair to look for an old relic."

"And why did he do that?"

Razz squinted at Bezeal. "Uh . . . because you told him to."

The crowds exploded in discussions, mutterings, grumblings, and even a few shouts. The thunder-gavel sounded. Silence resumed. Undaunted, Bezeal said, "Yes, Archer and I made a deal, so he went in search of this relic. Why didn't you join him?"

Here it comes, Archer thought.

Razz frowned. "Because Master Gabriel commanded Archer not to meddle with the Lurker."

Bezeal's Cheshire grin reappeared. "Did Archer go see the Lurker? Did he defy his Dreamtreading commander?"

"Yes."

"Ladies and gentlemen of the jury," Bezeal said, the lights in the courtroom dimming as he spoke. "I submit to you that Archer impudently turned from his Dreamtreading path. He rebelled. He forsook Master Gabriel's command and defied him. Let us see the Eternal Evidence."

Archer felt his skin begin to crawl, especially on his scalp. It felt like a hundred tiny electric ants were parading upon his head. The lights went out altogether, and a strange, white cylinder appeared in the air between the two galleries. Suddenly, the cylinder came to life with moving pictures—not film, but memory. Archer was suddenly looking at himself. He was standing on his Dream surfboard on the eastern border of Archaia, and Razz was perched on his shoulder.

But he wasn't just watching. That prickling sensation on his scalp intensified and continued for the duration. And, though he was still seated at his table in the courtroom, he could feel the motions of the memory as it played out. The movements felt dreamy and kind of suppressed, more like involuntary flinches than regular motion. It was a most peculiar sensation, and Archer thought it could have been fun . . . if it weren't for the fact that he was on trial for his life. With trepidation, he watched as the scene unfolded.

The on-screen Archer seemed to stare, his eyes fixed on some point to the west. But he and Razz were talking, the conversation growing more and more animated as it went on.

"What are we waiting for?" Razz squeaked. "Let's go get that puzzle relic thing!"

"What about the Lurker?" Archer asked.

"We'll deal with him if we have to, right? You have plenty left in the tank, don't you, Archer?"

"Yeah, sure," he said. "But there is one more thing."

"Uh-oh."

"Gabriel told me not to go, not to get the relic."

"What? Why?" Razz drifted to the stump and curled up.

"He wouldn't tell me," Archer said. "But I think he's worried about me getting hurt."

"I guess that settles it then," Razz said.

"You don't want to go now?"

"Are you crazy?" Razz yelled. "No one, I mean no one, defies Master Gabriel."

Archer sighed. He'd been so hopeful Razz would travel with him. "I have to do it," Archer said. "I have to try. The Nightmare Lord has been going after my friends, my family, even Kaylie. I've got to stop him."

"Yes," Razz said, "we do need to stop him, but not by going against Master Gabriel."

"I'm going," Archer said quietly.

Razz frowned, leaped into the air, and flittered in Archer's face. "Well, you can count me out then. I won't cross Master Gabriel. Not now. Not ever."

The last visual to be displayed for the whole court to see was Archer's catching an Intrusion wave right to the edge into Archaia. After discarding the board, Archer crossed the border, stepping defiantly onto the blood-red soil of that desolate country. The screen went blank, the darkness feeling like a door slamming shut.

A cell door.

TWENTY
CHEAP WALLPAPER

KAYLIE STOOD IN HER BEDROOM DOORWAY AND FELT A chill. It was actually quite a mild day for January, so it wasn't from the weather. She was dressed warmly; she had no other symptoms of cold or flu; and she'd eaten a nice warm breakfast. Yet the chill was there.

At just eight years of age, Kaylie possessed a superior intellect. Beyond simply being a genius, she had tested off the charts and out of regular school classes long ago. She understood the nuances of Einstein's theories. She could do advanced calculus in her head. She found Oxford's online literature classes overly simplistic. So when her intellect failed to determine a reason for the cold, it was a big problem.

She felt certain something was different. Some variable had changed, but what? Patches, her scarecrow doll, was in his usual spot, sitting on the bed among the pillows arranged just so. Her laundry was folded, stacked neatly on her hope chest. Every dresser drawer was closed tight. Nothing seemed out of place. The shade was drawn down low, and the drapes were just as she'd left them in the morning.

The window.

Kaylie smiled at her own foolishness. Clearly, the chill was coming from the window. Obviously, someone had opened the window and failed to close it tight, and a chill breeze had seeped in. "I'll take care of that," she muttered.

Kaylie bounded across the floor, detoured a moment to scoop Patches from the bed, and then scuffed across the carpet with enough force to generate a visible static spark when she touched the metal latch on the window. "Ouch," she whispered, plopping the zapped finger into her mouth.

The chill's dramatic increase seemed to confirm Kaylie's theory, but when she tried to shut the window, it wouldn't budge. It couldn't budge, actually, for it was already shut and locked into place. The uncanny chill was still there.

She clutched Patches tighter and looked from the doll to the window and back. Some kind of connection had been made between the window, Patches, and the precise spot where Kaylie stood now. It was like closing a complex circuit. The chill. A monstrous shadow. Sickly green eyes, glistening with malice.

Kaylie let out a high squeak and hurriedly backed away from the window. She squeaked louder when she backed into something near the door, and strong hands gripped her shoulders.

"Kaylie," he mother said gently. "Sweetie, what's the matter? You're shaking."

Kaylie spun around to hug her mom but stopped and backed the other way.

"Honey, what's wrong?" she asked.

"Um, nothing . . . nothing, Mom," Kaylie said, trying to play it cool. "I just caught a chill, that's all. Well, I better get back to the books. Studying, you know."

"Kaylie, are you sure?"

"Totally sure, Mom." Kaylie flopped onto her bed and snatched a physics book off her bedside table. "I'll be down in a bit." She flipped open the book and pretended to teach Patches part of the lesson, all the while waiting for her mom to disappear from her doorway.

Once the coast was clear, Kaylie ran to her door, shut, and locked it. At last, she thought she understood the cold. It wasn't a drafty window, nor any natural phenomenon. It was supernatural. Hearing Archer the other day talking about their mother's cancer taking her life had terrified Kaylie. But worse still, it somehow rang true.

Then, the icy feel of her room had vexed her until she stood next to the window. Something had happened there. Something with Archer and a dark intruder, a towering force of evil, and it had happened right there in her room. But she still wasn't able to call the memories back to put it all together. Not until colliding with her mother just now.

When Kaylie had turned to look into her mother's gentle eyes, there was no comfort to be found there. For just a moment, her mother had no eyes at all . . . just swirling ash. Soon, little bits of gray, like flurries of ashen snow began . . . bit by bit rebuilding her face. The entire process of restoring her eyes had taken just a few seconds, but Kaylie wasn't about to second-guess what she had seen.

There wasn't just something wrong. Everything was wrong. Kaylie sat on her bed, saw her Patches dolly, and then she remembered. She remembered the Nightmare Lord breaking through the Dream into the Waking World. She remembered Archer struggling to protect her. And she remembered the awakening of her own Dreamtreading power and how she'd used Patches against the evil intruder that night.

Like the simplest geometric proof, all the pieces came together.

The Rift.

"So this . . . is what it does?" Kaylie muttered, standing and walking slowly to the bedroom window. "But it's fake. All . . . fake."

Kaylie flexed her will to call up a massive amount of her mental power, focusing it like a laser on the window glass. She reached up and with her fingertips pinched until she caught hold of something feathery. She diverted her will to that spot and began to pry mentally at it. Soon, she had a firm grip on . . . something. She began to peel it upward, a disorienting thing to see the reality peel away like some kind of cheap wallpaper. As she removed a shred and then another, she could see clearly that there was another world all around her.

The real world.

Dreamtreader Creed, Conceptus 13

In previous eras, a Nightmare Lord has always occupied the throne at No. 6 Rue de La Morte. In fact, rarely has that dark seat lain empty for more than a few years.

Dargan was the first Nightmare Lord. His was a short-lived but fiery reign. Under his fist, the first instances of insanity entered the Waking World. And as a result of his meddling, the Dreamtreader Order was founded.

It was by the very first trio of Dreamtreaders—Aurora, Olin, and Fortescue—that Dargan was thrown down. It cost them their lives and set a high standard for all those who would follow in their place.

Dreamtreader, always be conscious of this: the Waking World and those you protect are very much worth your own life. Do not surrender it foolishly, but if you must in order to succeed in your calling, then cling to it not.

TWENTY-ONE
A Nasty Sandwich

NICK BUSHMAN LUNGED TO PROTECT HIS LITTLE BROTHER. The old nutter had shown up in his kitchen spewing about dreams and different worlds—lunatic-grade material. That was all surprising and awkward, but didn't seem particularly worrisome, until the maniac drew a sword.

"Look, mate," Nick said, pushing Oliver backward toward the den, "I don't know what you want, but I've got some money and some electronics you could sell for a fair bit. We don't want any violence here."

"No," Master Gabriel replied, "and that is part of the problem. You are seeing what you want to see because you do not want the violent truth. And because of that, I have no choice. I must open your eyes no matter the pain it causes."

The intruder took up his broadsword, and Nick swallowed. This was no costume weapon. This was cold, wickedly sharp metal. Nick's mind flew into calculations. Before he knew what he was thinking, he'd already sized up the intruder and calculated the best angle of attack.

His kitchen was narrow, so the maniac had a very limited space for any sort of slash or swing. That left a thrust. Nick felt certain he could sidestep the impaling attack, roll toward the cabinets, and take the man down with a 'rang to the throat.

Nick blinked. He'd seen the whole thing in his mind, and it would work—he was sure of it. But here was the baffling thing: he had no combat training. How would he know the first thing about this sort of hand-to-hand fighting?

"Again," Master Gabriel said, "I am sorry. This will be quite . . . *disturbing* to you."

"Oliver!" Nick grunted, lowering to a crouch and readying his countermove. "Get outside. Get on your bike, ride to Dunny's place. Ring the police."

"No, Nicky," Oliver protested, "I can't leave ya!"

Nick used his body as a shield. He kept his eyes riveted to the intruder, but continued to nudge Oliver back. "No time for heroics, Ollie. Get yourself to Dunny's like I said. Go!"

"This is for the best," Master Gabriel said, raising the sword high.

"Go!" Nick commanded, and to his relief he heard Oliver pound across the den floor and crash through the screen door. But the maniac wasn't going for a thrust after all. He'd expertly maneuvered the blade vertically and held it now like a major league slugger.

Nick instantly changed tactics. He'd bull-rush, duck under the chopping stroke, and take the bloke down to the kitchen floor. From there he'd give the bitzer a bit of knuckle to chew on.

But Gabriel moved the sword faster than Nick thought possible. With strength and fury, the intruder carved a wicked gash across . . . the cabinets.

Nick dodged, and he banged into the pantry. A bag of flour fell off a shelf, hit the floor hard, sending up a white cloud at Nick's feet.

"Dooley!" Nick cried out. "What're ya doing?"

Master Gabriel paid Nick no mind but thrust the sword into a walnut-colored cabinet, plunging the blade in almost to the hilt. He jagged to the left, carving a carpenter-straight line across the rest of the cabinet and then through the metal of the stove's overhead microwave oven.

Nick stood up straight and stared. "How crazy are ya?"

Master Gabriel sheathed his sword. Turning to the furrow he'd just carved, he took hold of an edge and began to pull it away from the wall. But it wasn't the actual cabinetry pulling away from the kitchen wall.

"That's not possible," Nick said, gasping for words. "This isn't real."

"Quite the contrary," Master Gabriel said, continuing to peel away. "What you will see behind this facade is reality. See for yourself."

With a great, wrenching pull, Master Gabriel yanked the cabinets, the counter, the microwave, and the stove—at least, a two-dimensional print of them—and tore them down to the kitchen floor.

Behind it was quite a different sight. The cabinets were still there, but only a blackened skeleton of them. The wall behind them had been partially ripped out, exposing the studs and in some spots allowing the outside to be seen.

Nick gawked, his mind registering the scene and wrestling with its meaning. He stared through the jagged porthole and saw Queensland. While it was broad daylight in the kitchen, the view through the destruction showed night. There were fires, patches of angry flame that didn't belong in his beloved countryside, and there was something else, something wrong on the distant Glass House Mountains.

Nick craned his neck to view the vista from multiple angles. He counted. "Blast it," he muttered. "There have always been eleven. Now, there are just eight. How do three mountains just disappear?"

Master Gabriel sighed. "Do you understand now?" he asked. "Do you remember?"

"Remember?" Nick scoffed. "Only thing I remember is that there used to be eleven mountains. That's what I . . . I . . . I'm a Dreamtreader, aren't I?"

Master Gabriel unloaded a large sigh of relief. "Thank the Almighty," he whispered. "I was afraid we'd lost you. Yes, Nick Bushman, you are a Dreamtreader."

"And Archer . . . Archer Keaton, he woke me up the first time, right?"

"That's right."

"But we failed," Nick said, closing his eyes. "That's what all this is. We failed, the Rift finally happened, and the world's gone spewing mad."

"You had a great deal of help. You had powerful enemies who wanted the Rift to happen."

Nick muttered, "Kara."

"And others," Master Gabriel confirmed. "Archer suspects you have Kara to thank for this lovely fantasy you've been living in."

"Kara?" Nick barked. "Wouldn't surprise me. Spewing mad, she is."

"By the way," Master Gabriel said, "were you really going to eat that?" He gestured.

Nick looked and found the stove was now misshapen, dented, and corroded with some crust that looked like battery acid. And then he saw the roast beef sandwich he had just made for himself. In the peeled skin of fantasy, the sandwich still looked delicious: medium-lean roast beef, Muenster cheese slices not melted but drooping deliciously, crisp lettuce still wet from washing, and those ripe heirloom tomatoes—mouthwatering in total.

But when Nick took a step forward and looked past the failing fantasy to the reality, he retched and nearly lost the contents of his stomach.

"Dooley! What . . . is that?"

With a nostril-flaring sneer, Master Gabriel said, "Filet of rat, I believe."

"All right, then," Nick said, steadying himself. "I'm officially gobsmacked. Remind me to thank Kara for this little bit of madness. So how do we fix this, Master Gabriel? How do we end the Rift and turn the world back?"

Master Gabriel did not answer.

"We can fix this, can't we?"

"The Rift *might* be repaired," Master Gabriel said slowly. "How that might be accomplished will be your task. But the Waking World, as you knew it, may never be the same again."

"I don't like the sound of that," Nick said. "No better time to start than now, I guess. Where's Archer?"

Master Gabriel paused once more. "I have more bad news, actually . . ."

TWENTY-TWO
PROSECUTION

AFTER BEZEAL'S DEVASTATING ACCUSATIONS, ARCHER STOOD. He had to make a good impression here. He left the defense table and strode to the witness box. Razz stared at him and shifted uneasily, still perched upon the rail.

"Dreamtreader Keaton." Chief Justice Michael the Archelion's expression was an odd combination of curiosity and indignation. "May I ask, *what . . . are . . . you . . . doing?*"

Archer blinked and found that most everyone in the courtroom was staring at him. "Um, I'm approaching the witness," Archer said. "I have questions. I think it's called cross-examination, right? Or—"

"I *suppose* it would be natural to make such an assumption," the judge said, "but this court doesn't work that way. The prosecution has the opportunity to present its full case. Only then may the defense respond."

If Archer had been back in school talking to a teacher about procedures or some such thing, he might have considered making some kind of polite counterargument. But in the presence of Chief Justice Michael, Archer had seen already this judge was not someone to be trifled with.

"I'm sorry," Archer said quietly, hurrying to take his seat. "I misunderstood."

"Thank you, your honor," Bezeal said. Archer felt like he could hear the sneer in his opponent's words. The beady-eyed merchant spun on his heel to face the gallery once more. "This is but one case of direct disobedience. There was also the time when Archer, with unmitigated gall, attempted single combat with the Nightmare Lord himself."

The cylinder screen came to life once more, showing the rampart leading up to No. 6 Rue de La Morte, the Nightmare Lord's fortress home. And there was Archer somersaulting high over the mounted enemy. Archer's fiery blue sword flashed as he hewed one of the horns from the Nightmare Lord's fearsome helm.

"And then," Bezeal continued, "there was the time Archer refused to take care of the Lucid Walkers, the trespassers to the Dream—even though Archer knew their presence in the Dream caused damage to the fabric. How many times did the Walkers go in and out? That, I cannot say, but this Dreamtreader's failure to secure the Dream's borders clearly led to the Rift."

When Bezeal finished, he had his Cheshire grin cranked up to eleven. He sidled over to the witness stand once more, turned to Razz, and with an arrogant wave of his three-fingered green hand, said, "Witness, you are dismissed."

Razz crossed her arms and disappeared in a puff of purple smoke and blue sparks. She reappeared next to Archer and whispered heatedly, "I'll dismiss you, ya little hooded nitwit."

"Shush, Razz," Archer warned. "Not now."

"And so we see, ladies and gentlemen of the jury," Bezeal addressed the court, "Archer, in direct defiance of his commanding officer, none other than Master Gabriel, the Chief Dreamtreader himself, did travel into Archaia. Against all better judgment, Archer did enter the lair of the Lurker, and he did procure the ancient relic. He placed his own personal ambitions above the expressed command of his superior. This is insubordination in its purest form, repeated often since!"

Bezeal gave the court a long, contemplative pause. Archer felt it: the weight of his own poor choices condemning him. Bezeal was right, in essence, and Archer knew it.

"For my next witness," Bezeal said, his tone morphing in an

instant from triumphant to grim, "I would like to call two former Dreamtreaders. But, alas, I cannot because they are dead."

The jurors murmured and shifted in their seats. Archer knew what was coming next.

Bezeal waltzed slowly around the courtroom. "Three Dreamtreaders," he said, "always three, and they are intended to work in concert not against each other. When Archer Keaton was inducted into the Dreamtreader fold, he joined two veteran Dreamtreaders, the seasoned and well-respected Duncan and Mesmeera. This, you'll note, was during the same time period in which Archer directly disobeyed Master Gabriel. Those events led to this little scene . . ."

Bezeal gestured to the cylindrical screen. The lights dimmed once more. A vast cobblestoned courtyard appeared. On the far side of it, two trees towered, each one occupying its own significant place as if it were an object of great worship. In the foreground, a gigantic hound lay writhing, and Archer dropped to the ground just on the other side.

"Oh, I can't watch!" Razz squeaked, and then vanished.

Archer didn't want to watch either, but he couldn't tear his eyes away. Somehow it felt right to see what he had done; it was the very least he could endure for his wrongs.

The on-screen Archer stood before the first of the two trees, this one similar to a great oak. Fire crackled in Archer's hands. It seemed to be surging and pulsing . . . growing. The fireballs glowed with increasing ferocity, became great molten globs around Archer's wrists and hands. Suddenly, Archer screamed and threw up his arms. There was a fearsome red-orange flash. The on-screen Archer was thrown violently backward even as a wall of fire shot forward and engulfed the tree.

In the courtroom, Archer braced himself for what he knew would come next:

The screams.

The agonizing shrieks filled the courtroom. Archer shut his eyes while they endured. He knew all too well the scene that transpired.

He'd defeated two more of the colossal hounds, and then torched the second tree in like manner as he had the first. When Archer opened his eyes, the screen went blank. The lights came up.

Bezeal said, "The screams you heard came from Duncan and Mesmeera, Archer's partners. They were imprisoned within the two trees, yet Archer killed them anyway. He burned Duncan and Mesmeera alive."

The resulting uproar in the courtroom required four gavel strikes from Chief Justice Michael. When an uncomfortable silence ensued, Bezeal spoke up once more. "The loss of Duncan and Mesmeera is indeed disturbing," he said, "and while Archer may try and persuade you that he acted in ignorance, I contend there is no excuse for this sort of gross negligence. None of this would have happened if Archer had simply done as Master Gabriel commanded."

Bezeal again paused, and the horrible truth took its toll on Archer. He was grieved to the point of trembling.

But Bezeal was not finished. "Archer Keaton is guilty of these charges," he said. "Of that, there can be no doubt. But there is more. And this, perhaps, is the most deplorable of all. A Dreamtreader is sworn to protect the people of the Waking World. He is never to use his powers to harm a human being, especially not one who could not possibly defend himself."

Bezeal gestured. The room darkened. The screen came alive. There was the medical suite in Rigby's basement. And there was old Doc Scoville looking frail, sickly, and unconscious. He was hooked up to dozens of machines. The lights in the room blinked, and then Archer was there. He approached Rigby's uncle and seemed to stare.

Back in the courtroom, Archer remembered the scene all too vividly. He didn't need Bezeal to narrate, but Bezeal did.

"What you see here," he said, "is Archer after he had broken into Rigby Thames's home, and, against Rigby's expressed wishes, entered this basement laboratory. Why is Archer there you might ask? Why is he doing this?" Bezeal hesitated, leaving the question to hang for several moments, while he strolled to and fro in front of the jury box.

Then, his eyes flashing, he cried out: "Revenge! Revenge was on Archer's mind. You see, Rigby Thames had threatened Archer's little sister. Archer decided he had to take matters into his own hands. Here, watch! Watch as Archer's hand goes perilously close to that thick black cord—the very cord that supplies the power to keep Doc Scoville alive. He planned to pull that cord, to use attempted murder as a threat against Rigby."

Archer watched the on-screen Archer reach for the cord, hesitate, and then reach more. The lights in the lab blinked again, and suddenly Doc Scoville was very much awake and standing beside Archer.

Bezeal gestured. The screen went blank. "Fortunately, Doctor Scoville awakened from his catatonic state," he said. "Just in time to save his own life. Archer Keaton did not succeed in his murderous plot, but a murderous plot it was. This was premeditated and in complete opposition to the Dreamtreaders' sacred Creeds.

"Archer Keaton's actions and thoughts reveal him to be inexperienced, defiant, deceitful, and dangerous . . . for these and many other reasons, you must convict Archer Keaton. The prosecution rests its case."

TWENTY-THREE
SEEING DOUBLE

RIGBY HAD NEVER SEEN SCOVILLE MANOR LOOKING SO beautiful. "It's January," he muttered. "And the spring flowers are already up." But that wasn't all.

The hedges were trimmed. There was a metric ton of new, dark mulch in all the flower beds and around the trees. The stonework on the mansion's facade and turrets looked to have been recently power-washed. The windows were all sparkly clean—even the half-wagon-wheel windows projecting from the slanting roof way up high.

"Fat chance anyone would wash those in real life," Rigby muttered. Still, he had to marvel at the magnificence of it all. Somehow, Kara Windchil had not only figured out how to make the Harlequin Veil work, but she'd perfected it. Now, the big question was: how did she do it?

The Victorian mansion that had been Rigby's home for so many years seemed so foreign in its pristine condition he was nearly tempted to ring the doorbell. He didn't. But as he entered his home, he did so very quietly. There was no telling what he might find. Three steps into the foyer, Rigby heard voices coming from the kitchen. Familiar voices.

". . . must insist." The first voice sounded like Uncle Scoville. "The devil's in the details, my boy."

"I don't understand," came a reply. "We've never been enemies. Why would you do this?"

Rigby squinted. The second voice had an English accent. "No," Rigby whispered. "It can't be."

"Consider it an experiment," Doc Scoville said. "And as you well know, one must repeat an experiment again and again to make certain the results are reliable."

"No," the other voice protested, growing higher and frantic. "Please, please don't!"

Then Rigby heard a gunshot.

In retrospect, Rigby thought himself rather daft for running *toward* the sound of the gunshot, but that's what he did. He found Doc Scoville sitting at the kitchen table with an iced tea in one hand and a rather formidable looking pistol in the other. There was someone slumped over in the chair across from his uncle.

"Uncle Scovy!" Rigby exclaimed. "You . . . you've shot someone!"

If his uncle were surprised to see Rigby or even surprised to be caught in the act, he showed no sign of it. He simply replied, "Yes, but it's all for science."

Rigby blinked, trying to wrap his brain around what he'd just experienced. If this were the Harlequin Veil, how had such a tragic thing occurred? "What 'ave you done? Who 'ave you killed?"

Doc Scoville looked back as if a third arm had grown right out of the middle of Rigby's forehead. "Well," he said, "I've shot you . . . that's who."

Rigby stared at the body, took in the physical characteristics. Indeed, it was him: a perfect copy. "That is me!"

"Told you," Doc Scoville replied rather casually. "And I'm rather afraid I'll have to shoot you as well as . . . uh . . . the other you. Unless, of course, you can show you're not a drone."

Rigby stared at the gun in his uncle's hand. "A what?"

"A drone," he said. "Well, that's what he is." He gestured to the dead Rigby. Then, he pointed the gun back at the living Rigby.

"I am most certainly not a drone, Uncle," Rigby said, at last piecing things together. "I am not a manifestation of the Veil. That is what you're talking about, aren't you? The 'arlequin Veil?"

"Ah, good," Doc Scoville said, putting down the gun. "So you got free from that Kara girl at last, did you?"

Before Rigby could answer, the dead Rigby sat up.

Rigby backpedaled and slammed into the pantry door. "What?" he blurted. "'e's still alive?" He stared at the fake Rigby who, only a moment before, had lain dead from a gunshot wound.

"What?" the fake Rigby said, mockingly. "Of course, I'm alive. Don't know what your problem is, mate—aye, you look a wee bit familiar."

The real Rigby glowered. "A wee bit," he repeated drolly. "Quite."

Doc Scoville cackled hysterically. "Oh, isn't this a hoot?" He slapped the table with his free hand. And then he nonchalantly lifted the pistol and shot the fake Rigby again.

The fake Rigby fell over, but this time, the real Rigby noted, there was no blood. No visible wound. The fake Rigby just slumped over. "Wait a second," Rigby said, "do you mean to tell me . . ."

"That's right, lad," Doc Scoville said. "Don't react; don't feel. Think."

Rigby let the wheels of his mind spin until the proper combination formed. "So this is how the 'arlequin Veil treats violence," Rigby said. "Yeah?"

"Not a spot of blood," Doc Scoville replied. "She's got the Veil so amped up . . . it won't let anyone abide pain or violence for very long."

"What if someone dies?" Rigby asked. "You know, beyond the Veil?"

"Died, kidnapped, imprisoned—makes no difference," Doc Scoville explained. "The Veil replaces you with a drone. I've shot this version of you nine times."

"Yeah, and I'm getting right tired of it," the fake Rigby said, sitting up. His eyes blinked a few times . . . slow motion blinks that gave the real Rigby the creeps. "Now, Uncle," the fake Rigby said, "shall we take that walk, then?"

"Persistent," Doc Scoville said. "I'll give him that. Now, listen, Rigby Number 2, you go on and take that walk. I'll catch up later if I can."

"All right, Uncle," the fake Rigby said. He stood up, brushed past the real Rigby, and exited via the front door.

"Okay," Rigby said, "that's just creepy."

"Isn't it, though?" Doc Scoville asked. "Creepy and impressive. This Kara friend of yours has taken the Harlequin Veil to new levels. It's almost too effective for its own good."

"What do you mean?" Rigby asked.

"Well, it's too good to be true, isn't it?" Doc Scoville asked. He took a sip of iced tea. "That's what woke me up. I turned on the news: no death, no crime, no violence. Everything's unicorns and rainbows, for heaven's sake."

"You've seen what's really going on, then?" Rigby asked.

And at that question, Doc Scoville removed his wire-frame glasses and placed them on the table. When he looked up, tears were already streaming down his cheeks.

Alarmed, Rigby sat down beside his uncle and went to embrace him, but Doc Scoville held up a hand.

"No, no," he said, "I've got to face up to this—we've—got to face up to this." He swiped his coat sleeve across his eyes and continued. "When we put this thing in motion, Rigby, I swear to you, I thought we were doing the right thing. The Dream seemed like the final unexplored frontier, and it seemed such a dire shame that everyone couldn't experience it."

"That's the way the Dream is, Uncle, you were right."

"That's Harlequin Veil talk, boy," Doc Scoville said. "And I'll have no more of it. Heaven knows I dished out plenty to you and even fooled myself. I thought it would free everyone, allow humanity to use its brains to the full potential. I thought it was the next step in evolution."

"Uncle Scovy, please . . . please don't talk like this. Without the Rift, you'd never 'ave come back. You'd never 'ave awakened from the coma."

"Would'a been better that way," Doc Scoville said quietly. "Don't you see what we've done? By ripping open the Rift, we've given people extraordinary power . . . power they weren't meant to have. Worse still is Kara's version of the Harlequin Veil. It's not keeping people safe like we designed it. It just makes people think they're safe. Behind the Veil, people are killing each other and themselves—and they don't even know it. The nice old lady down the street thinks she's taking a walk but goes right off a cliff. Meanwhile, her poor old husband welcomes his wife home a few minutes later and has supper with a drone."

Rigby sat very still. There wasn't much to say when the person he most looked up to in the world had just taken a hammer to his priceless crystal dream. *Power . . . they weren't meant to have?* Rigby pondered furiously. *What does he mean by that?*

"We have to stop her," Doc Scoville said quietly, replacing his glasses. "We have to shut it all down."

Rigby stood up so abruptly that he almost sent his chair to the floor. He grabbed it and gently slid it up to the kitchen table. "Don't worry, Uncle," Rigby said. "We'll stop Kara. I've been inside, remember? I've seen the new Dream Inc. Tower, and I know where to look."

"Nephew, we aren't just going to stop Kara," Doc Scoville said. "You know that, right? We've got to put it all back together the way it was . . . the way it was always meant to be."

Rigby winced. There was that odd phrasing again. *Meant to be? Meant by whom? Surely not the Dreamtreaders.*

"This can't wait," Doc Scoville said. "We've got to do this now."

Rigby's attention came flying back. "I believe you're right, Uncle," he said. "When Kara had me locked up, she said something . . . something that made me think there's a time component to all this."

"What? What did she say?"

"It was quite puzzling, really," Rigby explained. "I told 'er that you'd come to rescue me, and 'er reply was something like 'Well, 'e'd better do it soon because if 'e waits too long, neither of you will care anymore.' Do you know what she meant by that?"

Doc Scoville's eyes narrowed. "I know that it troubles me," he said, looking away. "And I know Kara and her version of the Harlequin Veil must be stopped."

Rigby was quiet a moment. "I've given this a great deal of thought," he said. "We can beat Kara. I'm certain of it. And if we can find the broadcast source of the 'arlequin Veil, I believe we can simply turn it off. But what I do not know . . . is whether the fabric between the Dream and the Waking World can ever be repaired."

Doc Scoville nodded sadly. "We were so foolish," he whispered. "We destroyed the balance; we tore the fabric and caused this Rift. We must find a way to mend it."

"First, we need to get inside of Dream Inc. Tower," Rigby said. "With all the equipment there, I'm certain we'll think of something."

"I hope so," Doc Scoville said, "for all our sakes."

TWENTY-FOUR
SURPRISE WITNESSES

AFTER BEZEAL COMPLETED THE CASE FOR THE PROSECUTION, Archer watched Chief Justice Michael the Archelion. He watched closely, wondering how the judge would react. But at first the judge said nothing. The eagle-glare in his large eyes still smoldered with ferocity, and the set of his granite jaw was still firm.

The courtroom had gone silent too; no murmur or whisper was heard. All was still and solemn. What this lack of reaction meant, Archer could not fathom. But whatever it was, it wasn't good.

"Dreamtreader Keaton," the judge declared. "The defense may now state its case."

An icy trickle worked its way down the center of Archer's back. The evidence against him had been so terrible even Razz had felt the need to vanish. He whispered, "Razz, are you coming back? I could really use the support. Razz?"

There was no answer, so Archer pushed away from the table and stood, feeling very much alone. He took a deep breath and thought, *Anchor first; anchor deep.*

"Your honor," he said, "as my first witness, I would like to call . . . myself."

The galleries rumbled with disapproval. The judge readied his gavel and waited, but the noise died down without the need for thunder.

"Dreamtreader Keaton," the judge said, "this is highly irregular. Not illegal, but very unorthodox."

"I'm sure that it is, your honor," Archer said. "But the truth is, I have very few witnesses to these events, and Razz—er, Ms. Moonsonnet—seems to have reconsidered her presence here. The Eternal Evidence cannot be deceived, can it?"

"No," the judge replied, "the Eternal Evidence is a flawless rendering of what transpired."

"So even if I wanted to deceive you, even if I wanted to alter certain details or even whole scenes of my life, I couldn't do it?"

"No, Dreamtreader, no power of yours can impact the truth of what has happened."

"That being the case," Archer reasoned, "I'd like to call myself as a witness and let the Eternal Evidence bear witness to my testimony. Could I do that?"

"Objection!" Bezeal cried out. "The accused cannot possibly be objective toward his own situation."

"Nor can anyone," the judge replied curtly. "We all have biases, do we not, Bezeal? But the Eternal Evidence cannot lie. Objection overruled."

Bezeal plopped down in his chair and crossed his arms. Archer walked a slow, circular trail so he could, at turns, make eye contact with both galleries. When he began his defense, he wasn't certain what he would say, but the first sentence came out: "Ladies and gentlemen of the jury, your honor, I am guilty of many things. When I began Dreamtreading, I was inexperienced, foolish, ambitious, and, at times, disobedient. But as my Dreamtreading Master would say, I was young and stupid, but not evil. I want to take you back to the incident with the Nightmare Lord."

The lights dimmed. The cylinder screen gleamed to life. There were the ramparts of No. 6 Rue de La Morte coming to life. But this time, the Nightmare Lord had not yet emerged. The on-screen Archer stood under the boughs of a deep and gnarled forest, the Drimmrwood, and a great crowd of villagers, armed with pitchforks, hammers, and torches went racing up the ramparts toward the Shadowkeep. But they didn't get far. Merciless guards appeared, and they hacked their way through the villagers, dropping them to the street or sending them sprawling from the ramparts to a perilous drop into the chasm below.

"It was foolish of me to come to No. 6 Rue de La Morte that night," Archer said. "But when I saw the tyranny of the Nightmare Lord as he sent all those people wheeling to their deaths, I felt like I needed to act."

"Objection!" Bezeal shouted. "The villagers in the Dream were not really dying! They were just figments of their human counterparts' sleeping imaginations."

Chief Justice Michael nodded. "Sustained."

"I agree," Archer went on undeterred. "But I did not know the villagers weren't actually people dying. I'd always heard that dying in a dream meant dying in reality."

"Objection!" Bezeal called out again. "Does the accused really expect us to believe that a seasoned Dreamtreader wouldn't know something as vital to the Dream Realm as that?"

Archer looked up to the judge and said, "Your honor, Bezeal doesn't need to believe me. He can see it for himself."

"Overruled, Bezeal. We'll see the Evidence."

The screen left the ramparts of No. 6 and flashed to Archer's bedroom where Master Gabriel was pacing across the floor and gesturing wildly.

"You have no idea how relieved I am that you survived . . . relatively unharmed," Master Gabriel said, his voice mercifully gentle. "But it was not worth the risk. Not yet."

"But the villagers . . . they were storming the Shadowkeep. They couldn't get through the guards. They were being slaughtered."

"Dispatched, you mean," Master Gabriel muttered. "They should not be in any mortal danger, not really. When will you understand that?"

Archer continued to stare at the ground.

"At worst, one of your kind might awaken with a bloody nose," Master Gabriel went on. "He might be . . . haunted by irrational fears or even develop a severe sleep

disorder. No, those people who became villagers in the Dream would not likely die. The fabric keeps them safe enough physically. But this layer of protection does not exist for you. Oh, no . . . not for the Dreamtreader. You might have been killed . . . or worse. Noble intent, Archer, but foolish . . . foolish actions."

"I'm sorry," Archer muttered.

The screen went blank, and the lights came up. "As you can see from the Eternal Evidence," Archer explained, "I thought that attacking the ramparts of No. 6 was the only way to save lives. I was foolish to get that close to the Shadowkeep, and even more foolish to attack the Nightmare Lord when he later emerged. But I did so, not out of defiance, but rather out of the desire to save people."

A muted buzz flowed through the courtroom. Archer seized the momentum and went on. "For my next witness," he said, taking a deep breath, "I'd like to call Bezeal."

The outraged merchant shouted, "Objection!" But the clamor of the two galleries drowned out everything else. Everything but Michael's thunder-gavel, of course.

After the flash-bang of that mighty hammer, order was instantly restored . . . for the most part. Bezeal was still livid, hopping up and down, and crying out: "You can't put the prosecutor on the stand! I can't be forced to testify against my own case!"

"Dreamtreader Keaton, I am afraid I lean toward that argument," Chief Justice Michael said. "But I will at least ask why I should allow you to put Bezeal on the stand."

"The prosecutor built part of his case on my defying Master Gabriel to go and get that relic from the Lurker. By showing what came before that scene, I believe the court will see there were other interests at work here, things beyond my control."

Chief Justice Michael the Archelion stared hard at Archer. Contemplation danced on the judge's brow. Now and again, he cast a sideways glance at Bezeal, who seemed to be on the edge of his seat, waiting breathlessly for the decision.

Archer felt it too. So much of his strategy hinged on what happened next. For Archer wanted far more than to simply prove his case, more even than victory for himself. It had occurred to him in a quiet moment in his cell, long after Master Gabriel had gone.

In thinking deeply about his own case, about his own evidence, so many events—so many disasters—circled back to Bezeal. If Archer's strategy worked, it might just take care of Bezeal for good.

The courtroom galleries began to stir. Judge Michael the Archelion's posture became very rigid, his expression—if possible—more stern than before. He was about to speak, about to deliver his decision.

TWENTY-FIVE
A Slim Hope

"No Archer," Nick muttered. He paced the half-torn reality of his kitchen back in his Queensland home. "Well, what about Kaylie?"

Master Gabriel sighed and said, "I am not actually certain about Kaylie. Archer told me that she, too, was under the illusion that all is right with the world."

"Why come after me first, then?" Nick asked. "Kaylie's stronger."

"That is precisely why I came to you first, Nick Bushman. It seemed to me that you might take longer to come to your senses."

"Well, now," Nick said, "don't I feel a bit like a toady?"

"Spare yourself such nonsense," Master Gabriel grumbled. "We will need Kaylie and you at the top of your games if we are to have any hope of winning."

"Just the two of us," Nick whispered. "Dooley."

"I am afraid so," Master Gabriel replied, moving the filet-of-rat sandwich to what was left of the sink. "Until Archer's trial is resolved, you and Kaylie are on your own. The Rift, Kara, the ravaged Waking World, and all its needs . . . are your concerns now."

"But Archer will get freed, right? He hasn't really done anything bad, has he?"

"The court will decide," Master Gabriel said. "But I cannot help but wonder at the timing of the charges against Archer as well as the agent through whom these charges have come."

"What do you mean?" Nick asked.

"If Kara's ultimate goal was to cause the Rift and thereby assume power over the newly fused world, she has certainly done that. Why send Bezeal to press charges now? After all, Kara has what she wanted."

"You think Bezeal is acting on his own?"

"There is no telling what Bezeal is doing. He is as devious as they come, and we know he has, at times, advised both Rigby and Kara. But it is of little import to us whether Bezeal has attacked Archer with such sudden zeal alone or by Kara's command, for we already know why."

"We do?" Nick asked. "Well, I'm gobsmacked, so you'd better fill me in."

"Back to the timing, Nick," Master Gabriel explained. "If the Rift and this maddening fantasy world are permanent, there would be no need to incarcerate Archer. Whether it's Kara or Bezeal or both, someone wants Archer out of the way and right now. And that means . . ."

Nick got a chill as the idea dawned on him at last. "You ripper!" he exclaimed, gesturing wildly as he paced out into the living room. "It means there might be time yet to fix this thing. I see the plan now: take Archer off the board straight away to cripple us."

"But Bezeal was wrong," Master Gabriel said. "His efforts will slow us down, but we will keep fighting. What we cannot know is how much time we have. That is what I want you and Kaylie to discover. And we ought to be leaving as soon as possible."

"Wait," Nick said, "one thing before we go."

"Yes?" Master Gabriel asked.

"What about Oliver?" Nick said, staring from the living room picture window. Oliver was leading his neighbor Dunny across the field in haste. "My brother . . . I've been talking to him all the time. Do you mean to say he . . . him there . . . he's not really my brother?"

Master Gabriel nodded, looked through the glass at the boy bounding over tufts of grass, and explained, "That Oliver is a mental projection of your brother. He's all of what you remember him to be, but, no, he's not the real Oliver. Did you not notice how young Oliver appears?"

Nick shook his head. He hadn't noticed before, but he noticed now. He looked through the window and smiled. There Oliver was, just a hundred yards away, but it wasn't really him. In fact, the beautiful day, the gorgeous view of the Glass House Mountains—none of it was real. Nick had seen the fake world peel away like a curtain, revealing a harsh and dangerous place. *And I'm a Dreamtreader,* he thought. *And I fell for it. I feel for the poor blokes who don't know any bet*—"Wait!" he said aloud. "What about the real Oliver? Where is he? I've got to look after him!"

"Calm down, Nick," Master Gabriel advised. "Your Oliver is safely occupied by a certain crab apple tree in your grandmother's front yard."

"My anchor?"

"Yes," Master Gabriel replied. "Oddly enough, the tree itself seems unaffected by the Rift, though in your Oliver's mind, your grandmother yet lives."

"I don't blame him," Nick said. "I'd like to see Granny again. You're certain Oliver will be okay?"

"He will be as safe as possible," Master Gabriel replied. "I have left a few friends to keep Oliver occupied . . . and safe."

"Friends?"

"Like your Dream companion, Taddy, and Archer's Razz," he explained. "Oliver should have great fun as his new playmates are extraordinarily fuzzy."

"What are we going to do, then?" Nick asked. "The fake Oliver is coming back, and he's bringing my neighbor Dunny with him."

"I am afraid we must depart," said Master Gabriel. "And I . . . wait." The Master Dreamtreader went very still. His eyes widened. "I'm feeling something."

"What? What's wrong?"

"I am not certain," he replied. "I am feeling something pulling at me. Ah, yes! I know what it is, and very good timing, I must say."

"You've lost me," Nick said. "Pulling at you, uh . . . how? And from—"

The front door flew open, and there stood Oliver and all six-foot, five-inch Dunny, Nick's closest neighbor. He had a boomerang in one hand and a bush knife in the other.

"Oy, just what's goin' on here?" Dunny asked.

"Oh, uh . . . nuthin," Nick stammered. "Oliver, sorry! False alarm, fair Dinkum."

Dunny's and Oliver's eyes went big as saucers. Blue light shone out from the kitchen. Nick heard a strange muted buzzing and felt a very strong hand grab his arm. "What? Master Gabriel, what are you—"

"No time to explain," he replied. "Suffice it to say, I am taking you with me."

Nick gave a little wave to the fake Oliver and to Dunny, and then the blue light flooded the house until there was nothing else but the blue light.

TWENTY-SIX

OF FOOLS AND VILLAINS

THE JUDGE HUSHED THE GALLERY, THIS TIME WITH A WAVE of his hand rather than the thunder-gavel. "This is highly out of the ordinary," he said, "but, then again, most of this case is highly out of the ordinary. Given that both the accused and the accuser were actively involved in the events that transpired, given that we have already delved into Archer's memories for Eternal Evidence, I will allow you to call Bezeal to the stand."

"Objection!" Bezeal shrieked.

"Overruled!" the judge declared. "Bezeal, take the stand."

Archer turned to the merchant and dared to hope. Bezeal did not disappoint.

"I won't do it," Bezeal muttered.

The galleries exploded in cries of shock, outrage, and even a few jeers. Chief Justice Michael struck with the thunder-gavel, not once, but twice. Even then, it took a few moments for silence.

"What did you say, Bezeal?" the judge asked.

The merchant plopped back in his chair, crossed his arms, and muttered once more, "I will not do it. I will not take the stand."

A strange glint flickered in Chief Justice Michael's eyes. "You will take the stand, Bezeal," he said, his words clipped and tight with threat. "The court compels you."

"This court cannot compel me," Bezeal replied, his voice suddenly changed . . . deeper but not distorted, resonant and as different from Bezeal's wheedling, scheming voice as it could be.

Archer remembered that voice. He'd heard it once before and, like before, he had a powerful urge to flee, to get as far away from Bezeal as he could.

Chief Justice Michael, however, actually stood up from his judge's bench. "Guards," he whispered sternly, "please escort the accuser to the witness stand and then, if need be, chain him to the seat."

Bezeal hissed and leaped to stand upon his chair.

Archer had what he wanted. "Objection!" he cried out.

This exclamation froze everyone in the courtroom. The judge, eyebrows raised to a comical height, turned. "You . . . object?" he said quizzically. "Dreamtreader Keaton, to what do you object?"

"I'm sorry, your honor," Archer said. "I wasn't sure how to speak up, but it's okay. Bezeal doesn't need to take the stand."

"It is most certainly not 'okay.' Bezeal will stand witness."

"He's already done that, sir," Archer said. "By refusing. I take back my request. I no longer need Bezeal to take the stand."

The judge was very quiet. Bezeal continued to murmur and hiss, but Archer could not make out his words.

"Very well," the judge said, his scowl oddly lopsided. "You have a brief reprieve, Bezeal. A very brief reprieve. Dreamtreader Keaton, how do you wish to proceed *now*?"

"I would like for the court to view another memory I have," he said. "A memory that will shed light on many of the accusations made by my opponent this day."

The judge nodded. The lights dimmed, and the cylindrical screen came to life. It was Kurdan's marketplace in the Forms District of the Dream. The on-screen Archer strode with purpose toward a seller's stall in the middle of the market. Bezeal was there, scraping a few coins off of the table and grinning as usual.

This was the memory Archer had planned to drag from Bezeal himself, but since the merchant refused to take the stand, the action showcasing Bezeal's duplicity for all, Archer would reveal it through his own memories. The beauty of Eternal Evidence was it revealed not only the actions that took place but also Archer's attitudes and intentions.

"Dreamtreader tall, how come you to my stall?" Bezeal asked. "Can I . . . help you at all?" Bezeal's eyes shrank to the tiniest pinpricks of light.

Archer had been mentally rehearsing how he would approach Bezeal. The little, hooded merchant was very clever and deceitful. If Master Gabriel were correct, no intelligent person would underestimate Bezeal. Archer wasn't about to. It would tax his mental will fiercely, but Archer was beyond caring. He would endure no trickery, no foolishness from Bezeal. Not this time.

Archer grabbed a fistful of Bezeal's hooded cloak just below his neck and flung him one-handed into a high-security bank vault. The vault hadn't been there a second before, but Archer's will made it happen just in time for Bezeal to crash into it.

Archer raced inside the vault just as the multilayered-titanium steel door slammed shut. He used his will to spin the inner tumblers, and the vault was locked tight. There was total darkness except for Bezeal's tiny eyes and the angry red smoldering in Archer's hands.

"What is this foolish thing you do?" Bezeal squeaked. "We're trapped just us two. Release me now; I'm warning you."

"You lying, scheming scab!" Archer yelled, fire flaring in his fists. "You tricked me into getting the Karakurian Chamber. You knew all along it was the stolen Shadow Key, and you used me to get it."

Bezeal's eyes grew, and a tiny white glimmer of his smile appeared. "Of course I knew it was the key. It was right where I wanted it to be. But I needed you to give it back to me."

"You used me," Archer repeated. "Come to think of it, you used Duncan and Mesmeera too. Because of you, they're dead."

Bezeal's laugh startled Archer. It was a crackling sound, low, and full of malevolent glee. "As I recall, it was you who killed poor Duncan and Mesmeera."

Bezeal's sudden lack of rhyme unnerved Archer. The Dreamtreader took an involuntary step backward but then grew angrier for his own cowardice. "You listen to me, runt," Archer growled. "I want the Shadow Key back, and I want it now."

Archer felt a pulse in his will, a throbbing kind of strength, aching to be exercised. He decided to make a statement. He turned his palms down toward the floor and set loose streams of flames that hit the floor and slithered across to widen at Bezeal's feet.

As Archer stepped toward Bezeal, the flame rose a little higher until at last it encircled the merchant and rose to form a cage of flame.

Bezeal's voice was shrill and fearful. "Do not burn your faith . . . your faithful servant. I have not the key, no matter how much you chant. The key to give you, I—I can't."

"I'm through playing around, Bezeal," Archer said. "Give me the Shadow Key."

With a sound like a scream, all the fire blew out. The vault plunged into total darkness.

"Ah, the sweet smell . . . of arrogance," came a voice Archer didn't recognize. "You have no idea what real fire is."

In court, Archer said, "I accept responsibility for my actions. Your honor, ladies and gentlemen of the jury . . . I want to make that perfectly clear. No matter what Bezeal or anyone else did or said, I made the decisions that led to my actions. I never should have trusted Bezeal to begin with, but I did. And as a result, terrible events transpired . . . events that will haunt me the rest of my life."

"At least," Bezeal muttered, "you have a life. Poor Duncan and Mesmeera. Poor, poor—"

"Be quiet!" Archer commanded. "If you won't take the stand, the least you can do is keep your mouth shut."

Bezeal squirmed uncomfortably in his chair but said nothing.

The judge nodded to Archer. "Continue."

"I place myself at the mercy of this court," Archer said. "Whatever you decide will be just. But I want the court to see Bezeal has lurked behind the scenes in almost every step of this process. Bezeal, by his own admission, put the Shadow Key relic into the Lurker's hands. Bezeal, through lies and temptation, set me on the path to get that relic back for him. Bezeal also tricked Duncan and Mesmeera into a course of action that would lead them directly into the Nightmare Lord's hands. And it was Bezeal himself who told me the only way to destroy the Nightmare Lord was to burn the Trees of Life and Death, the trees where, unbeknownst to me, my friends had been imprisoned."

The court murmured. Many turned to stare at Bezeal.

"Order," the judge said curtly. "This instant."

Archer continued, "And so if there's a fool here, that fool is me. But if there's a villain here, that villain is Bezeal."

TWENTY-SEVEN
TAG TEAM

"KAYLIE," MASTER GABRIEL LAUGHED. "I AM SO VERY GLAD to find you awake."

"Gabe!" Kaylie squealed. She raced across Archer's bedroom and hugged the Master Dreamtreader. "I was afraid you wouldn't come."

"I cannot tell you how wonderful it was to sense the Summoning Feather," Master Gabriel whispered as he lowered Kaylie back to the floor. "I knew it had to be you doing the summoning."

Kaylie stepped back a pace. "But . . . it might have been Archer . . . or Nick, right?"

"I'm right here," Nick said, stepping out from behind Master Gabriel. "You got two for the price of one."

Kaylie bounced over to Nick and gave him a hug too. But even in his embrace, Kaylie felt something wrong. She backed up and looked from Master Gabriel to Nick and back. "What about Archer?"

"I am sorry, Kaylie," Master Gabriel said, "but Archer is unavailable. Have a seat. There is much to explain."

Frowning and nervously twiddling one of her red pigtails with her fingers, Kaylie took a seat on the bed.

Master Gabriel told the story of Bezeal's bringing charges against Archer, that the charges needed to be addressed in court, and that, in the end, he wasn't certain when or if Archer would be able to return to his Dreamtreading duties.

"Poor Archer," Kaylie muttered. "Isn't there anything we can do to help him?"

"No," Master Gabriel said, "Archer must face his opponent in court and let justice take its course. But there is something you must do, the both of you."

"What?" Kaylie and Nick chorused.

"The two of you have awakened from this insidious spell," he said. "Whether it is simply the Rift or something Kara Windchil has created, Kaylie, you and Nick will need to put a stop to it. The Waking World is no longer awake, and it is dying from a lack of truth."

"Where do we start?" Kaylie asked.

"That is the easy part," Master Gabriel said. "Baltimore."

"What's in Baltimore?" Kaylie asked.

"What *is* Baltimore?" Nick asked.

"Baltimore is one of Maryland's most beautiful cities," Master Gabriel explained. "As for what you will find there . . . Dream Inc."

There were many skyscrapers in Baltimore, but none was taller, none more grandiose than the Dream Tower. Occupying a triangle of land roughly the size of a professional baseball stadium, the tower glowed like a deep blue flame and loomed high in the cityscape as if it were some gigantic ancient stone. It was shaped like a pillar from Stonehenge too, just a thousand times bigger.

Having flown to Baltimore, Kaylie and Nick decided to wait for nightfall, when the tower was lit from within by myriad lights but was otherwise less busy than during the day. Whether it was the tint of certain windows or the type of light inside certain rooms, Kaylie couldn't tell, but the building had a lighter, nearly turquoise pattern crisscrossing its way all the way to its pinnacle.

"Fair beautiful," Nick said, "if I didn't know what it stands for."

"It is," Kaylie agreed. They stood in the plaza just outside of the spray from a vast, sparkling water fountain. "The whole city is so full of light. Reminds me of the Emerald City from Oz."

"It's not really so nice though, now, is it?" Nick asked. "Master Gabriel . . . I don't know how he did it, but he used his sword and cut away the fake world so I could see reality . . . the reality left behind by the Rift."

"I don't like to look," Kaylie muttered. "But sometimes I think it's best."

"Wait," Nick said. "You can do it too?"

Kaylie nodded. Then, her brow furrowed in concentration, she reached up and pinched the air. To Nick's astonishment, there was something there, something tangible for her to grasp. Kaylie's pinching motion caused the view of that space to distort, bend, and stretch. Then there was a tear . . . a small rip at first, but it grew as Kaylie exerted will and effort. A fold of existence peeled away, revealing darkness.

"Look," Kaylie said. "Look through here."

Nick dropped to one knee to peer through the window torn into the air. He gasped. The contrast was that stark. Through the window, the city of Baltimore lay in darkness but for the great fires that burned wildly in spots, that and a strange greenish glow that seemed to be coming from the harbor. But in the midst of all the darkness and destruction, the Dream Tower stood . . . just as grand and as perfect as it appeared outside of Kaylie's window.

"That's creepy," Nick muttered.

"And sad," Kaylie agreed. She clutched Patches close to her chest, and her lower lip trembled. "We need to fix this."

Nick took her by the shoulders and steered her away from that dark window. "C'mon, then," he said. "Time to get ready for business." Battle fatigues replaced his jeans. A tactical vest full of boomerangs and other weapons materialized over his chest. A massive steel chain looped once around his neck and hung down like a scarf.

Kaylie raised an eyebrow. "My turn!" She bounced once, her pigtails dancing, and she suddenly wore a hooded cloak. Beneath the cloak, she was covered in some kind of interlocking slate-gray armor. It wasn't metal, but seemed rather to be a carbon fiber composite, something closer to Kevlar. She wore a gold utility belt with more gadgets than Batman ever dreamt of. And slung over her shoulder was a glistening silver and black crossbow.

Then, to Nick's surprise and amusement, Kaylie made a full-length mirror appear. She twirled in front of it once, a second time, and then she stopped and frowned. "I don't think this gold belt works," she mumbled. But it wasn't gold for long. In an instant, the belt and all its gadgets became slate black.

Kaylie nodded at her reflection. The mirror vanished. "Let's do this."

Nick led the way, crossing the plaza in a will-infused instant. Kaylie readied her crossbow and trailed just behind, staying at an angle so she could fire past Nick if needed.

Nick held up a hand and stopped just outside the sensor range of the automatic doors. He held up five fingers, then one. Six guards.

Kaylie rushed up and slid to a stop beside him. "I'm having second thoughts," she whispered.

"About going in?"

"No," she said, rolling her eyes. "If we go in and start a fight right away, we're going to get caught."

"Right," Nick said. "We need information. Best to be stealthy."

"I have an idea." Kaylie reached into the air with both hands, took hold of reality, and grunted. Then, straining the whole time, she tore corners from the air and continued to pull until there was a five-foot door into reality. "C'mon," she said. Then she stepped through the door.

His expression slack and eyes wide, Nick hesitated for several moments. He stood blinking until Kaylie's hand appeared and she gestured for him to follow.

Once Nick was in, Kaylie used her will to seal the door closed. As before, the Dream Tower looked pretty much the same. The colors and lights might have been a bit muted, but that was all. Inside the doors, the six security guards remained.

"Um, what . . . where are we?" Nick whispered. "Is this real?"

"Actually, yes," Kaylie replied. "I tore a door through the fantasy world so we can travel through the same space and time in the real world."

"Won't they still see us?" Nick whispered.

"I don't think so," Kaylie replied. "Look at them."

Nick stared. Each of the security guards wore a blank expression . . . as if recollecting some fond memory. A few of the guards were pacing the interior, but their movements were strange, slow, and languid, punctuated by odd hitches. "Here goes nothing," Nick said, taking a step forward and triggering the door's motion sensor.

The doors parted and glided open. Nick and Kaylie pressed inside, and none of the guards changed expression. "Excuse me, sir," Kaylie said to one of the guards at the front desk. But the man stared straight ahead, oblivious to anyone being present nearby.

Nick waved a hand in front of the man's eyes. "Wow," Nick said. "You were right, Kaylie. Nobody is home."

Kaylie grinned.

Nick picked up one of the blue binders on the guards' desk and began to flip through it. "Kara's private quarters are at the top," he whispered. "There are an awful lot of executive suites. But which one?"

Kaylie scanned the binder. "I don't think any of those," she said. "At least not yet. I think this is what we want." She pointed to Research and Development.

Nick nodded, and they headed for the elevator. Once inside, Kaylie opened the reality door and stepped back into the false world. Nick did the same and hit the button for the correct floor. It was a long, long way down.

Dreamtreader Creed, Conceptus 14

At this advanced point in your studies, you no doubt have questions, more intelligent questions than you ever could have asked prior to your calling to Dreamtread.

And while it is true that you are ready to ask these higher questions, it is not true you are ready for all of the answers. There is, however, something of a historical fact of which you must now learn. There is a reason the first Nightmare Lord came into being.

For many ages, the Waking World slept in peace with no fear for darkness intruding upon its slumber. But mankind was not content with that which was provided. Man strove for more and got precisely what he asked for.

And this is the Tragedy of the Ages.

Dreamtreader, you must not look in disdain at this tragedy . . . as if to ask, "Why, oh, why did mankind commit an act of such tragic foolishness?" Had you lived in the beginning and had you faced the same situations and choices, you likely would have committed the same . . . or worse. And do not think yourself safe now either.

That same temptation exists for you now. You have been provided with amazing powers. You have been granted access to a world that others of your kind quite literally can only dream about. Be content. Do not reach above your station. Do not pine away for more than you have been given. And do not plot to take more than you are allowed. There is an order to things, and if you violate that order, you will either provide a tool for our enemy to use, or you will become the enemy.

TWENTY-EIGHT
THE VERDICT

THE COURTROOM WENT SILENT AS ARCHER'S CLOSING words hung in the air for several moments. The jurors on both sides had shifted their scrutiny to the hooded prosecutor. Nobody dared speak. Well, almost nobody.

"Ridiculous!" Bezeal cried out to the courtroom. "I am not on trial here."

"Perhaps you should be," Chief Justice Michael quipped. "I find it a great and terrible irony that you have brought charges against Archer Keaton's actions when you yourself have acted to influence most of those actions! Think that you are as clever as to deceive even me? You have cast a dark cloud over Archer's mind, but you have not deceived me. Yes, oh yes, I think I know who you are. And given the notes I have in your file here, I have become even more certain of my guess."

The merchant seemed to shrink a size. "You have a file on Bezeal?" he asked meekly.

"We have files on everyone. And for reasons I cannot reveal here or begin to understand, you are not to be imprisoned. Be glad that—for now—my hands are tied where you are concerned. Otherwise, Bezeal, to put it in terms Archer might appreciate: I would open up a galactic-sized can of whoop-your-behind!"

Bezeal did not respond directly. In fact, he seemed deep in some conversation with himself. The court had become so entranced and silent that all could hear the merchant's words. "Misbegotten fool that I am, I should have just delayed the trial! I should have taken the time to gather the evidence. You wanted to put him away for good, but all you needed was six days. Now, you've ruined it. You've ruined everything!"

"Enough!" the judge roared. "You will not make a mockery of my court any longer. Bailiff, toss this miscreant out on his ear."

The bailiff and a few armed guards moved toward Bezeal. The merchant shrieked. His eyes turned blood-red and tripled in size. He held up his sickly green hands. Red flames rose up and encircled him. The entire courtroom trembled. The chandeliers swayed overhead and went out.

That foreign, otherworldly voice rang out. "Guilty! You are all guilty! And I will render sentence upon you all!"

The flames intensified. There came a sharp crackling, and the floor beneath Bezeal's feet dropped away, and, in a split second, he was gone.

Archer raced the bailiff to the scene and peered over the edge of the smoldering hole in the courtroom floor. He gasped. There was no sign of Bezeal, but a snaking tunnel, painted with rings of fire, plunged downward and away. Archer couldn't see the bottom . . . nor did he wish to.

"Ladies and gentlemen," the judge announced, "you are all bound by what we have seen here. And much will be made of it . . . at the highest levels. But for the purposes of this case and this trial, I declare this a travesty!"

The crowd cheered, but Archer had no idea what the judge meant. "Sir," he asked, "what is a travesty?"

"In your vernacular, it means, I have declared a mistrial. Archer, you are free to go. Please, return to the Waking World, rejoin your comrades, and put a stop to the anarchy occurring there now."

"I will, sir," Archer replied. "Thank you."

"But before you go, Dreamtreader," the Chief Justice said, "I have for you two warnings. The first is to beware of yourself."

"Sir?"

"The accusations Bezeal brought against you were inflamed, some of them coerced even. But you are not guiltless in all this. When you place your desires above your Dreamtreading duties—and orders—you are begging for tragedy. And should this court see you accused once more, I fear the verdict would not remain so sympathetic. Do you understand me, Dreamtreader?"

Archer nodded vigorously. "I understand, sir. Loud and clear. And the other warning?"

Michael the Archelion's eyes narrowed to slits. "Beware of Bezeal. He will not give up."

"Thank you, your honor," Archer replied. "Neither will I."

TWENTY-NINE
UNSTOPPABLE FORCE

NICK AND KAYLIE HUNG BACK WHEN THE ELEVATOR OPENED to Research and Development at last, more than six hundred feet below the surface. A pair of guards was waiting, of course, but when no one came out, the guards went to investigate. The two Dreamtreaders waited until the guards inevitably looked inside. Nick dropped the first one with a quick boomerang blow to the back of the head, and then dragged him inside the elevator. When he turned to inspect the opposite side of the elevator, he found the other guard sitting cross-legged, wide-awake, and with the goofiest look on his face Nick had ever seen.

Nick whispered, "What did you do to him?"

Kaylie shrugged. "I happified him."

"Glad you're on my team, mate." Nick shook his head and slid outside.

Before Kaylie followed, she quickly hit each and every button inside the elevator. "I love doing that," she said.

Research and Development was a world of brushed steel. There were massive curving pipes overhead, spider webs of cables running up the weight-bearing pillars and shrouded in the eaves, and approximately every ten feet was an immense bank of winking and blinking fiber-optic servers.

Nick and Kaylie slid in and out of corridors, ducked around corners to avoid the lab-coated scientists who seemed to roam everywhere, and came at last to a pair of pressure-sealed, smoked glass doors. There were four guards there: two seated at matching computer stations across from each other and one on either side of the doors. All were dressed in spotless white uniforms and wore a strange silvery sidearm.

Kaylie ripped a door into reality and passed inside, with Nick right behind her. When Kaylie sealed the false reality behind them, she bent over at the waist. "Just a second," she whispered, breathing heavily. "Doing that takes a ton . . . of will."

"I don't think there's any other way," Nick said. "For this part, anyways. Sealed up tight. At least the Rift helps us recharge, eh?"

They waited in silence until Kaylie finally sighed. "I'm good." They walked right past the two seated guards, who didn't stir an inch. Neither did the two guards at the doors. Nick reached for the brushed metal handle on the door and pulled, but nothing moved.

"I don't think I can hide us for much longer," Kaylie whispered, sweat trickling down her forehead. "Hurry."

Nick tried the other handle, but the door was shut tight. He looked right and left. Just past the guard to the right, there was a keypad and some kind of optical scanner. "Hmm," Nick whispered. He snagged the ID badge from the guard and swiped it across the scanner. There was a hiss of air, the doors parted, and the two Dreamtreaders slipped inside. "That was just in time," Kaylie whispered. She peeled open the reality door, and they rushed beyond its threshold. Kaylie swayed a little.

Nick picked her up and carried her behind a bank of servers. "You going to be okay?" he whispered.

"Yeah," she said, clutching Patches. "I think so . . . it's exhausting."

The lab they'd stepped into was flush with noise: muted buzzing, regularly spaced tones, and a warbling beep that sounded like an alarm clock going off underwater. On top of all that, there was a constant pressurized hissing sound.

Nick leaned around the bank of servers to get a better look. Through a panel of crisscrossed wires, he saw what appeared to be a kind of command station. It was composed of wide rectangular tables arranged like the top half of an octagon, and upon those were strange pyramid-shaped white pods—each with a single, blinking red light and at least a dozen large flat screens. "We've got to get a better look," Nick whispered.

"Let's go up," Kaylie replied. She flexed a little of her will and began to rise.

Nick followed suit and said, "Oh, I see. That's genius, Kaylie."

Kaylie winked. The ceiling was an absolute labyrinth of pipes, cables, cords, filters, and scaffolding amidst the computer monitors. They found crevices to fit into and, though they trusted none of it to support their weight, they could hold themselves there by force of will.

"My view is blocked here," Kaylie whispered. "What do you see?"

"I dunno what I'm lookin' at," he said. "There's a wicked strange series of graphics on one screen. Trying to make out the data here. It looks like 1900 MHz in one corner of the screen, but then a series of different colored bars are moving up and down like a stereo equalizer."

"Are there any numbers beneath the colored bars?" Kaylie asked.

"Dooley, there are!" he replied. "Beneath each bar is the word *cell* followed by a number. One is 65°; the next 92°; and the next 37°. Temperature? Is Dream Inc. monitoring climate for some reason?"

"Possibly," she replied. "Anything else?"

"Yeah, but the rest of the screen makes even less sense . . . to me anyway. I see some abbreviations: MHz, GHz, and Rf quotients, whatever those are. Still, I'll wager it's important to Dream Inc."

"I'd better look," Kaylie said. "Let's switch." Like astronauts in zero gravity, the two Dreamtreaders floated out of hiding but only as long as it took to exchange spots.

"Much better," Kaylie said. She saw all the numbers, graphs, and figures Nick had described but instantly became spellbound by a graphic representation of the earth. She'd seen the type before. There was the globe and a pulsing line plunged north to south, showing the spin axis, and springing out east and west from that were concentric circles of differing colors. These circles, she knew, were magnetic field lines, estimates based on the earth's rotation.

What Kaylie didn't understand was why there was a second throbbing line forming a perfect cross through the center of the earth. It was as if there was a second axis. Another entirely different set of magnetic field lines extended out from this horizontal pivot, these circles radiating outward to the north and south. Strange, blinking pulses showed up intermittently as the graphical globe rotated to show North America. It reminded Kaylie of a deep-sea submarine's sonar making contact. At that moment, another little blip showed up in the northeastern United States.

Next to that display was another, but this one was filled with a single, bright, white point that bounced and danced across the screen, much like the pulse of a heartbeat monitor. Beneath the ever-gliding blip was a numerical interface. It read *138.42.15.07*, but it was counting down.

Some of this began to crystallize in Kaylie's mind. "Nick," she whispered. "I think we'd better go."

He hovered over to join her by a huge duct. "I don't understand any of that," he said.

"I think I do," she said. "And it's not good. We need to get back. We need to talk to Master Gabriel again."

They left the same way they'd come in, and once more Kaylie was nearly tapped of her will. Nick had to carry her back around the corner to the elevator.

"I can stand," she said, and he put her down gently.

Nick hit the elevator button, and they waited for what seemed like an eternity. "You had to hit all the buttons," he said, "didn't you?"

"Yeah, sorry," she replied. "Not my best plan."

When the elevator doors finally parted, the guards were gone. In their place stood two people: Rigby Thames and his uncle, Doc Scoville.

THIRTY
DARK NEWS

KARA WINDCHIL LOVED SEEING THE MOON'S LIGHT reflecting off Baltimore's Inner Harbor. She lay atop her California king bed and stared through the crystal-clear glass of her penthouse window. The way the lunar gold shimmered on the dark water was entrancing.

Something glimmered in the sky to the west. Kara turned, shifting on the bed just in time to watch the light dust tail of a shooting star fade in the dark canopy of night. *Ha,* she thought, *I made that.* It had been a simple thing, really. Just a few lines of code and *voila!* Twenty percent more comets visible in the western hemisphere. Next month, she planned to give northern lights to North America. It made sense.

She flipped over onto her back and sighed, happily marveling at just how far she had come in the last few years, particularly the last. It had been close at times, but she'd managed to stay one step ahead of them all: Doc Scoville, the Nightmare Lord, Rigby, Archer, and all of the other Dreamtreaders.

Kara bounced off of the bed and strode toward her double-wide closet with mirrored doors. She watched herself twirl, and in the first spin she wore the stardust white dress, the same one she'd worn when she danced with the Nightmare Lord in the sky. With another whirl, she became adorned with the gray cloak she'd always clothed herself in for visits to the Inner Sanctum of Garnet Province. There, she'd learned so many interesting things. Thinking they were assisting a Dreamtreading Master, the Sages had been ever so helpful.

She reversed course and spun back toward her bed, clothing herself in what had become one of her very favorite visages: the bold, rose-red dress of Lady Kasia. "Oh, Archer Keaton," she purred, "you are so very gallant. But you simply must stay for tea." Archer had bought the act—hook, line, and sinker. That silly Nick Bushman had as well.

Just before passing the last mirror panel, she changed into the garb of the Wind Maiden, a spectral gown created from long, flowing translucent petals, each one moving as if from a different breeze. Kara had loved that role.

As she flew to the bed, she changed into an oversized hooded sweatshirt and comfortable jeans. She landed softly on the bed and reminded herself that none of her roles were gone. She could be those and any other she wished now. The world was better with her in charge and so much more interesting.

"Wait," she said to her reflection. "You're doing it again." She shook her head. "I . . . I am doing it again." Gloating, mocking, reveling in her superiority to them all—her stomach turned. *But maybe,* she thought, *maybe it's not so bad.*

The thought had hardly left her mind when Kara heard muttering from the hall that led to her private elevator. The voice stopped, but she heard the familiar swish of small feet on the carpet. Bezeal entered the room, his cloak fluttering like the gossamer pectoral fin of a sea skate ghosting across the ocean floor. The merchant paused in the middle, his beady eyes glimmering, but it was a cold glimmer, like ice on steel.

"I'm glad you've come back," Kara said. When she sat up on the bed, she was again dressed in an exquisitely tailored business suit. "We need to talk."

"I am here to listen, Kara, my friend. Here with my cunning mind to lend. Here for you . . . until the end."

"Rigby Thames is dead."

Bezeal's eyes glinted, grew a size, and then shrank again. He did not smile. "Are you certain?" he asked, a tremble in his voice.

"Of course, I'm certain," she said, a little off-balance from Bezeal's lack of rhyme. "He's dead, so I can't ask him about the Veil."

Bezeal turned away from her and ventured slowly toward the window. He seemed to shake a moment. Then he grew still and said, "There is another we could query about the Veil. One of greater knowledge we can assail. Fear not, my lady, your plan won't fail."

"Scoville," she muttered. "I thought about that, and I've taken measures to make certain he doesn't discover his nephew has died. If we can just get past this . . . this boundary, it won't matter anyway. Speaking of which, how's the court case going? You're sticking it to Keaton, I hope."

Bezeal did not reply at first.

Kara took a deep breath. "Bezeal?" Kara whispered. "Is it done? Is Keaton out of the way?"

He still didn't answer.

"Well, Bezeal?" she asked. "Don't keep me waiting."

"Archelion, so high and mighty," he muttered, "clings to his *justice* ever so tightly, and dealt with Bezeal most unkindly."

"I don't get it," she said, her voice taking a hard edge. "Stop with the riddles. What's going on?"

"My lady," he said. "My queen, alas, I bear news of the terribly obscene. The high court was not high, only mean."

Kara stood up. "You blew it?" she barked. "How did I know you would mess this up?"

Bezeal bowed halfway and said, "The judge was unjust; he was not fair. Though Archer was guilty, he just didn't care. He wanted Bezeal on trial . . . something I just could not bear."

For ten minutes, Kara continued to interrogate Bezeal. In his rhyming, roundabout way, he communicated several frustrating pieces of information:

Master Gabriel had not been in the court to represent Archer.

Archer had defended himself by turning the court against Bezeal.

And Bezeal had just barely escaped being incarcerated himself.

Kara threw up her hands. "I can't believe it. We had the evidence stacked so high against Archer that you could see it from Kansas. Do you know how hard I worked to set this all in motion?"

"Clearly, your design was from beginning to end. Your plan was profound, I must defend. But, alas, not all comes about as we intend."

"So what's up with Archer?" Kara asked. "Did the judge just let him go?"

"I do not know. I could not stay to see. In fear for my life, I had to flee. But I expect, yes, young Archer is free."

"You couldn't even keep him locked up for six days?"

Bezeal shook his head.

"Six days, Bezeal?" Kara raged. "That's all we needed. Six days. Couldn't you have just delayed the trial six days? I thought . . . I thought that's what you intended to do."

Bezeal did not answer, but his eyes shrank to pinpricks of light.

"What are we going to do—?"

Kara stopped mid-sentence and stared at her windows. The interior seam of all her penthouse windows glowed bright red. "Something's wrong. Somebody's coming." She glared at Bezeal. "This is your fault. It's probably Keaton banging on the Dream Tower's front door."

"So what if it's him?" Bezeal queried, his voice low and wispy. "Why act so grim? You've beat him before. You'll do it again."

Kara ran to her security console, hit the touch screen, and flew through a dozen different interface windows. "The Harlequin Veil is still fully operational," she muttered. "Pole stations are clear. No, no, it's definitely here, definitely the Dream Tower. They are *inside!*" She turned and sent a flurry of hate darts screaming toward Bezeal. Only with Kara, these weren't figurative hate darts. They were real.

Bezeal deflected them all with a flick of his hand, and the darts buried themselves in the penthouse ceiling.

Kara went back to the touch screen. "I'm going to scan with EMF." After a few finger taps and one finger slide, she hissed. "I'm getting four signals, Bezeal. Four! Three of them are approaching Tesla strength and . . ." Kara went very still. "And one of them is close to Halbach level. That'll be Kaylie. I can't believe this! How did they get in? And, wait, who else? Archer, Nick, Kaylie . . . and who else?"

Bezeal joined her by the security console and said, "I do not know why there are four, but this time, Kara, it's time to make sure. We must usher them all through death's door."

Kara caught her breath. Kill the Dreamtreaders? For a moment, it seemed the wickedest thing she could imagine. But, somehow, with Bezeal by her side, it didn't seem such an unusual conclusion. Everything she'd worked so hard to do, the beautiful new world she'd provided for people to enjoy, these—intruders—were coming to tear it down. They were guilty of trespassing and sabotage . . . and worse. They needed to be stopped. They needed to be ended. Kara turned to the merchant. "For once, Bezeal, I totally agree with you."

THIRTY-ONE

IMMOVABLE OBJECT

"WELL, WELL," RIGBY SAID, STEPPING FROM THE ELEVATOR. "Fancy meeting you two 'ere."

"Really, mate?" Nick quipped. "Could you be any more clichéd? Wait, wait. Could you twirl a black mustache and finish with a fiendish laugh?"

Rigby raised an eyebrow and scratched at his sideburns. "What are two Dreamtreaders doing here?"

"We were wondering the same thing about you," Kaylie said. "I thought Kara had you captive—" Kaylie froze. "Doctor Scoville?"

"Yes," he said. "I am 'ere too, though, I imagine you wish I were not."

Kaylie frowned, remembering the doctor's attempts to enslave her with gort. She remembered the things he'd asked her to do while trapped in the Dream. "I'm stronger now," Kaylie said. "A lot stronger."

Doc Scoville swallowed. "No need for that," he said. "I've changed, heh-heh. But we might pick a better place to chat, hmm?"

"Right," Kaylie said. "Let's get out of here."

"What?" Rigby gawked. "We're not leaving. We're 'ere to take care of Kara and stop all this."

"Stop it all?" Nick blurted. "But you helped cause this whole thing. I ought to chuck a Jackie at ya."

Rigby tilted his head comically. "What?"

Nick clarified, "Hit you in the jaw."

"Look," Rigby said. "To say we screwed up is a light-year from 'ard enough. We've made a royal mess of things. Now we're trying to make amends. We want to set things right."

Kaylie eyed them both suspiciously. "Well," she said, "if that's true, you won't find Kara down here."

"But this is Research and Development," Doc Scoville said. "She's got to be here."

"We've been over every inch of the labs," Nick said. "She's not here."

"She talked about a penthouse apartment," Rigby said. "Bet she's there." He slipped back into the elevator. "Get in."

The slim elevator car was a little more than cozy with all four of them in there. The door shut. Rigby went to reach for the elevator buttons.

"We're not going after Kara," Nick said, blocking Rigby's hand. "Not yet."

"What?" Rigby objected.

"We've got to," Doc Scoville said. "Time is ticking."

"What does that mean?" Kaylie asked.

Rigby raised his voice, saying, "It means that if we don't get this thing turned around soon . . ."

"We won't ever repair the Rift," Doc Scoville finished.

Rigby reached for the highest button, but again Nick blocked him. "Look, mate, if there's something you know, you better tell us."

"We don't know exactly," Rigby said. "We know that time is running out, and we don't know 'ow much time is left. That's what's so frightening. And Kara's running this 'arlequin Veil . . . and it's all gone wrong."

"Harlequin Veil?" Kaylie asked.

"Long story," Rigby said. "But, look, we're going with or without you." He slammed the highest button.

"We saw things in the lab," Kaylie blurted out. She tunneled around the legs of the much taller men, and then slammed the button for the ground floor. "We've got to think this through. And, honestly, I think we need Archer."

"Oh, come now," Rigby sighed. "We'll be just *fine* without—"

"Wait!" Nick shouted. "Shush it. The elevator's not moving."

"We crossed it up," Rigby said, "smacking the two buttons."

"That doesn't make sense," Kaylie said. "You're supposed to be smart."

"Watch it, half-pint!"

Then the elevator did begin to move. But it was going down.

"How can it go down?" Nick asked. "There's nothing below this floor."

"Hit the emergency stop!" Doc Scoville shouted.

Nick reached around the others and slammed the emergency stop button. "Nothing," he said. "We're still going down."

Rigby didn't move. The ferocity of his expression melted away to an angry smirk. He looked like a chess master whose brilliant move had just been countered.

"I'll stop us," Kaylie said. She called up her will and created a powerful updraft beneath the elevator car.

But still the elevator went down.

Kaylie frowned and intensified her will, putting a physical barrier beneath the elevator car. "Oh!" she gasped.

"What?" Nick asked, kneeling to her level. "What's going on?"

"There's something down there," Kaylie said. "Something stronger than I."

Nick frowned. "But nothing's stronger than you."

Doc Scoville asked, "What's down there, Rigby?"

Rigby blinked. "Kara's down there," he said. "Kara and the Scath, and, apparently, she wants us to join 'er."

"We're not ready for this," Kaylie said. "I told you."

"Whether we are or we aren't," Rigby said, "we've not much choice now."

"All together," Doc Scoville said. "Focus your will on the door. No telling what that minx will throw at us."

The elevator drifted down for a few more seconds before coming to a startling rest.

"Whoa!" Kaylie gasped. "That was strange."

"I felt it too," Nick said. "We passed through something. Felt like a layer of skin just got pulled off, fair Dinkum."

"The Veil," Rigby muttered. "It doesn't extend down to this sub-basement."

Kaylie asked, "That's the second time you've mentioned a Veil. What's going on?"

"No time to explain," Rigby said.

Doc Scoville barked, "The doors aren't opening!"

That's when the lights went out.

Kaylie didn't scream, but she did react. "I'm not waiting," she muttered, focusing her will on the front left corner of the elevator car. Fire, lightning, thunder, smoke, and wind flew from her hands, burst through the metal and plastic, opening a nine-foot gash in the elevator and the stone shaft beyond. "We can fly out. Follow me!"

Nick darted out behind her with Rigby right behind. Doc Scoville was last, muttering, "I can't believe I'm following this half-pint."

The four of them skidded to an awkward halt as a slate-gray fog bank rolled toward them. As it neared, it began to undulate. Shreds of darkness peeled away from the mass and streaked in all directions.

"Scath!" Rigby yelled, but he wasn't in a panic. He was angry. Kaylie couldn't help but stare as a top hat appeared in Rigby's hand. With a flourish, he rotated the hat up smoothly onto his head. His eyes began to crackle with red electricity as he thrust out both hands, and then hurled a wide chain mail net at the oncoming horde. The second it left Rigby's hands, the net glowed white-hot as if it had just been taken from a forge. It scooped up a squirming knot of Scath and carried them to the wall on the far side of the cavern, where it seemed to adhere to the stone.

Kaylie felt a sharp pain in her shoulder. She spun just in time to see a vision of shadow and teeth streak away. "Oh, no, you don't!" she cried, reaching over her shoulder for her crossbow. She winced at the pain, took aim, and fired. The projectile wasn't an arrow or dart, but rather a bolt of violet light. It flashed across the cavern, struck the Scath in midair, and reduced the creature to a swirling eddy of ash.

"Hooroooo!" Nick cried out as he sailed over Kaylie's head, his chain flashing to and fro like a whip. He was deadly accurate with those thrashing links, each snap reducing a Scath to ashes . . . at least until Nick dropped to the ground, rolled, and then bashed into a stone wall that hadn't been there a moment ago. The Dreamtreader slumped to the ground with his chain piling up on his back.

"Nick!" Kaylie cried, but Doc Scoville was already racing across the chamber. He knelt at Nick's side, only to be struck so hard by some unseen force that he was bodily launched thirty yards backward.

Rigby cried out, "Uncle!" He loped across the chamber and dove toward Doc Scoville's body.

Kaylie hesitated, not knowing whether to help Doc Scoville or go the longer distance to Nick. She never got to make a choice. There came a sudden vacuum of sound, something like the heart-pounding moment right after a nearby lightning strike. A supernova of brilliant white light filled the cavern. Kaylie dropped to a knee and shielded her eyes with her arms. But the light was a tangible thing. She could feel it on her wrists and palms at first; it was an unnerving fizz that intensified to heat . . . and then it burned.

In the midst of the white light, Kara Windchil appeared. Arms outstretched, silken white-blonde hair flailing violently, she descended, but her scalding brilliance kept Kaylie from watching for too long.

"Hear me!" Kara demanded, her words heavy and impossibly resonant. "Dreamtreaders, bow to your knees! It is your due penance before you die!"

Kara drew her arms in toward her body and seemed to be taking a deep breath. Her brilliance flickered, dimmed, and then surged into her body, giving her the appearance of some figurine lit from within. Her eyes flickered with red lightning. A moment later, she threw her hands forward and screamed.

THIRTY-TWO
WALKING WOUNDED

FORCE.

That is what Kara Windchil wielded like a hammer. When she unleashed her will into the chamber, Kaylie didn't see it coming. She felt it. Waves of irresistible power crashed into her, knocked her off her feet, and sent her cartwheeling violently along the chamber floor.

The pain of the initial impact was immediately eclipsed by the turbulence of being thrown about like a doll. Kaylie lost her crossbow and nearly lost Patches as she tumbled with the force waves. Then something took hold of her arm. The grip was iron-tight. It yanked her sideways out of the power tide and drew her down to a heavenly motionlessness.

Kaylie didn't even realize she was crying until she looked at her rescuer and said his name. "Rigby."

"Don't get used to it," he said with his usual smirk.

They were huddled behind a ridge of stone so black it might have been obsidian. It was shelter from Kara's force wave, but Kaylie knew it wasn't going to last. Doc Scoville lay on his side groaning and holding his ribs. "Your uncle?" she mumbled. "He'll be okay?"

"Uncle Scovy's tough as an old tree root," Rigby said. "You'll see."

"Right, then," Kaylie said through her sniffles. She wiped away the last of her tears. "I'm going after Nick." She stood up, using her will to deflect Kara's force wave, like a stone dividing a river current.

"What are you doing?" Rigby whispered urgently. "Get down."

Doc Scoville cried out, "No, Kaylie!"

But Kaylie was already moving toward Kara. "Why are you doing this?" Kaylie screamed, no hint of fear or sadness, only fierce indignation. "What's wrong with you, Kara?"

Kara drew back her arms, descended to the ground, and strode toward Kaylie. Her tide dissipated in an instant. "There is nothing wrong," Kara said, her voice simmering. "Look at me."

Kara's form was suddenly surrounded by green fire. Her aura grew to a blinding flame, and then faded to reveal Kara in a breathtaking gown. Sapphires, onyxes, and other dark stones glistened along her sleeves, at her neckline, and in clusters upon her full-length skirt. She moved with languid grace, confidence, and purpose. "You see?" Kara asked. "I'm perfect."

"But you used to be so nice," Kaylie muttered.

There was a slight hitch in Kara's step.

"Archer had a crush on you," Kaylie said. "Did you know that?"

Kara stopped. "Where is your brother? Why wouldn't he join you here?"

Kaylie didn't answer. "You've got to stop this, Kara," she said. "It's bad. It's really bad. People are dying out there."

"I am sorry, Kaylie," Kara said, clenching her fists. "But this is for the best." She was about fifty feet from Kaylie when she unleashed another blast of force.

Kaylie was ready this time. She pushed up a massive amount of will as a shield and tossed Patches to the side. The doll pinwheeled through the air and started to grow. Patches landed on his feet, doubled and redoubled his size, and then rammed into Kara from the side. She landed in a jumbled heap. When she pushed herself up from the floor and looked up through mussed hair, her eyes crackled with red electricity. "You little snot!" Kara rasped. "You might be strong for your age, but you're no match for me!"

Kara levitated back to her feet. Shimmering steel armor replaced her black dress, and she drew a wickedly curved dagger in each hand.

She flung a dagger at Patches, stabbing deep into the oversized doll's back. Patches staggered to one knee, and then exploded in a ball of red light.

Kaylie covered her eyes, and when she looked again there was nothing left of Patches but piles of singed fluff.

"Playtime is over," Kara hissed. "My turn—"

A blur. Something moving very fast barreled into Kara, knocking her sideways.

"Pick on someone your own size!" Rigby snarled. He adjusted his top hat, and then held out his hands, each palm full of red lightning.

Kara flopped over and rolled to one knee. Her eyes became huge and haunted. Her mouth hung agape. "Rigby . . . it can't be. Y—you're dead."

"Come now, Kara," Rigby teased. "You're smarter than that, aren't you? It was a ruse. A little trickery, you know."

"I saw your body," Kara muttered. "You weren't breathing."

"How 'ard do you think that was to fake? Never would 'ave worked, though, if the Scath 'adn't 'elped. You enjoy their Something Really Scary game?"

"The Scath wouldn't allow this," Kara muttered. "They are loyal to me."

"Let's just say I appealed to their fundamental nature." Rigby suddenly turned away from Kara for a moment. Perplexed, Kaylie watched him put one hand up to his mouth as if he might shout. But he didn't make a sound. A silvery bubble appeared at his lips. It looked very much the same as a bubble made with chewing gum, only shimmering with a metallic sheen. Rigby seemed to release a strong breath, and the bubble sailed across the cavern, whirling and bobbing like some will-o'-the-wisp. It even managed to hop over the stone that hid Kaylie and Doc Scoville.

When the bubble popped, Kaylie distinctly heard Rigby's voice say, "Uncle Scovy, you and Kaylie get out of 'ere. I'll keep Kara busy so you can escape. I'll do my best to get Nick out too. Run! Run now and don't stop 'til you're free of this place!"

Doc Scoville groaned as he sat up. "You heard the lad. We're leaving, Kaylie."

"But you came here to defeat Kara," she argued. "I don't understand."

"We bit off more than we could chew," he muttered. "That's become a rather tiresome habit of ours. In any case, there will be another day to fight. We need to go now while we can."

"How do we get out?"

"The elevator."

"But I blew up the elevator."

"And . . . why is that a problem? You are a Dreamtreader, aren't you? There are other ways, right?"

"Oh," Kaylie said. "Duh." She stood up and gave a mental command to Patches. The doll reassembled itself and came running in their direction.

Rigby, meanwhile, stood his ground before Kara. He summoned up an ornate walking cane and began to twirl it. Red lightning crackled with each revolution of the cane, and Rigby said, "The trouble with being so smart, Kara, is you can overlook the simple solutions to certain problems."

He'd not even finished the final syllable when he pointed the cane and unleashed a fist of feverish red electricity. The power surged into Kara, lifting her from the ground and throwing her backward. She struck the rear of the cavern with an audible crack.

The sound was so sudden and shocking Rigby thought that, perhaps, he'd done it. He'd caught her off guard and hit her with such a powerful attack he'd knocked her out or at least disabled her. But Rigby, too, had learned from some of his past mistakes. He wasn't about to play games with Kara.

He summoned up his will, dredging up a portion much larger than usual, and began to build. Stone by six-ton stone, Rigby built a crypt over Kara's prone form. The weight alone should have kept Kara down. But then Rigby created a chain net, draped it over the crypt, and secured it by pounding twelve-foot stakes into the cavern's solid rock floor.

Half-spent but exhilarated by the successful attack, Rigby bounded to Nick's side. He knelt down. "G'day, mate!" Rigby announced cheerily. "Or whatever you blokes down under say. Come on, then. Up with you."

But Nick did not stir. Rigby's breath caught in his throat. Trickles of blood were coming from the corners of Nick's eyes. Rigby put his ear close to Nick's face. "C'mon now, Nick, you can't let her take you out this easily!"

Rigby waited anxiously for a breath. And it came. It was a faint breath, somewhat irregular, and positively reeking of garlic, but it was there. "Nick, you there?"

"*Rak-ta, Shak-ta,*" Nick muttered, "come . . . come to me."

"What?" Rigby said. "Speak English, would ya? Nick, snap out of it."

"Bonzer, mate," Nick whispered, his eyes springing open. "I feel like I was hit by a Mack truck."

Rigby sat up little, breathed a sigh of relief, and said, "Glad you pulled through. Next time, remember: a little defense goes a long—"

A sound stopped Rigby in mid-sentence. It was a rumble, but not a deep thunder sort of sound. More like a churning of many stones turning over and over and over.

Rigby stood up and prepped his will. The ponderous chain net still covered the crypt, still secured it to the cavern floor. It wasn't trembling. There was no evidence it was moving at all.

"What an amateur," came a voice from behind, and Rigby felt himself picked up by the seat of his jeans. He flared up red lighting from his fingertips and from his walking cane, but it did nothing to stop him from being manhandled, slung around, and hurled across the cavern.

Rigby had the presence of mind to recognize his body's trajectory. He used his will to exert force against the opposite wall of the cavern, to slow his approach. But even as he slowed down and defeated the possibility of being pulverized by the wall, something tore the shoulder off his jacket.

No, it had cut through the jacket, his shirt beneath, and opened a burning gash in the flesh of his shoulder. Rigby landed in a crouch just in time to see a dozen more of Kara's daggers flashing toward him. Rigby held out his top hat, and it turned into the shield. A few daggers careened off the shield. Several others buried themselves hilt-deep.

"Playing for keeps now, are we, Kara?" Rigby said, casting away the shield. His top hat reappeared in his right hand, and he swept it upon his head. "I didn't think you 'ad it in you."

Red electricity sparking all around her, Kara appeared from thin air over Nick's prone form. "You want the Australian, Rigby? Come get him."

In spite of his better judgment, Rigby strode toward Kara. Halfway there, he froze. There in the shadows, just over Kara's shoulder, were two sparkling eyes and a Cheshire grin.

"Bezeal," he muttered, taking a hesitant step backward.

Kara began to laugh. She dropped to a crouch and reached forward. Rigby couldn't tell what she was doing. When she stood, she held the end of a six-foot wide strip of stone. With will-augmented strength beyond anything Rigby had ever imagined, Kara whipped the stone as if it were a blanket. The motion sent a quaking tremor rolling across the cavern floor. Rigby tried to leap out of the way, but it took his feet out from under him and sent him cartwheeling into the air. He came down in a heap near the stone where Kaylie and Doc Scoville had been hiding.

Rigby rose to a knee and nearly blacked out. He blinked and rubbed the back of his head. "Ah, they got out," he whispered. He glanced across the cavern to Nick. "Sorry, mate," he said. "I'm not up to this. Not yet."

Rigby fled. He sprinted to the torn-down elevator shaft, and began climbing like a frenzied spider. Kara's voice followed him the whole way. "Run, run, Rigby! It will all be over soon!"

THIRTY-THREE
A House Divided

"Did you see that?" Kara asked as she waltzed around one of the medical clinic's recovery rooms. "I beat them. I beat them all."

Bezeal paced in front of the cobalt cube, putting his own finishing touches on the prison Kara had created to imprison Nick Bushman. "Careless fight," Bezeal muttered. "Rigby's appearance was such a fright, and you've yet to face the Dreamtreaders' full might."

"Don't be morose," Kara muttered. "They were toys to me."

"They were supposed to be broken toys," Bezeal hissed. "And yet . . . they live." The merchant became very still. His arms hung at his sides, his hands clenching and unclenching.

Kara stopped twirling. She had seen Bezeal in this mood on only a few occasions. Though she wouldn't allow herself to be afraid of Bezeal, something about his dark moods troubled her. Sometimes it was just the lack of rhyming, ominous in its rarity. But very rarely, it was almost like a second personality came to the surface, a menace hidden beneath that hood.

"Need . . . I . . . remind . . . you, Kara," Bezeal said, his voice dropping octaves with each word, "they bypassed your vaunted tower's defenses. They toured your precious Research and Development sector for half an hour before you were even aware of their presence. And what of Rigby? You claimed he was dead."

"He was dead," Kara bristled, "by any human standards, anyway.

It was the Scath's fault. They were supposed to serve me alone. I am their master."

"They call you master," Bezeal muttered. "But the Scath cannot be mastered, not entirely. They will do as you command, but they live for mischief. You should have known this. You should have made certain with Rigby."

"Like you made certain with Archer?" Kara quipped. "You were supposed to keep Archer Keaton occupied. Six days were all we needed, Bezeal. Remind me again how you messed that up?"

"Be silent!" Bezeal's voice dropped to such a low that it became a vibration, shaking the concrete and steel foundations, the glass panes, and electronics panels. When he turned, his pinprick eyes had grown to dark red gouges. "You dare stand in judgment? Over me? Fool! No one is Bezeal's judge. Do you understand?"

Kara swallowed and nodded, but within, she smoldered. She'd seen Bezeal's little scary song and dance many times before. *So the little beast thinks he's top dog now?* she thought. *Go ahead and believe that . . . for now.*

Bezeal's eyes returned to their normal flickering points of light floating in the inky black beneath his hood. "Now, sweet Kara, it is time for your power to pour. We must end this game; we must make sure. At last, it is time for us to make war."

"War?" Kara echoed. "I don't understand. We've won the war. All we need is to keep them at bay for a few more days."

"Are you so certain your plans will not fail? The Dreamtreaders have already learned to pierce your Veil. From decisive action we must not quail."

"They broke through the Harlequin Veil, but only for a time. They don't know our secrets. They don't know . . ." Her voice trailed off. She thought back to her conversations with Rigby while he had been her prisoner. Under the assumption that he would never escape, how much had she told him?

She began to pace the medical center. What if Rigby had made the proper inferences about his cobalt shackles? Combining that with what he already knew about the Rift and the Harlequin Veil . . . well . . . that could mean serious trouble.

"We've got to get rid of Rigby and his uncle," she said at last. "They are too smart for their own good." The moment the word *smart* passed her lips, she felt a chill.

Kaylie.

Kara hung her head and closed her eyes. Kaylie would be a problem also. She was astoundingly brilliant and perceptive. And she'd had a look around Research and Development. If Kaylie and Rigby compared notes, it would only be a matter of time before they unraveled the whole thing.

"Fine," Kara said, opening her eyes. "We take the fight to them. You and me, Bezeal, we finish it."

"Nay," Bezeal said. "Not just we two. Not enough to see this through. But I believe an army will do."

"An army?" Kara replied. "Where will we get an army?"

Bezeal drew a green finger across Nick's cobalt cube and sidled closer to Kara. "We might find some . . . *willing* to play," he said. "Soldiers many, fearless, and tame—the Nightmare Lords discovered a way."

Kara put it together in an instant. "I'll call Frederick. It's so simple, really. And it won't take long." She laughed, and her eyes crackled with familiar red electricity.

She stopped a moment and stared down at the cobalt cube. "Gort won't be enough for this one," she said. "Do you think Nick would respond to one of your whisper treatments?"

"Everyone responds," Bezeal replied, "maybe sooner or maybe later. Even the strongest make no debate. Surely it will cure the Dreamtreader in the crate."

Nick Bushman had been in a lot of fixes. Just walking around Australia's outback could be a threat to one's health and life, what with all the poisonous spiders and snakes that made the region their home. But he couldn't ever recall a predicament quite like this one.

"They put me in the dunnie this time, haven't they?" Nick muttered to his cramped quarters. "S'truth, they tossed me in a box like some kind of a pet."

That was a rather large insult to his already-injured pride. He couldn't believe the ease with which Kara had taken him out. *The Rift,* he thought. *We all got stronger after the Rift. But Kara . . . she's off the charts.*

Worst of all, Nick thought, was getting an ear-bashing from Kara and Bezeal, hearing all about their plans for an army to use against Archer, Kaylie, Rigby, and the Doc—but not being able to do a thing to warn them. He'd tried. He'd searched deep within his mind for just a little bit of Dreamtreader will, something that might let him create a message to send out . . . or even make some kind of telepathic connection. He didn't know if such a thing were even possible for a full-strength Dreamtreader. There was no mention of such a thing in the Creeds, at least in the parts he'd read so far. He'd tried, anyway, tried hard with every bit of concentration and screaming hope he could muster.

Nick slammed his hand into the side of his prison. A sharp strike of pain made him wish he hadn't. He closed his eyes and bowed his head. At least he could still pray, he thought.

"Whoa," Nick blurted as his prison cube began to move. "Hey, take it easy out there!" he yelled, but there was no reply. He slapped his hands against the walls to no avail. The cube shook and wobbled and tilted. Then it became steady again and began a long, slow march forward.

"This might be it," he muttered. He closed his eyes, ducked his head, and went back to prayer.

Some time passed. Nick wasn't sure if he'd fallen asleep or was still awake. It was dark as ever in the box. But he thought for certain he'd heard something. There had been a shriek in the distance. Surely, somewhere outside of the box, outside of the lab, and maybe even outside of the building. But what had it been? There was a familiarity to it.

Another sound. This much closer, a rumbly, growling sound. But Nick didn't jump. It didn't frighten him. "Can't be," he whispered. "Can it?" Nick closed his eyes and probed the depths of his thoughts.

Rak-ta, he voiced in his mind, *Shak-ta? Soonerian, se?*

A few tense heartbeats later, foreign thoughts invaded Nick's mind, and he was everlastingly grateful. "Yes," two voices said in unison, "we are coming."

THIRTY-FOUR
ALLEGIANCES

ARCHER SAT DOWN ON THE EDGE OF HIS BED AND STARED through his window. Old Jack was back.

"Why is it back now?" Archer wondered aloud.

What really troubled him was Old Jack's face. Before the Rift, the clock showed the Dreamtreader's allotted eleven hours, missing only the six due to Sixtolls, the randomly occurring hour of the Nightmare Lord's chaos. Now, Old Jack showed only six hours. And rather than counting forward in time (one leads to two, leads to three, etc.), Old Jack now seemed to be counting down from six.

Archer thought he knew what Old Jack was counting down to now, but if he were right, it was a frightening prospect. The ancient clock face already showed half past four.

Archer pulled himself away from the window, sat up, and tossed the Summoning Feather into the air. Master Gabriel did not delay. To Archer's relief, he did not appear to have guards or handcuffs with him when he arrived.

"It is about time," Master Gabriel grumbled, stepping from the closet. His Incandescent Armor already burned brightly. "Archelion Michael informed me of your release. I would have expected a call from you sooner."

"I'm sorry," Archer said, "I needed to come home first. I needed to check on my family."

"And?"

"The same," Archer said, lowering his eyes. "They're under some kind of spell, wandering about the protective vault I built around them."

"I am sorry, Archer," Master Gabriel said.

"Kaylie's gone now," Archer said with a sigh. "Did you wake her? What about Nick?"

He took a deep breath. "I propose an exchange of information. Tell me about your court process. I will update you on Kaylie, Nick, Kara, and more."

Archer nodded and began to detail his court battle with Bezeal, leading ultimately to the merchant's banishing from the court and subsequent escape. In turn, Master Gabriel spoke of waking Nick from the post-Rift, perfect-world illusion. He informed Archer of Kaylie's self-awakening, and the two Dreamtreaders' plans to infiltrate the Dream Tower.

"But I do not know the results of their mission," Master Gabriel explained. "Kaylie has yet to summon me."

"Should I be worried?"

"I do not believe so," Master Gabriel replied. "They were not planning to confront Kara, not yet. Their mission was infiltration and reconnaissance."

Archer nodded, glancing through the gap in his curtains. "Old Jack is back." He pulled back the curtains.

"So I see, but with six hours?"

Archer shook his head. "I'm not sure it's hours this time."

"Why?" Master Gabriel replied. "What else could it be?"

"Days," Archer said. "After the court case, Bezeal was so enraged that he began muttering to himself, something about needing only six days. It sounded like he wanted to keep me out of action for at least that long."

Master Gabriel spun on his heel. "This . . . this is encouraging, Archer!"

"I don't see how. Look at Old Jack. It's counting down. If I'm right, we've only got three and a half days left."

Master Gabriel frowned. "You are looking at the wrong side of this, Archer. If you are right, and it is six days—now down to a little more than three—remaining, ask yourself, three days until . . . what? Why would it be so important to Bezeal for you to be unable to fulfill your Dreamtreading duties for such a limited time?"

Archer wished he had an intellect as quick and deep as Kaylie's. His thoughts felt like churning butter, slow and sloppy. Then, like the parting of a curtain, the idea came to him. His eyes sprang wide open with brows raised, and he even dared to smile. "Do you think?" he asked. "There's still a chance?"

Master Gabriel nodded. "I do."

"Snot rockets!" Archer shouted. "I've got to find Kaylie and Nick!"

"I suggest you try Scoville Manor."

"Scoville Manor?" Archer barked, incredulous. "Why would I go there?"

"Aside from the fact that it is my advice to you, you just might find Kaylie there."

"Oh, no," Archer groused. "Rigby doesn't have her captive, does he?"

"No, no," Master Gabriel explained. "Nothing like that. Just go and see. Oh, and Archer, keep an open mind."

Archer didn't knock. He didn't ring the doorbell.

He stood on the front porch, focused his will for a thunder-stomp, and blew the door off its hinges. He stepped through the wreckage and cried out, "Rigby! Where are you? What have you done with Kaylie?"

There was no answer. Even the pets in the basement were silent. They should have been barking, screeching, yipping, and yapping their heads off. "Rigby!" Archer yelled. "Doctor Scoville! Where are you?"

After a quick search of the upstairs, he raced down to the basement zoo, but the zoo wasn't there anymore. In its place was a magnificent and very futuristic laboratory. No test tubes and beakers sitting on Bunsen burners—it clearly wasn't that sort of lab. Instead, there were banks of slender computer servers, touch screens, tablets, styluses, and a vast array of flat-screen monitors, the smallest of which had to be at least ten feet wide. Those were just the things Archer could identify.

More amazing still were massive rolls of fiber-optic lines that reminded Archer of gigantic bundles of glowing yarn. Up above, thick tubes formed a dizzying labyrinth. Some were clear and full of bubbling liquid; others were more metallic. On the far side of the vast laboratory was what Archer originally took to be a kind of vault door. Full of chrome and brass components and thick circular slabs, it looked like something out of a federal bank. Archer stepped a little closer and noticed it was in motion. The centermost circle, where the spindle on a bank vault would be, was a radial dial turning slowly clockwise. Not clockwise, but oscillating. Large screens flanked the strange apparatus and showed various digital views of the earth.

"This place is crazy," Archer muttered. "It almost looks like—"

"Dream Inc."

Archer whirled around to find Rigby had appeared on his right.

"It's very close to the original blueprints, along with a few upgrades we observed at Kara—"

With will-augmented speed, Archer flew into Rigby and pinned him against a pillar of concrete and steel. "Where is she, Rigby?" he demanded. "Where's my sister?"

"I'm right here, Archer," Kaylie grumbled. "Put him down. We're friends again."

"Friends?" Archer barked. "Friends? Kaylie, don't you know what

Rigby was going to do . . . to you? Don't you know what happened at the hospital?"

"I know," Kaylie said. "Rigby and Uncle Scovy told me all about it. But Kara lied. Did you know that? Rigby never pulled out that plug."

"What?" Archer gasped.

"It's true, Keaton," Rigby said through clenched teeth. "Now, be a good lad, and set me on my feet."

Archer lowered Rigby to the floor. "I don't believe you," he whispered. "I saw it. I saw it in your eyes."

Rigby stared at the floor. "I'm not proud of that night," he said, his voice uncharacteristically shaky. "I was desperate. All my plans, everything and everyone I ever cared about seemed to be slipping through my fingers."

Archer tightened his fists on Rigby's jacket. "She's a little girl, Rigby."

"No, I'm not," Kaylie insisted. "I am a Dreamtreader and a strong one too."

"Anyway, Keaton, like I told you. I never pulled the plug. I went there in a fit of madness, and I almost did . . . well . . . I almost made a tragic mistake. I guess you wouldn't know about that, would you?"

Archer released Rigby and wandered a few paces away. He remembered being in this very basement, albeit before it had become a space station. He remembered staring at Doc Scoville's comatose body, his shriveled form kept alive by a dozen machines. One flip of the master power switch. That's all it would have taken.

"I know something about tragedy," he whispered. The Dreamtreader turned on his heels and went face-to-face with Rigby once more. "Swear to me, Rigby," he snarled. "Swear to me you never pulled that plug."

"Okay, okay, Keaton," Rigby muttered. "I swear, okay? Good enough?"

"For now," Archer said, but he was far from certain. He'd be watching Rigby carefully. And he'd be ready if Rigby showed any sign of treachery. He stepped away and gestured to the machinery and electronics. "So what's all this? Had to take a lot of mental energy to build something so huge . . . and so advanced."

"Wasn't so tough, Keaton," Rigby said, "when you've got three of us working on it."

Kaylie nodded. Archer sniffed the air. "Where'd all the critters go? I can't even smell 'em."

"They're two levels down, Archer," Kaylie said. "It's like a great big terrarium down there. We built that too. You should see it. The animals are much happier now. I think Dr. Who misses you. And did you know Old Jack is back? Weird, he only has six numbers—"

"Where's Doc Scoville? Where's Nick?"

"We 'ave a lot to talk about," Rigby said. "Good news and bad."

"We're onto something, Archer!" Kaylie squealed. "Something big. And I mean really, really, really, really, really, really—"

"I get it," Archer said, putting his hands lightly on her shoulders. "Something big, but what?"

"Nothing certain yet," Rigby explained. "Promising, but not certain. We 'ave more research to do, more tests."

"This is torture!" Archer grumbled. "Research and tests for what?"

"Magnets!" Kaylie squeaked. She bounced up and down so much her pigtails did a little dance.

Archer frowned. "O . . . kay, magnets? For what?"

"Silly," Kaylie replied. "For fixing the Rift!"

Dreamtreader Creed, Conceptus 15

If your Master should present to you a Dream creature, think of it as more than a pet. For really, the creature can be a very able assistant. Whether as a messenger, a breach-spotter, breach-stitcher, or even for entertainment, these mercurial creatures will make your Dreamtreading less of a burden.

What sort of creature, you may wonder? It is different for each Dreamtreader, but you will likely find the creature suits you in some way. Often, the creature will help cultivate a character trait you are currently lacking. They may even try your patience, but remember: they are there for your own good.

That is, of course, when they choose to come at your call.

THIRTY-FIVE
RESEARCH AND DEVELOPMENT

"SNOT ROCKETS, KAYLIE!" ARCHER EXCLAIMED. "THAT'S the best news I've heard in a long time."

She leaped into his arms and squeezed like a grizzly bear. Well, like a grizzly cub. "Isn't it great?" Kaylie asked, snuggling under Archer's chin. "We'll have Dad back and Buster and Amy and—"

"Didn't you 'ear me, Keaton?" Rigby asked. "I said it's not all good news."

Archer put Kaylie down. "Kaylie, I want to hear all about the magnets and Rift-fixing, but uh . . . maybe I should hear the bad news first."

Kaylie stuck out her bottom lip. "Kara took Nick," she said.

"I tried to get 'im back," Rigby explained. He stared at the floor. "But Kara was too strong."

Archer's eyes narrowed. He'd heard stories like this from Rigby before. "You mean you conveniently left Nick?"

"That's not fair, Keaton," Rigby growled. "You weren't there. You didn't see what Kara could do."

"Rigby took on Kara so Uncle Scovy and I could escape," Kaylie said. "If it weren't for Rigby, I'd have been caught too."

"Kara's that strong?" Archer asked, blinking. "Even compared to us? Even with all the extra power we have due to the Rift?"

Rigby sneered. "It's galling, actually," he said. "I don't know what she's gotten into, but she's ten times stronger than she ever was."

Ten times? The thought hit Archer like an ice ball to the temple. *How'd she get so strong?*

Doc Scoville darted out from a corner of the lab. "Ah, Archer's back at last!" he said. "You couldn't have come at a better time. We're about to run the test!"

Archer was lost again. "What test?"

"Well, Anchor Protocol, of course," he said, adjusting his glasses. "The test of tests, heh-heh."

"I helped name it," Kaylie said, beaming. "C'mon."

As Kaylie led Archer into another wing of the lab, Archer couldn't help feeling a little surreal. He and Kaylie were walking side by side with Rigby Thames and Doc Scoville, known in the Dream as the Lurker. Betrayals, failures, lies, destruction—so much of it due to the actions of these two. *And yet here I am playing friendly again,* Archer thought. *I won't get fooled this time. Never again.*

In the next room were more monitors, these humming with graphical motion. Servers lined the right-hand wall, with some kind of glassed-in workshop on the left.

"Take a seat," Doc Scoville said.

The four of them rolled their chairs over to the center monitor. It was running some kind of split-screen application, but Archer couldn't make heads or tails of any one of the screens.

"Ready for the test?" Doc Scoville asked anxiously.

"Wait," Archer said. "You need to catch me up a little bit first. All I know is that it has to do with magnets."

Doc Scoville looked crestfallen. "But the test?"

"It's okay, Uncle," Rigby said. "We just need to back up a little for Keaton 'ere."

Doc Scoville frowned and nodded reluctantly.

"Okay, Keaton," Rigby said. "So this started when Kara and I were running Dream Inc. out of the Antietam Creek Building . . ."

"Back when you were selling Lucid Walking trips to the highest bidders?" Archer asked. "And tearing holes in the Dream fabric? Is that what you mean?"

Rigby folded his arms across his chest. "Look, Keaton, are you just going to keep throwing cheap shots, or are you going to listen?"

Archer didn't answer but motioned for Rigby to carry on.

With a slight shake of the head, Rigby explained, "Some of the customers tried to bring things back . . . back from the Dream. You know, a souvenir from the journey, that kind of thing? Thing is, whatever they brought back played 'avoc with our electronics. Didn't matter if it was big as a pirate ship or as small as a gold doubloon, the thing was ultra-magnetized."

"Did anyone really bring back a pirate ship?" Kaylie asked.

Rigby raised an eyebrow. "Uh, no, I was just saying . . . but they brought back plenty of other things. We didn't know why they came out magnetized, but we were easily able to catch anyone who tried to smuggle something out. The magnetic field gave them away."

"So what's this have to do with fixing the Rift?" Archer asked.

"It's all about electromagnetic fields," Doc Scoville cackled. "I don't know how we missed it all these years."

"Easy, Uncle," Rigby said. He typed a few commands on the keyboard, and then took hold of something that looked like a flight simulator joystick. "Let's prove we're right first."

"Don't you see, Archer?" Kaylie asked. "There's a powerful magnetic force in the Dream."

"I get it," he said. "But I still don't get it."

"Don't worry, Archer," she said. "I didn't get it either until we were snooping around in Kara's research center. She had some machines and computer applications that I'd never seen before. But when I saw she was measuring magnetic fields, especially the strongest magnetic fields, I figured it out."

"Okay," Rigby said. "So watch the screen." Rigby's fingers flew on the keyboard, and a wire-frame representation of the earth appeared.

At least, Archer thought it was the earth. Dotted-line rings circled the planet, like the planet Saturn. But not quite, these rings passed in and out of the planet's mass. Rigby kept typing, and two points appeared.

"Know what these are?" Rigby asked.

Archer guessed, "North and South Poles?"

"Close," Rigby explained. "These are the magnetic North and South Poles, distinct from the geographical poles, y'know, like the actual locations South Pole and North Pole on the map. Heh-heh. Santa's place, right? The geographical poles don't move, but the magnetic poles do. And these circles are the electromagnetic fields of the earth as they normally are. Now watch this."

He clicked a few more buttons. Archer blinked at the screen. There were a lot more dotted-line circles, but these were horizontal.

"Now this," Rigby said, "is earth after the Rift. Right now, as a matter of fact."

"I—I—I don't understand what I just saw," Archer admitted. "It looks like there are two more magnetic poles, only the two new ones are going east and west."

"No, no, you got it," Rigby said. "Don't you see? The Rift gave us new poles."

"Yes, yes," Doc Scoville said. "And this is the very thing we need to test. We've just gotten the data in to run a simulation."

"What data?" Archer asked.

"Fluctuations in the earth's electromagnetic field. Fluctuations over the last two years, leading up to the Rift," said Doc Scoville.

Archer sat up rigidly. "You mean since you started Lucid Walking?"

Rigby didn't say anything, but he nodded slowly.

"Run it, Rigby," Doc Scoville urged.

"Roger that," he replied, his fingers rippling over the keyboard like a pair of frenzied spiders. He clicked once more. "And 'ere we go."

THIRTY-SIX
THREE DAYS

ARCHER STARED AT THE SCREEN. HE WASN'T ENTIRELY sure what he was looking for. The digital earth appeared once more, the magnetic North and South Poles looking pretty much as before, the rings circulating north and south. Then, just a few seconds in, the North and South Poles appeared to shift. It was more of a wobble, Archer thought, the rings shifting a little one way and then the other.

"How much time is passing?" Archer asked.

"A week per second," Rigby said.

The magnetic fields of the digital earth continued to waver. A few seconds passed. Then the whole screen flickered.

"Wait!" Archer said. "Did you see that?"

"Back it up three weeks, Rigby," Doc Scoville said.

Rigby did. "Oh, now *that* is peculiar," he said.

There had been a rogue fluctuation. A new ring of electromagnetic energy had formed for just a moment.

"Point of origin?" Doc Scoville asked. "Looks like the UK."

Rigby clicked away. "Glasgow, Scotland."

Archer frowned, something itching at the back of his mind, but nothing he could identify.

Rigby pulled up a picture within the main screen. "This field," he said, "will monitor for similar magnetic spikes." He tapped a few keys. "Going forward now."

Archer lost count of the rogue spikes, but became mesmerized by the way the north and south fields were bouncing. One minute they were steady. The next, the graphic looked like a Slinky bent in half.

"Getting into this past autumn," Rigby said. "That's . . . that's just incredible. The movement . . . so far."

"There!" Doc Scoville said, pointing.

The east and west fields made their first appearances. They flickered and were gone, but in a few seconds they returned . . . and they remained. More and more rings appeared. They too began to wobble violently. Then there was a flash, and the screen froze.

Archer asked, "What happened?"

No one answered right away. Doc Scoville knelt to give Kaylie a high five, and then he yanked Rigby out of the chair and hugged him.

"What?" Archer groused. "You wanna tell me what's going on?"

"There's still a chance," Doc Scoville said.

"I think Kaylie's plan will do it," Rigby said.

"But we haven't much time," Doc Scoville said. "Reverse the algorithm. Reduce the frequency and go from the Rift to this very moment."

"Right," Rigby said, leaping back into his chair. "On it."

Archer was fit to be tied. "Would someone please tell me—"

"Shhh!" Rigby, Doc Scoville, and Kaylie cut him off.

Another data field appeared on screen. As the digital earth's EM fields jumped around, the numbers rolled on the new field. Then it all stopped again.

The number field read:

78:24:46:02

"How long is that?" Doc Scoville asked. "I'm too excited. I can't think straight, heh-heh!"

"It's a little over three days," Rigby said, his tone much soberer than a moment ago.

"That's a tight window," Doc Scoville grumbled. "I still have so many tests. We'll have to factor in travel. There's so much to do, and just three days . . ."

"It matches up with Old Jack," Archer muttered, leaping from his chair and trotting to the lab's nearest window. "Yup! Three days left, and it looks like to the minute."

"Old Jack?" Rigby echoed thoughtfully. "The clock tower you Dreamtreaders use, kind of like Big Ben in London, right?"

"Yup, yup," Kaylie agreed.

Doc Scoville looked up from a notepad filled with calculations. "But I thought that was only in the Dream."

"It just showed up again," Archer explained. "But it's keeping time differently. Not hours, but days."

"How peculiar," Rigby said, squinting. "And it's at three days? Like the chronometer?"

Archer nodded, returning to his seat.

"Where does the clock—Old Jack—where does it come from?" Rigby asked.

"I don't know actually," Archer replied. "Master Gabriel has never said."

"Not in the Creeds either," Kaylie said. "Not the cause of it anyway."

Rigby shifted uncomfortably in his chair. "Is it like Dreamtreader will, maybe something out of your subconscious?"

Archer shrugged. "Like I said, I don't know."

Doc Scoville looked up from his calculations. "Has it . . . has Old Jack ever steered you wrong? You know, showed the wrong time or . . . uh . . . put you in danger?"

"*No,*" Kaylie said emphatically, drawing out the word. "Never."

"Why so interested in Old Jack?" Archer asked. "It's harmless."

"Well," Doc Scoville said, "whatever it is, it managed to survive the Rift."

Save for the quiet hum of the servers, the laboratory went silent.

Archer had never really given much thought to Old Jack. The old clock was pretty much a part of the scenery of the Dream, a landmark like the Empire State Building or Mount Rushmore. The fact that Dreamtreaders could always see Old Jack no matter how far away it was—well, that was strange. But then again, so was most of what happened in the Dream.

"So three days," Doc Scoville muttered as he scribbled on the notepad once more. "If we position the anchors correctly, it should push the magnetic fields back."

"What happens after three days?" Archer asked.

The room grew very quiet. Kaylie frowned, Rigby's eyes seemed to glaze over, and Doc Scoville said, "In three days, the earth's magnetic field will be set in its normal position."

"But you said it moves all the time," Archer said.

"It moves a little, but not like it has with the Rift. The thing's all out of whack, but it's still swinging with the Rift's initial push. If we wait past the three days, we'll still be able to move it, but we won't have the momentum from the Rift. We'll never push it far enough. The Rift and all its consequences will become permanent."

"As in there'll be nothing we can do?" Archer asked.

Rigby rolled his eyes. "As in the normal meaning of *permanent*, Keaton."

"Let's not think that way," Doc Scoville said. "It's simply a deadline."

"We can do this," Kaylie said. "Archer? Do you hear? Anchor Protocol is going to work. Archer?"

But Archer didn't answer. He couldn't answer. He was no longer aware of anyone in that room. A high shriek had pierced his consciousness, followed by a regal, melodious voice, speaking in a language Archer at first did not understand.

Te voxis, Kae-ah-tohn. Te voxis borundum entrar mil se bonis. Skandar belli, skandar vin thel te mourna xivis . . .

It was an unearthly language, proudly spoken, but desperate to be understood. Archer trembled, gasped, and then convulsed so terribly he fell out of the chair. As he thrashed about on the cold floor, at last he began to understand the message.

THIRTY-SEVEN
WHISPERS AND FLAME

"THESE NUMBERS," KARA SAID, FLIPPING BACK AND FORTH through the packet Frederick had given her. "Are these right? We have that many people coming in?"

"Baltimore is a large city," Frederick replied, gesturing with a sweep of his arm to the vast metropolis beyond the window glass. He sat on the edge of the conference table, adjusted his ever-dark sunglasses, and said, "Six hundred thousand people and counting—there's bound to be a healthy supply."

Kara frowned and tilted her head. A ribbon of her silky black hair swung down over her eyes like a pendulum. With a curt wave of the hand, she tossed it back, and said, "But there are fifteen hundred names here."

"Not enough?"

"More than enough," Kara replied incredulously. "Far higher than our initial projections. Can we treat them all in time?"

Frederick whipped out his phone. "We're already at 66 percent," he replied. "Thanks to Mr. Bezeal."

Kara shook her head in amazement, both at this extraordinary news . . . and at Frederick's calling her merchant *Mister* Bezeal. "He is kind of a miracle worker," she said. "When can we expect full strength?"

He didn't answer right away but scrolled on his phone, his fingers swishing back and forth as if he were tracing an inverted cross. "By tomorrow morning," he said. "At the latest."

"I want to see them," Kara said.

"Let's go," Frederick replied, springing off the table. "I think you'll be pleased."

Archer stopped convulsing. He lay very still and lost any concept of where he was. "Archer, Archer! Please wake up!" came a voice.

Archer felt movement around his body. Someone said, "Nephew?"

"It wasn't me!" someone exclaimed. "I didn't do anything!"

In a warbling storm of sound, the world came back to Archer. He coughed, spat, and tried to sit up.

"Easy, Archer," Doc Scoville cautioned.

"No, can't," Archer coughed. "Nick . . . I . . . the valkaryx . . ."

"What? Keaton, you're not making any sense."

Archer blinked. "Help . . . help me up." Rigby and Doc Scoville each took one of Archer's arms. Kaylie hovered around like a mother hen.

"I know of the valkaryx," Doc Scoville muttered. "Majestic creatures in the Dream."

"No," Archer said. "Here. They survived the Rift, at least Nick's pair did. Rock and Shock, he calls them."

"What happened to you, Archer?" Kaylie asked, a worried quiver still in her voice.

He looked at her. "I . . . I don't know exactly. But Rock and Shock, they found Nick at the Dream Tower but couldn't get to him, couldn't rescue him. They could speak to him, though. And through them, Nick . . . he sent us a message."

"Well, out with it, lad!" Doc Scoville said. "Honestly, you've gone ghost-pale, Archer. What was Nick's message?"

Archer blinked. "Kara knows where we are," he said. "She's tracked us somehow."

"Magnetic signature," Doc Scoville mumbled.

"Gotta be," Rigby confirmed.

"She's building an army," Archer whispered, "not to capture us but to wipe us out."

Kaylie's hands flew to her lips. "Oh!"

"It's worse than that," Archer muttered. "Kara and Bezeal are going to do something to Nick . . . something . . . I don't know, something that turns him against us. They're going to use Nick as a weapon against us."

Kara's private elevator dropped below Research and Development and came to a gentle stop at the recently repaired section of the shaft in the region she called Beneath. It was a gaping, open space with an arched, stalactite-ridden ceiling hidden in shadows far overhead. The Karakurian Chamber was there, as was her throne. It was her area. *But it is no longer private, is it?* she thought. *Bezeal knows. The blasted Dreamtreaders know. Rigby and his uncle know. And now Frederick knows.*

But when the elevator doors opened, Kara quickly realized a few more people were now aware of the Beneath. An army of fifteen hundred was now using the cavern as a mustering point. Even more were on the way.

The vast chamber lay in a shadow, but the soldiers were unmistakable. "Breathtaking," Kara whispered.

Frederick smirked. "You haven't seen anything yet."

"What do you mean?"

"Take the stage," he said, gesturing forward. "Bezeal told me he left you something on your throne that will be of interest to you . . ."

Kara raised an eyebrow and strode toward the mass of soldiers. When she stepped within ten feet of them, the entire troop came to simultaneous attention. In unison, they made a quarter turn inward and opened a six-foot aisle for Kara. As she marched between them, Kara couldn't help but marvel at her army.

They were outfitted in armor that looked equal parts medieval and science fiction. It gleamed as if it were made of black glass but had some kind of beveling on the surface, giving it depth and weight. Each warrior wore a bulbous oval helm, connected by thin tubes that disappeared over an articulated mantle of shoulder plates. Futuristic weapons crisscrossed each warrior's breastplate. Additional guns, rifles, blades, and blunt objects were attached at each soldier's hips and again at their thighs.

Every third warrior possessed some kind of pike weapon, something Kara couldn't readily identify. They were a little too thick to be spears, a little too long to be staffs, and they weren't tapered like jousting lances. And yet there was still something very menacing about them. Kara made a mental note to ask Bezeal later.

She strode up the stairs to the waiting stage. *Odd.* Bezeal must have redesigned the space in here. The stage area and the stairs were all new. Her throne had a much higher vantage now. She stared out over the soldiers, amazed at how silent they could all be. Of course, they were under the influence of a rather concentrated dose of gort, a dose they'd all willingly taken, thinking it was medicine to relieve their Rift disorientation.

Kara stopped suddenly, gaping at the object that lay on her seat. It was curled in a tight spiral like a sleeping snake. But Kara knew it was far more powerful and dangerous than any serpent. It was a thick whip made of braided strips of dark leather that might have once been the color of rust, but through use and staining, had turned dark but for its orangey fringes. Perhaps three inches down its baton-sized handle it tapered around and around in the coil. A tiny skull of glistening copper was affixed there. It was eighteen feet of coiled malice, and Kara knew its name.

"Vorcaust," she whispered, taking up the baton handle. "The Tongue of Fire."

The moment she allowed it to uncoil to its full length, she felt a *whoosh!* Crimson fire raced along its entire length, but it did not burn her hand. This was meant for others, for control. Swooning with power from the weapon that had once belonged to the Nightmare Lord himself, Kara lifted the fiery whip and slashed it through the air. The resulting crack shattered the silence.

All at once, the helms, shoulders, and breastplates of all fifteen hundred warriors flared to life with a spectral, molten light. It was as if Vorcaust had spat liquid flame upon the armor, for it did not flicker or lick up like fire. It pulsed, dimming slowly to almost nothing, and then flaring once more.

Kara flicked her whip again. The soldiers, so well-equipped, raised their lances high, and the molten light danced eerily from weapon to weapon like webs of melted steel.

"Tonight we are strong!" Kara cried out, "Tomorrow, when the rest of our army has come, we will be unstoppable. And tomorrow . . . we go to war!"

The lights flickered overhead. Nick had been strapped down to some kind of medical table and left for what felt like hours. But now he was no longer alone.

"Dreamtreader, Dreamtreader, caught in a trap, what a surprise to fall into our lap. Tell me, how does it feel to have your power sapped?"

"Bezeal!" Nick yelled, struggling at the restraints that with his normal Dreamtreader strength he should have been able to snap like rubber bands. Now, he couldn't. Something was keeping his will in check. The bonds held him tight. "Ya blasted shark bait, what have you done to me?"

Bezeal did not answer, but the tip of his hood bobbed up and down at the edges of the table. There came a series of metallic clicks, and then a long whirring sound.

Gray, sloping panels descended from the ceiling. Seemingly made from some sort of fibrous material, the irregularly shaped, geometric pieces came together to form a solid rectangular surface just inches above Nick's face. Additional panels clicked into place at forty-five degree angles to his shoulders. The shape wasn't quite the same, but Nick felt as if he'd been put into a coffin.

"Bezeal," Nick growled, "you don't need to do this, this . . . whatever it is. You're not a monster. Dooley, ya gotta let me out of here."

"Quiet now, quiet oh Dreamtreader prone. You've entered into my whispering zone. In moments your will shall be mine to own."

A thump startled Nick and echoed away. "Bezeal! Stop this, ya rash bludger!" There came a rasping sound. It seemed to circulate around him . . . a shushing, undulating murmur of hissing breath. "Bezeal! No! If I ever get out of this, I'll come for you! No, no!"

Nick began to thrash wildly. It felt like ten thousand ants were crawling all over him—on his arms, his face, beneath his clothing.

Bezeal's Cheshire cat grin appeared suddenly by Nick's face. "Listen to the whispers," he said. "Just listen . . . to the whispers."

THIRTY-EIGHT
The Ready Room

"What do we do?" Kaylie asked.

"We defend ourselves," Rigby replied. "We'll make our own army."

Archer didn't reply. It wasn't that he had nothing to say, but at the moment he didn't trust himself to say anything at all without further thought. The wheels of his mind spinning, he gazed around the table in the part of the laboratory Rigby called the Ready Room. It was a round, low-ceilinged chamber with a central meeting table, two computer workstations, and enough flat-screen monitors on the walls to encircle the room completely. It reminded Archer of the kind of room in the movies the president always went to when he had to talk to generals and the Joint Chiefs of Staff to try to prevent World War III. *If only it were that simple.*

Doc Scoville sat nearest the door, his eyes glued to the tablet computer he held. Kaylie seemed to be lecturing Patches on something, gesturing animatedly and making a variety of facial expressions. Rigby had his palms flat on the table, and his eyes seemed to be bulging.

"Well?" Rigby asked. "Isn't anyone going to respond to my idea?"

"I've got it," Archer said. "I know what we have to do."

"Well," Doc Scoville replied, "out with it, then."

Archer leaned forward and said, "We need to make an army."

Rigby rolled his eyes. "Earth to Keaton: that was my idea ten seconds ago."

"No," Archer said. "Not like that. Not with gort. We aren't going to put innocent people in harm's way even if, in the end, it's to help mankind."

Rigby shifted uncomfortably in his chair. "Well, what do you mean then?"

"I mean . . . we literally need to *make* an army. We'll use our collective mental will and create warriors to fight, ones that won't hurt anyone."

Rigby made a face as if he'd just eaten a bug. "It's a war, Keaton," he said. "People are going to get injured. People die."

"But not from our end," Archer said. "We can equip our soldiers with some kind of stun weapon. Something like a Taser, but stronger."

"That's ridiculous," Rigby grumbled.

"No, it's not," Kaylie said. "I know how to do it too."

"'ow do you know?" Rigby asked.

"It's what I did to the guard in the elevator at Kara's fortress-thingy. I happified him."

"'appified?" Rigby echoed.

"Oh," Doc Scoville said, "I remember now. The guard with the goofy look on his face. You did that?"

Kaylie nodded vigorously. "Nick hit his guy with a boomerang, but didn't wanna hurt anyone."

"That's exactly the kind of thing we want," Archer said.

"Kara's going to wipe the floor with us," Rigby muttered. "And you can bet she won't be happifying anyone. She'll be playing for blood. She'll kill us all, and we'll never fix the Rift."

Archer squinted. "She's really that strong?"

"She threw an entire cavern floor at me," Rigby muttered. "And I got the feeling she was just warming up."

That silenced Archer for a few moments. Rigby wasn't the type to show his fear openly of . . . well . . . anything. Kaylie and Doc Scoville were backing him up, so clearly Kara had become a force with which to be reckoned. Archer didn't understand it. After the Rift, Kara should have grown stronger the way everyone else did. How did she manage to get supercharged? *Before we tangle,* Archer thought, *I'd better find out.*

"Time's wasting, Archer," Doc Scoville said. "The test results here are extraordinarily promising, but we've still got many variables to analyze."

"Okay," Archer said. "But you think we can do it? You think we can repair the Rift?"

"I do," he said. "I've been tinkering with calculations, but I think Kaylie's Anchor Protocol will work. If we put all our power together at certain strategic points, we may be able to push the earth's electromagnetic fields back to their original position before the Rift occurred."

"Okay," Archer replied, nodding slowly. "Okay, so here's the plan: Doc Scoville's on the technical stuff. He'll get the Rift repair details all figured out. Rigby and Kaylie, think you two can dream up an army?"

"Of course," Rigby replied. "I'll fix up a wicked bunch of warriors."

"Just not too wicked," Archer cautioned. Rigby sighed, but Archer continued. "What about you, Kaylie?"

"I'm going to make a Patches army," she said. "And they'll happify everything Kara throws at us."

"Excellent," Archer said. "You guys might want to fortify Scoville Manor too. Make it as hard as possible for Kara."

"Wait a minute," Rigby said. "'ow come you get to call the shots?"

Archer sighed. "Look, is it a good plan or not?"

Rigby shrugged. "It's okay."

"Fine, then."

"But, Archer," Kaylie said, "what are you going to be doing?"

"I need to talk to Master Gabriel," Archer replied. "Something's been bugging me, especially now. And . . . I want to check on Dad and Buster . . . Amy and her mom."

"Say hi to Gabe for me," Kaylie said brightly.

"I will," he said, shaking his head. *Gabe . . .*

"Wait," Rigby said. "I feel like we should make a contract or something. Something to make our partnership official. You know, like a pact?" Rigby held out his hand to Archer.

The chill Archer felt blasted his memory back to another handshake offered. "No," Archer said firmly. "I'm through with pacts. Let's just do our jobs."

In a flurry of spiraling sparkles of blue and white, Master Gabriel appeared just outside of Archer's closet. "Ah, Archer," he said. "What have you discovered?"

"It is three days," Archer replied. "Old Jack was right. We have three days to repair the Rift or it becomes permanent."

"How can you be certain?"

"Doc Scoville, Rigby, and Kaylie did all the calculations," Archer explained. "It has something to do with magnetic fields, but I'm letting them handle that part."

Master Gabriel raised an eyebrow. "You and Kaylie are working with Rigby and his uncle? Happily?"

Archer shrugged. "I wouldn't say that, but I don't see any other way."

Master Gabriel said, "I must confess I had hoped it would be so."

"You did?" Archer sat down hard on his bed. "Why?"

Master Gabriel's eyes grew distant as if reliving a memory. "Rigby and his uncle may be enemies," he said, "but they are people. Their lives matter, and no one is expendable. And that includes Kara Windchil."

"Kara's why I summoned you here," Archer said.

"Really? Why?"

Archer recounted the story of Kara's dominant victory at the Dream Tower and how powerful she became.

"Ah," Master Gabriel said, "you are wondering how Kara got so strong."

"That's part of it," Archer replied. "I mean, together the four of us might be able to counter Kara's power. But how do we counter her motives?"

"I do not follow."

"I mean, Kara's just a teenager . . . like me, right? But somewhere, something went wrong. It had to. I mean, she's planned this whole thing out for years. What she's done—and people are dying because of it. So many people. Why?"

Master Gabriel's expression sagged. "Why?" he echoed. "It is the question of mankind. Tell me, Archer, is there any cause—any element of a human life—that would justify the evil that people do? Anything at all that can justify what Kara has done?"

"Well, not justify," Archer said. "She made choices. She—"

"Precisely, Archer," Master Gabriel said. "She chose. And so have all who have committed evil. There is no tragedy of the past to justify what is done in the present. Everyone is accountable."

Archer sat very still, but his eyes wandered restlessly. He thought of his own poor decisions. He thought back to the court battle with Bezeal and the evidence presented. No matter the motives, no matter the good intentions, every step of the way, he'd still made choices.

"No justification," Master Gabriel went on, "but there is a matter of understanding. And that is worth something."

"What do you mean?"

"We will never excuse Kara's actions," he said. "But we can seek to understand. And this is what I believe you must do."

"But I've known Kara for . . . for forever," Archer said.

"Have you?" Master Gabriel countered. "Perhaps, you can explain how you really *know* Kara Windchil? Do you suppose that hours of texting and what you call social media actually allows you to know a person?"

"Well, no, but . . . we've ridden the bus together for ages. We've had classes together."

"That's a start, Archer, but only just a start," Master Gabriel explained. "Knowing a human being goes far deeper than what you can figure out from a person's public appearance. Tell me, how many of your Facebook friends know your mother died of cancer seven years ago?"

Archer looked down. "Well, Amy does."

"And Amy knows you from being online with you, does she?"

"No, not really," he said. "She kind of hates technology. She knows me because we spend time together."

"Exactly."

"But I can't call up Kara and just ask her to hang out," Archer groused. "We're kind of past that point."

"True," Master Gabriel said, "but there might be other ways."

"How?"

"When you lost your mother, Archer, it had a lasting impact on you. Such a thing still impacts the way you think. The well behind your home, it is your anchor, is it not?"

Archer nodded, slowly at first, but then faster as the idea took hold. "Thank you, Master Gabriel," he said. "I know just where I need to go."

THIRTY-NINE
INVISIBLE FRIENDS

ARCHER SLOWLY OPENED THE PRESSURE-SEALED DOOR OF the protection vault where he'd left his family and friends. It hissed but swung freely. Archer readied his will, but no threats appeared. He stepped inside and found things pretty much the same as the last time he'd checked on them.

Archer's father stood at the workbench. His eyes were open and active, and he made subtle movements with his limbs. A knee would bend, a hand would clench, he'd lean or nod, but it was clear that Mr. Keaton was mentally somewhere else, somewhere beyond reality. Buster was sitting in an old beanbag chair, but he was the same: there, yet, not there. Mrs. Pitsitakas too. She sat on an old kitchen chair and seemed to be staring at her cell phone, but given the dark screen the battery had likely died long ago. The little shop television was still on, but the channel flickered between a test pattern and fuzz.

Where was Amy?

Archer crept into the chamber and checked every nook and cranny, but there was no sign of her. He hurried to the door, turned the corner, and came to a jarring stop. Archer recoiled. All he'd seen was ghostly pale flesh, a shrouded face, and red eyes. He readied a thunder-stomp.

"I thought I heard someone on the stairs," came a voice, and Archer put his foot down very slowly and withdrew the power that would have devastated anyone nearby.

"Amy?"

"Uh, yeah," she said. "Whom did you expect?"

"Well, I thought you'd still be . . . that is . . . everyone else is—"

"Brainwashed," Amy said. "Yep."

"But you're conscious. You're talking to me."

"Uh-huh," she said, rubbing her eyes. "Sorry, I think I'm allergic to all the sawdust down here."

Archer laughed at himself. *Red eyes, right?* "You have no idea how good it is to find someone else . . . awake," he said.

She put her owlish glasses back on and gave him a sideways frown. "Great. So you're happy to see anyone?"

"Not what I meant, Amy," he quickly corrected. "I'm glad it's you, but how'd you do it? The whole world is brainwashed."

"I stayed away from electronics," she said. "Whatever's going on, it's coming through the airwaves: through the TV, cell phones, pretty much anything that receives and transmits."

Archer shook his head. "How'd you figure that out?"

"Well, once you stuck us down here, pretty much everyone was watching TV or messing around on their tablets or phones. I just cracked open a book. I know I can have like a gazillion e-books loaded onto a tablet, but I still like paper."

"And you figured it out just from that? That's brilliant, Amy," he said.

"Well . . . uh, thanks, but I really put it all together when I saw everyone else went all zombie like that. Seemed like whenever I got close to the TV, I felt nauseous, so I went out. I've been sleeping on the couch in the den. I've read three books. Yep. No brainwashing for me."

"Rigby says it's called the Harlequin Veil."

"You're working with Rigby?"

"Long story," Archer said. "I'll explain on the way."

"On the way . . . uh, where?"

"To Kara's house."

"Um, okay. A few days back you wanted to keep me locked up in a vault, and now you want me to come with you?"

Archer felt himself reddening. "Okay, so maybe I was a bit hasty before—"

"Yep."

"But I just wanted to keep you safe."

"And you don't want to keep me safe now?" Amy stifled a laugh.

"No!" he said. "That's not what I mean. It's just . . . well . . . I don't know how this is going to go . . . and I guess I just want your company."

"Finally!" Amy said with a sigh.

"Wh-what?" Archer mumbled. "I didn't . . . well . . . what I meant was—"

"Don't sweat it, Archer," Amy said. "But I'm glad you said it. Yep."

Archer scratched his head. He wondered absently if Master Gabriel had any wisdom that would help him understand girls better. He shrugged. With a will-infused shove, he shut the protective vault. Then he took Amy's hand, and they raced upstairs and out Archer's front door.

"You want to fly there?" Amy asked.

Archer skidded on the icy sidewalk and ended up sitting in a snowdrift. "What did you just say?"

"I asked if you wanted to fly to Kara's house," Amy said.

Amy laughed and said, "Watch." Slowly, she began rising from the ground. Then she tilted horizontally and streaked over Archer. After looping over the telephone lines, she landed next to Archer and helped him to his feet.

"So how did you learn to do that?" Archer asked.

"Well, so, making a strawberry milkshake made me tired," she said. "You explained that since we're newbies to the whole Dreamtreader-ish stuff that any creation would wear us out mentally."

"Exactly," Archer said. "And flying is one of the most taxing things you could do. So many variables. And . . . well . . . if you screw up, you fall to your death."

"But I trained," Amy said. "I figured I just needed to build up my mental strength, so I started making things. Little things at first: pennies, blocks of wood, toys, food, etc. If I got tired, I went to sleep for an hour. When I'd wake up, I'd be stronger. I made a piano in your living room. Did you see that? That really took a lot out of me. Yep."

Archer didn't know whether to cheer for Amy or grumble. It had taken him years to fly. "Well," he said, "flying is faster. Are you sure you can make it?"

Amy rolled her eyes and took to the air. "Kara's house is just a few blocks away."

As they flew, Archer caught her up on most of what had happened since the Rift, especially concerning Kara, Rigby, and Doc Scoville. Finally, he explained why they were heading to Kara's home.

"I hope we can find something, Archer," Amy said as they landed in Kara's front yard. "But I don't think we will."

No one came to Kara's door. That was no surprise. Kara was no doubt prepping her army for the coming invasion. Archer knocked once more and waited a full three minutes, but still no one came.

"Do we go in?" Amy asked.

"We have to," Archer replied, exerting the tiniest fraction of his will to make the doorknob vanish. They pushed into the home and were instantly greeted by a variety of scents: cedar wood, cigarette smoke, vanilla, and something else . . . something foul that Archer didn't want to identify. They passed through a hallway lined with photo portraits of Kara at different ages. The sound of a television led them into a den where they found a woman in a long robe sitting in an easy chair and staring listlessly at the television. It was Kara's mother. She was younger than Archer remembered and had the same silky black hair and light eyes as her daughter.

Amy quickly switched off the TV. "Don't want any more of that."

Archer knelt by Mrs. Windchil. "We need to wake her up," he said. "But I don't know how this works."

"How what works, honey?"

Archer blinked. Mrs. Windchil hadn't moved. Her expression was still completely slack, her eyes vacant.

"Mrs. Windchil, can you hear me?" he asked.

"Of course I can," she said. "I'll be right in with a tall glass of lemonade."

Archer and Amy exchanged looks. "No, that's okay, Mrs. Windchil," Amy said. "We just came to talk."

"That's fine," Mrs. Windchil replied.

"This is creepy," Archer whispered.

Amy shrugged and signaled with her eyes as if to say, "Yeah, but what can we do?"

"Mrs. Windchil," Archer said, "may we ask you a few questions about Kara?"

"Is that you, Kara?" Mrs. Windchil asked.

"No, it's Amy, Kara's friend? I live around the corner."

"And Archer too. Archer Keaton. Oh well," she said. "So glad you're here to see Kara. Been quite a while."

"Too long," Archer said. "Mrs. Windchil, do you know any reason why Kara might be behaving strangely lately?"

"Strange girl," Mrs. Windchil replied. "Always has been."

Amy grabbed Archer's arm. He nodded. Maybe they'd learn something after all.

"What about recently? Has anything changed?" Archer persisted.

"Nope," she said. "Well, there was one thing, but it really started about three years ago."

"What?" Amy asked.

"Well, Kara was always a studious child. But a few years back, she took to studying incessantly. I mean, I'd walk by her door at two or three in the morning, and there she would be with the scientific journals, books, and her laptop."

"Why is that odd?" Archer asked, rubbing his temples.

"Her grades," Mrs. Windchil replied, eyes still blank as marbles.

"Her grades just weren't that great. You'd have thought, all that studying, she could do a little better. Test anxiety, I always thought."

Archer asked, "Did she ever say what she was studying?"

"Science was all I got out of her." Mrs. Windchil laughed, which was a strange thing to behold because her facial expression remained frozen. "She actually told me off one night. 'Science, Mom, that's all you need to know,' she said to me."

"I know this is a personal question, Mrs. Windchil," Amy said, "but did Kara take any kinds of medicine?"

"No, no," she replied. "Kara was very careful about what she put into her body. So health-conscious . . . well . . . except for her sleeping habits."

Archer gestured, and he and Amy met in a corner by Mrs. Windchil's kitchen. "This is like looking for a needle in a haystack," Archer said. "I don't even know what to ask her."

Amy said, "Yep. So she studied a lot. Big deal."

"No, that's something," Archer said. "It squares with all the Lucid Walking research she's done."

"True," Amy said, "but what we're looking for is something that had a big emotional impact on Kara, right?"

"Right."

"Okay, let me try," Amy said. "Girls are better with emotional stuff. Yep."

Archer was about to argue but stopped himself quickly. Even if he disagreed, it wouldn't solve anything. Besides, his approach was getting nowhere. They were back at Mrs. Windchil's side in an instant.

"Mrs. Windchil, has anything happened to Kara?" Amy asked. "Anything that really upset her?"

"Yes," Mrs. Windchil said. "Yes, there was. Just about a month ago, we went by the mall, and her favorite taco place had closed up. She was so frustrated I thought she might cry."

Amy frowned. "That's very sad," she said. "But what I meant were more serious issues, like issues she might get counseling for."

"We tried that once, you know," Mrs. Windchil said. "That was after Bill left. Didn't do any good."

"What was Kara going to counseling for?" Amy asked.

"Oh, it was a weird kind of attention disorder," Mrs. Windchil said. "They didn't have a name for it really. Wasn't that big of a deal, but we wanted to make sure."

"Make sure of what?"

"When Kara was little, and I do mean little, she used to make up imaginary friends. You know, she'd set a place at the table for one and serve him a plate. It was cute at first, but we thought she'd grow out of it. And she did, for a while. When she was nine, though—and that was right after Bill left—she began doing it again. I'd walk by the door and hear her talking all kinds of nonsense. So I took her to counseling. They told me it wasn't too uncommon when a kid has a parent run out on the family. You know, the child pretends the parent is still there."

"Did losing her father hurt Kara?" Amy asked.

"Doctors said yes, but I don't really know. To be honest, I didn't really care that Bill left. I hate to say so, but he was a bit of a leech. Not the best with kids either. I made enough money, so it didn't kill me to see him go."

"What about Kara?" Archer asked. "Were the doctors right? Did she start talking to her invisible friend again because her father had run out on her?"

"I thought so at first," Mrs. Windchil explained. "Heck, for a while there, I thought she'd named her imaginary friend Bill. I'd walk by her room or stand at the top of the basement stairs, and I'd hear 'Bill this' and 'Bill that.' It was tiresome."

Amy adjusted her glasses and glanced at Archer. "You said, 'At first,' Mrs. Windchil, like at first you thought she was troubled over her dad leaving."

"But she wasn't, turns out," Kara's mom replied. "Tell the truth, I think she got over not having a daddy far faster than what was good for her."

"What do you mean?" Archer asked.

"Well, Kara never really got attached to much. When we moved into town, Kara was three, but she didn't cry about her friends in the old school. She didn't care. She was never content, always looking for a new . . . something."

"But the imaginary friend," Archer said. "Wasn't that all about her father?"

"Oh, no," Mrs. Windchil said. "I had that all wrong. Turned out, when she was talking to her invisible friend, she wasn't saying 'Bill.' She was saying 'Bezeal.'"

FORTY
TWO DAYS

"SCOVILLE MANOR," KAYLIE SAID, "IT'S TIME FOR AN upgrade."

It was a massive Victorian mansion, all dark wood siding, irregularly-shaped windows, and dragon-scale shingles. The ground floor was diamond-shaped with one pointed angle entirely made of a sprawling wraparound veranda. There were three stories, two protruding gabled roofs, two tall brick chimneys, some kind of sloping roof, and widow's walk. The spire had a dark, wrought-iron weather vane in the shape of a galloping horse.

"How could you live here?" Kaylie asked. "Well, here I go!"

Rigby held up a hand and said, "Remember, lil Keaton, we keep the basic structure intact. We build up around it. Wouldn't do to squash all the pets . . . or Uncle Scovy."

"Don't worry," Kaylie said. "I already have the perfect plan."

"Okay, then," Rigby said. "Impress me."

"Here," Kaylie said. She handed Patches to Rigby, pursed her lips, and beetled up her eyebrows. Then, her arms and hands moving in flourishes, she began to build.

A double wall of stone arose from the turf around Rigby's home and grew until the original structure could no longer be seen. Kaylie wiggled her fingers, and the top of the entire wall became crenelated. She pushed imaginary buttons with both her pointer fingers. Windows, arrow slits, and murder holes appeared at various strategic locations on the face of the wall.

Kaylie made a fist, and a wide rectangular keep arose in the section of the wall closest to the street that ran in front of Rigby's home. She punched her left fist three times into the air. Three circular towers arose. She bounced her right fist, and a series of smaller towers, each with a crayon-tip roof, suddenly protruded from the facade's right flank. Then, as if her silent symphony were coming to a dramatic end, she bent her knees, clapped her hands together, and then leaped into the air. From within the double wall, a massive square fortress grew. It was a mighty structure, an enormous rook, and it completely engulfed Scoville Manor.

Then, even though the sun was setting, a stark rainbow climbed from the distant woods and formed an arch over their new castle fortress. At the front gate, a white unicorn reared and released a proud neigh, followed by a mischievous nicker.

"There," Kaylie said, snatching Patches back from Rigby. "All done."

"Really? A unicorn and a rainbow?"

"What?" Kaylie asked innocently. "Everyone loves unicorns and rainbows."

Rigby frowned. "Not everyone."

"Don't be so negative," Kaylie said, batting her eyelashes. "You said to impress you, so there it is. I based my design off Corvin Castle in Romania. It's mostly Gothic architecture, but I borrowed a little Romanesque for the interior: arches, barrel vaults, columns, and such."

Rigby stared. "Sometimes, I forget 'ow much of a genius you are."

"That's okay," Kaylie said. "I'll remind you."

Rigby rolled his eyes and said, "C'mon, squirt, let us make 'aste to the inner bailey, for we 'ave an army to create."

"Why, yes, sir knight," Kaylie giggled, playing along. "Verily!"

Doctor Scoville heard the ruckus going on outside. It was next to impossible to ignore the forty-foot walls, eighty-foot towers, and half of a million tons of stone going up. Doc Scoville wasn't about to be distracted, though. Not now. Not when he was so close.

Back and forth, he ran the simulation showing the earth's magnetic field a few weeks before the Rift, during the Rift, and now a few days after the Rift. He watched the rings, the digital representation of the earth's magnetic fields, as they were buffeted by an unseen force. Soon, they were in motion, shifting violently as the Rift tore out the barrier between the Dream and the Waking World. And, in the days following, the rings continued to sway . . . back and forth. It was like a struck tuning fork, the metal tines vibrating so quickly and creating the loudest sound, but then the vibrations slowed. Just as they'd predicted.

While the magnetic field was still in motion, their team could reverse the Rift. If they could create their own magnetic tidal wave, it would send those rings back to their proper spot. But if they could not do so in time, and the waves ceased, the Rift—and all its consequences—would become permanent.

There were also those periodic burst-anomalies. "What are these things?" Doc Scoville muttered. He'd recorded the location of each. Just a few sites, really: Glasgow, Scotland, was the first; then Nice, France; a couple nearby in Maryland; and then one in Queensland, Australia.

Doc Scoville stopped typing and laughed at his own ignorance. "Of course!" he said aloud, slapping his knee. The anomalies, he thought, could be nothing else but the Dreamtreaders' bopping in and out of the Dream. Duncan, Mesmeera, Archer, Kaylie, and Nick—powerful magnetic signatures indeed. Maybe they would be enough to reverse the Rift.

Maybe.

"Who or what is Bezeal?" Amy asked as they passed by Archer's neighborhood and continued walking toward Scoville Manor.

"That's a little hard to explain."

"Try me."

Archer sighed. "He's some kind of being from the Dream Realm. He's been around forever. Everything he does—everything he influences others to do—it all turns to misery. Put it this way, he's messed me up more than once."

"Okay, so this Bezeal is no good," Amy said, thinking aloud. "And he was somehow with Kara when she was little?"

Archer clenched his fists. "I'm not certain what it means," he said. "But it's not good." He stopped in the middle of the street and gazed into the western sky. "Oh, no," he whispered.

"What?"

"Old Jack," he said. "We've only got two and a half days left."

"Old Jack?" Amy threw her hands up. "You realize, of course, I have no idea what you mean."

By the time Archer finished explaining Old Jack and the time remaining to reverse the Rift to Amy, they'd arrived at Scoville Manor, and it was night. The glowering, overcast sky reflected enough ambient light for them to see that the place had . . . changed.

"It's . . . it's a big castle now," Amy said breathlessly. "One big, big castle. Yep."

Archer saw the rainbow and then the unicorn. "I know Kaylie's work when I see it."

They came to the main gatehouse, and within twenty yards of the entrance, a swarm of red dots swam over them. "Get behind me!" Archer shouted.

Amy blinked. "What? Why?"

Too late. A beam of blue light flashed out of one of the gatehouse's many arrow slits and struck Amy right in the forehead. She started to fall, but Archer caught her. She was out cold, but still breathing. More than that, she had the goofiest look on her face that Archer had ever seen.

"Oh, crud," Archer muttered. "Sorry, Amy. You've been happified."

FORTY-ONE

An Evening at the Symphony

Once inside the castle gates, Archer found an alcove, and with the aid of a spray bottle of water, he managed to wake Amy up. Even so, she was wobbly on her feet for the next several hours and smiling like a maniac.

Just then, soldiers—on the alcove high above—turned, leveled crossbows, and took aim. Like some kind of electric measles, the telltale red dots of laser sights popped up all over him and Amy.

"Wait, wait, wait!" he cried out. "Don't shoot! It's me, Archer Keaton! And . . . and . . . Amy's a friend!"

In slightly staggered time, the knights stowed their crossbows and fell back into the alcoves. "Wow," Archer said. "Kaylie and Rigby *have* been busy."

"Y'know, Archer," Amy mumbled, blinking in a kind of sleepy slow motion, "I don't think your plan is going to work."

"What?" Archer asked. "What plan?"

"Plansies, plansies," Amy replied. "But I know you'll try hard. You'll fight for what's right. That's what's so great about you, Archer, you're brave. Brave . . . and cute."

Face burning, Archer coughed. "O-okay, Amy," he said, leading her ahead. "Try not to talk so much."

"Okey-dokey."

Moments later, after walking through a warren of passages, stairs, and semihidden doors, Archer led Amy into a huge courtyard, at the center of which stood the massive square bulwark they had seen from outside.

The courtyard surrounded the immense building, which Archer assumed, contained the original Scoville Manor—pets and Doc Scoville included. There were odd sounds coming from the structure's left side. Archer and Amy ran to investigate, and when they turned the corner, they arrived just in time to hear Rigby say, "Okay, squirt, now it's your turn!"

Archer and Amy skidded to a halt and could do nothing for several minutes but stare. Completely decked out in maestro garb fit for symphony conductors, Rigby and Kaylie stood on a raised circular platform. Kaylie had stepped upon a footstool before a narrow lectern. She cleared her throat and tapped a slim, white baton on the edge of the lectern. She waved her baton hand, and the music began. Archer didn't know where the music was coming from, but it sounded like an orchestra the size of a football field.

With each beat of Kaylie's hand, something new appeared in the courtyard. The first to materialize was hundreds of giant Patches doll soldiers, followed by camouflaged commandos, too many ninjas to count . . . and, suddenly, there were three frog soldiers wielding light sabers, a marshmallow warrior, and—finally—a dozen or more gleaming silver knights riding the ultra-fluffy, giant Siberian huskies.

The music rose in pitch. Rigby helped Kaylie down from the step stool, and then took his place at the lectern. He gently placed his top hat upside down on the lectern, lifted his baton, and gave a sudden sweeping gesture with both hands. A battalion of electric guitars instantly joined the symphony, not out of place, but rather in perfect melody and rhythm. Rigby certainly seemed to enjoy it. He began to move his head back and forth to the music, gently at first, but then with a powerful movement matching the beat.

"Is . . . is Rigby headbanging?" Archer asked.

Amy said, "Yep."

Rigby wasn't just getting into the music; he too was creating, albeit his creations were a little less *adorable.* In front of the ninjas and commandos, a team of warriors appeared. They wore spiked black armor with red visors on their helms, and they rode furry spider steeds as big as tanks. The arachnid creatures turned in unison, crouched low, and raised their bulbous abdomens in a threatening posture.

Archer and Amy gasped. There were eerie, glowing patterns in the short hair of the spiders' abdomens, ghostly, clownish faces. These things, Archer thought, would give the Nightmare Hounds a run for their money.

But Rigby wasn't finished creating. Beyond the spiky black knights and the ghoulish, clownish spider tanks, there appeared a phalanx of twelve-foot, flaming ogres. The music thrummed, a symphonic rock concerto, rising now to its climactic finale. Rigby thrust both hands forward. In front of the flaming ogres, appearing in ranks of twelve, came the Redcaps: sturdy, old, goblin men with red eyes, large crooked teeth, and talons for hands. Each creature held a long, gnarled-wood staff and, of course, wore a red cap.

Every single warrior or creature stomped its foot. The music came to an abrupt end. Rigby and Kaylie stepped to the edge of the platform . . . and took a bow.

Not knowing what else to do, Archer and Amy began to clap.

"Archer!" Kaylie squealed. She leaped down from the platform and sped across the courtyard to her brother and hugged him. "You're back! Yay! How's Dad and Buster and—hi, Amy!"

"Hiya, Kaylie!" Amy said. "That was quite a showsy, whoa-sy, concert thingy you two put on. Yep."

"Dad, Buster, and Amy's mom are safe," Archer said, "still inside the vault I built. They're still in the trance . . . or the Veil or whatever, but at least they're safe."

Rigby joined them. "Well, 'ello, Amy, you're out of the Veil too, eh? Keaton wake you up?"

"Nope, nope, nopity nope," she replied. Then she pointed at Rigby's face. "You have a funny nose."

"Uh-oh," Kaylie said. "Amy got happified, didn't she?"

Archer nodded. "She's getting better, but not quite out of it yet."

"So did you wake her up for a reason, Keaton?" Rigby asked.

"I didn't wake her at all," Archer replied. "She figured out the Veil on her own, but I'll let her explain it to you later. For now, let's just say we can count on her as one of our team. She's got a pretty strong will. She even flies."

Rigby's eyebrows went up. "Really?" he said, as if his thoughts were far away. "That's astounding."

Amy blushed and shrugged.

"Where'd you get the idea for the spider tanks?" Archer asked. "Those things are ultra-creepy."

"I dunno," Rigby said, shrugging. "I read it in a fantasy book, I think."

"They'd be kind of cute," Amy said, "if it weren't for the haunted clown faces on their abdomens and all those glassy black eyes. Not so cute at all. Nopity nope."

"Wait," Kaylie said. She whirled once and flung her baton hand forward. "They are a little too creepy, but this might help."

A peculiar clicking noise filled the room, and in a heartbeat all the spiders wore dark sunglasses.

"Better?" Kaylie asked.

"Much better," Amy said. "Yep."

Rigby frowned. "Oh, 'ey that's not fair." But he laughed it off.

They all were startled when a very loud voice came over a loud-speaker high above. "Attention!" Doc Scoville announced. "Report at once to the Ready Room. I think I've solved the Rift problem."

Doc Scoville had three of the huge monitors dedicated to his Rift research. The group crowded around them in the Ready Room, barely containing their excitement. Doc Scoville did not disappoint as he showed the animation of the pre-Rift, post-Rift electromagnetic field shifts. "This fluctuation," he explained, "is what we saw the other day. It's our hope, really. Heh-heh. Long as it's still moving, we can push it back to its original state."

"How?" Archer asked.

Doc Scoville said, "I'll let Kaylie explain this part."

"I didn't work it all out," Kaylie said. "We still need sources and locations."

"Not anymore," Doc Scoville said. "I've solved that problem."

Kaylie clapped and said, "Okay, so the magnetic fields are kind of swinging back and forth. What we need to do is catch one of those waves as it's swinging back, hit it with enough of our own, and use its forward momentum to knock it all the way back to its original position. But this isn't guesswork; it's absolutely precise. If our magnetic field is off by one tesla or any of our locations are wrong by a single degree of latitude or longitude, we'll be all messed up."

"What'll happen?" Amy asked.

"Well," Doc Scoville said, "if we aren't pretty close to perfect, the Rift—the Harlequin Veil, Kara, and all her plans—none of it's gonna matter anymore, 'cause we're gonna fry the world in EM waves."

Dreamtreader Creed, Conceptus 16

Congratulations, Dreamtreader. To ascend to this level, you must have a very powerful will indeed. As such, you must challenge yourself with new abilities. Perhaps, the most helpful of all advanced Dreamtreader skills is that of portalling.

In the Dream, distance is not measured distinctly as it is in the Waking World. All is related to time. For example, it may take you one hour of your time to reach the Markets of Kurdan from the mountains. And, as you know, an hour is no small thing. It is precious, not to be squandered.

Thus the portal.

A portal condenses time. Just as Dreamtreaders use ethereal silk to repair breaches in the Dream fabric, so may you also summon that fabric from afar. In effect, the Dreamtreader opens the fabric in one place, steps through, and exits the fabric in another place. It will save you time and, perhaps, much more.

But beware! As with all advanced Dreamtreading skills, portalling will tax your mental will fiercely. Use it sparingly and only at great need.

FORTY-TWO
BEST-LAID PLANS

"FRY THE WORLD?" ARCHER MUTTERED MOROSELY. "THAT'S not a good thing."

Rigby said, "You've got it figured out, though, Uncle?"

Doc Scoville slapped the palm of his hand to the table. "I think I do. Take a look." He gestured to the screen and began taking the data far back before the Rift occurred. "Remember those odd bursts of EM?"

Archer nodded. "I do," he said. "One of them popped up in Scotland, right?"

"Correct," Doc Scoville said. "Glasgow, as a matter of fact. And here it is."

Archer and the others watched as a small graphic explosion took place right over the UK. It was like someone had tossed a stone into a still pond, causing rings, one after the other, to surge outward.

"I went back through," Doc Scoville explained, "and I slowed down the frequency to make it a day per second rather than a week. Turns out, there was a ton more of those little bursts. And I say 'little' to mean they don't last long. But they aren't short of power. Heh-heh, no sir!"

"So what are they?" Rigby asked.

"Well, I pinpointed the locations, and I figured it out from there. Glasgow, Scotland . . . Nice, France . . . two separate signature bursts here in Maryland . . . and finally, Queensland, Australia. Sound familiar?"

"It's us," Archer muttered. "It's Dreamtreaders, right? Coming in and out of the Dream?"

Doc Scoville clapped. "That's right!" he said cheerily. "Lad, you're a whole lot smarter than Rigby gives ya credit for. Heh-heh."

Archer caught a sideways glance from Rigby but chose to ignore it.

"So we generate our own electromagnetic fields?" Kaylie asked. "I mean not like normal but great big powerful ones?"

Doc Scoville said, "That's right."

"But you mean Lucid Walkers too," Rigby said. "Right?"

"Not exactly," Doc Scoville replied, absently wiping a smudge from the tabletop with his index finger. "I'm afraid Lucid Walkers like us, well, we didn't produce much more EM than the average person."

"Oh." Rigby sat back heavily in his chair.

"Hold on," Archer said, "are you trying to tell me that all human beings produce some kind of EM fields?"

"It's really very simple," Doc Scoville said. "People have electromagnetic fields. If not, we'd die. It's one of the ways our cells operate and communicate. But the thing is, Dreamtreaders like you seem to have exponentially more powerful magnetic fields. No, metal won't stick to you, but the field is very strong."

"That's why you have such magnetic personalities," Amy said, snickering.

"Ooh, that was bad," Archer said, squinting. "I hope this happification wears off completely."

"There's a problem," Kaylie said.

Doctor Scoville sat up rigidly. "What? Where? Did I mess up my calculations?"

"Not that," Kaylie said. "It's the theory itself, what we called the Anchor Protocol. How can we Dreamtreaders produce enough EM to move the Rift? We don't enter or exit the Dream anymore."

Doctor Scoville's stricken expression melted away. "I thought of that already. All you have to do is make something really, really big.

The act of creation produces a ton of EM energy. Matter of fact, I was monitoring you and Rigby as you created your army. You were blasting out teslas left and right."

Kaylie frowned. "But did we move the earth's poles at all?"

"Some," Doc Scoville said. "Just not nearly enough at one time. We're going to need four Dreamtreaders to be the EM anchors, strategically positioned, all using their will to create something of a colossal but precise size, at precisely the same time."

"There's a pretty big problem with that," Archer said. "We don't have four Dreamtreaders." He sighed. "Right now, we don't even have three . . . unless we can get Nick back."

Doc Scoville looked gravely at all of them. "Rigby and I will step in as the third and fourth anchors."

Rigby sat up sharply. "Us?" he blurted. "But I thought you said we were pretty much EM weaklings."

"That was before the Rift, my boy," Doc Scoville said. "Now, we've got enough to pull this off." He glanced sideways, pointed to the leftmost screen, and said, "*Just* enough. See?"

Rigby looked at the rows of numbers below each of their names. He caught his breath, and his eyes widened.

"What?" Archer asked.

Rigby waved him off. "Nothing. Don't worry about it."

Archer let it go, but he wouldn't forget it.

"Where do we have to go?" Kaylie asked. "What are the positions for us to anchor in?"

Doc Scoville went over all the calculations and had Kaylie and Rigby check them on the screen. Once confirmed, Doc Scoville said, "As you can see, we've got to push the EM field the same direction, but from opposite sides. Archer and Kaylie, Rigby and I . . . well . . . we'll be paired up on opposite sides of the world from each other."

"Snot buckets!" Archer exclaimed. "How are we going to coordinate? You said we had to be positioned perfectly and build something just big enough and no more. How are we going to get all that figured out?"

Doc Scoville rubbed his palms together and got a mischievous glint in his eyes. "Well, since NORAD isn't exactly paying attention right now, I took the liberty of retasking all their satellites. I've created earphones, vest mics, sensors—the works. The EM's going to distort our signal a little, but since we'll have all the sats working for us, we'll be able to keep everything tight."

"We'd better," Rigby muttered.

"What about the Harlequin Veil?" Archer asked. "How do we shut that down?"

"That's the easiest part," Rigby said. "We just 'ave to blow up the Dream Tower."

"The whole thing?" Kaylie asked.

"We don't need to reduce it to dust," Rigby said, "if that's what you're thinking. No, we just need to take out her communication center. It uses the whole tower as a broadcast antenna."

"Okay, Doctor Scoville," Archer said. "What's our best order of operations here?"

"Well, the way I see it, Kara's the first priority," he said. "If the spy report from Nick is accurate, she'll attack come dawn. We don't need to beat her, not right off, anyway. We just need to repel her attack, knock her sideways, make her retreat to lick her wounds a little. That will give us time to get into position to repair the Rift. Once the Rift is fixed, we rendezvous at the Dream Tower and take out the Harlequin Veil."

Rigby nodded. "With the Veil down and the Rift reversed, we should 'ave no problem defeating Kara."

"Wait," said Amy. "I'm one of the team now. What do I get to do?"

Doc Scoville frowned. "I had no idea you'd be joining us," he muttered. Then, he smiled. "I know! I'll rig up a master command center here . . . as a backup, just in case something goes wrong with our communication out there."

"You sure you don't need me to go out there and fight stuff?" Amy said.

Kaylie frowned. "Amy, are you still happified?"

"No, I think . . . I think I'm okay now. I can fight. I'm ready."

"I hope it doesn't come to this," Archer said, "but if Kara's forces overrun this fortress, it'll be all of us fighting. Until then, Amy, I'd rather keep you safe. After all, you've only had a few days of experience."

"Close to a week," she mumbled.

"Still, not enough," Rigby said, his voice uncharacteristically gentle.

Amy smiled bravely, adjusted her glasses, and said, "Okay. I'll be the master command center, uh . . . person."

"What about Kara?" Kaylie asked. "What if Kara catches wind of what we're doing? Couldn't she just push back with EM pulses of her own? I mean, she's so strong right now."

"You're right, of course," Doc Scoville replied. "We just have to hope Kara doesn't figure it out."

Archer pinched the bridge of his nose, and then rubbed his eyes. "That's risky," he whispered.

Rigby muttered, "I don't know what choice we 'ave."

"And we won't get a second chance," Archer said.

Rigby looked at the nearest monitor. "You're right. Just two days left."

"We've got our plan, then?" Doc Scoville asked.

"I like it, mostly," Archer said. "But something's bugging me. I need to take a break and see if I can un-fry my brain. Let's meet back here in ten minutes."

"Anything I can help with?" Amy asked.

"No, no," he said. "I just feel like I need to think things through."

They exchanged nods and glances, and then departed the Ready Room. Archer ended up two floors down with a beautiful barn owl perched on his forearm. It was Doctor Who, Archer's favorite zoo resident. Somehow, having her with him again helped him think. The Dreamtreaders had their plan in place, but variables were way outside of his control: Kara and Bezeal chief among them. As he continued to pet Doctor Who, he had a few new ideas. Not fully realized, but seeds. That would have to do.

When the ten minutes were up, Archer and the rest reassembled in the Ready Room. The others sat, but Archer remained standing. "Okay," he said. "The bones of the plan are there. Doctor Scoville, your calculations might just save the world."

"Well," Doc Scoville said, holding up a hand. "It's not just me. It's a team effort."

"It is," Archer agreed. "But while we took that break, I was thinking . . . wondering if there might be a better way to utilize our team . . . and the time. We've so little time. We've got to use every minute or we're all done. I think I know how."

"Great, Archer," Rigby muttered. "You 'ad to go tinker."

"Hush, nephew," Doc Scoville warned. "What's your plan then?"

Archer took the next thirty minutes to explain his "tweak" to the plan. When he was finished talking, a lot of nervous looks were around the table.

"I don't know," Kaylie whispered.

Doc Scoville said, "It'll require twice as much coordination."

"It's incredibly risky," Rigby said. "But . . . it's a risk no matter what we do. I like it."

Archer nodded. "The only complication is Amy," he said. "This will likely expose her to greater danger, and I don't like it. But I've thought of something else we can do with Amy, especially if I can find Razz in time."

"I'm game for whatever," Amy said, "as long as I don't have to ride on one of Rigby's giant, clown spider things."

Rigby laughed. Everyone joined in. Afterward, Archer said, "No spiders for you. But . . . uh, you might get your wish, the one you mentioned earlier."

Amy's eyes widened in recognition. "Rock on. Tell me more."

Archer did. He outlined the rest of his plan concerning Amy, and in the end they agreed. They separated to get their gear ready and make other preparations.

In the hall, Kaylie raced over to Archer and almost made him trip. "Whoa, Kaylie," Archer said. "What's wrong?"

"Oh, it's awful, Archer."

"What is?"

"When we were on break," she began, "well, I didn't mean to, but I kinda eavesdropped on Uncle Scovy and Rigby."

Archer looked quickly up and down both sides of the hall. "They better not be planning to backstab—"

"No, no," Kaylie said, her lower lip trembling. "They were talking about the EM bursts we need to generate to reverse the Rift. They aren't Dreamtreaders, Archer. For them to make something big enough to generate a strong enough EM pulse, it could be dangerous."

"It'll weaken all of us," Archer said. "We know that."

"No, not weaken," Kaylie said. "It won't just weaken Uncle Scovy and Rigby; it could kill them."

Three hours later, long after all the gear had been packed, Archer stood on the high balcony in Scoville Manor's newly built main tower.

Amy wandered out of the inner stairwell. "Archer?" she called.

"Out here," his voice carried back from the balcony.

Amy appeared at his left shoulder. "You should be getting some sleep," she said, her voice oddly flat. "Four hours until dawn. The attack is supposed to happen then."

"I don't need sleep," Archer replied. He stared out into the gloomy night. Light snow had begun to fall, but the thickening clouds threatened more.

"What *is* that?" Amy asked, pointing out into the snow-flecked darkness.

"I see nothing of note," Archer said. "Range?"

"Four thousand meters," she replied.

Archer stared out, squinting to get to the proper distance. Then, he saw it: a distorted horizontal line in the night, and it was growing more distorted. Tendrils of white and violet lightning streaked around the line.

Suddenly, the line tore open, and glistening black figures began to pour out. They came by the hundreds and began to charge toward Scoville Manor. Their strides were superhuman, eating up great spans in each leap. Other things escaped the portal, flying things.

Archer turned and said, "Sound the alarm. Kara is here. And she is early."

FORTY-THREE
THREADS OF BATTLE

NICK AND BEZEAL HUNG BACK BY THEIR PORTAL WITH Kara as the last of her soldiers spilled over onto the road and raced away. The portal closed behind them with an electric snap.

"That is a sight to behold," Kara said, watching her soldiers loping up the street. Half invisible in the darkness and falling snow, her army looked like a sea of black glass shards, rippling away toward the fortress of Scoville Manor. "Bezeal, you outdid yourself on the armor and weapons. The Dreamtreaders won't know what hit them."

Bezeal bowed slightly. "There are very few subjects I know so well . . . as weapons, destruction, and all things fell. Eagerly, I await our foes' death knell."

"How long till we get in on the action?" Nick asked, his demeanor enflamed by Bezeal's treatments. "I'm fair raring to go."

Kara smiled at Nick's new enthusiasm. "We will let the ground troops break through the Dreamtreaders' defenses first. Then, we attack. And, remember, our main targets are Archer, Rigby, and Doc Scoville."

"What about Kaylie?" Nick asked.

"She is a target as well," Kara replied. "But I do not want her killed. I have plans for her."

Bezeal's pinprick eyes tripled in size. "What is this? You want the girl to survive? Nay, you cannot allow any enemy to thrive. We agreed there would be no Dreamtreader left alive."

"I changed my mind, Bezeal," Kara replied. "You did say your treatments would work on anyone. Kaylie's strength is too valuable to squander."

Bezeal's only reply was a quiet hiss.

"Dooley, look at that fortress," Nick said. "A fair bet they're expecting us."

"If they are, it's your doing," Kara hissed. "I don't know how you did it, but it could only have been you. Now keep your mouth shut unless I speak to you first."

Nick's expression didn't turn combative or angry. He nodded and said, "Yes, Mistress Kara."

She looked far ahead. Her soldiers were nearing the fortress' outer walls, their movement like a shadow tide approaching a shoreline. *And your castle,* Kara thought, *will fall like a sand castle. This, I promise you.*

With them in place, Kara closed her eyes and activated all fifteen hundred strings, the invisible mental tethers she'd established with each individual soldier. Through them, she could issue commands at the speed of thought, she could see through any one warrior's eyes, and she could even enter the consciousness of a soldier and take possession of it. It felt a lot like some of the more advanced virtual reality games, not that Kara really knew what that was like. She despised all video games.

For the moment, Kara took full control of a warrior about six rows back from the very front line. She gasped at the rush of adrenaline. It was exhilarating to flat out sprint into battle with so many allies running along with her. Kara leaped over a fire hydrant and a hedge, pausing just long enough to look up at the fortress. "Pretty good, Archer," she whispered. "Those walls look pretty solid. Pretty tall too. It's a shame the walls won't be good enough."

Eyes locked on the base of the forward wall, Kara watched as the rows of soldiers ahead of her didn't stop at the formidable walls. Like hundreds of frenzied ants, they found traction in even the slightest crevices between stones, and then clambered up. They didn't even break stride.

Kara willed her warrior to do the same and exulted as she ran up the side of the castle. It was Kara's last smile for quite some time.

Trumpets rang out overhead. Swarms of combatants issued forth from the high parapets. Kara skidded to a halt as a gigantic scarecrow simply dropped over the side and plummeted toward her. She yanked a laser-revolver from her breastplate and fired. For a breathless moment, the gun hummed and glowed with a rapidly increasing phosphorescent blue. Then it discharged a zigzagging bolt of destruction that instantly shredded half of the scarecrow's body.

The rest of it slammed into Kara's soldier body, dislodging her from the wall. She and the ruined scarecrow careened together and landed in a heap of other warriors. Somewhat disoriented, Kara shoved the broken scarecrow off and stood. It was just in time to see a strange, shriveled little man wearing a red cap. He grinned wickedly, revealing a set of crooked, yellow teeth.

Kara started to lift her weapon but was too slow. The dwarf cackled, spun around, and struck Kara's soldier squarely on the noggin with a staff. Through the thread connecting her to the soldier, Kara felt the blow. It wasn't pain as she expected but rather a rapidly increasing sense of numbness. She could still see through the soldier's eyes, but she could not will it to move.

"Oh, well," Kara muttered. "On to the next one."

She took control over a warrior who was cresting the outer wall. This was one of the soldiers who carried the peculiar lance-weapon. A trio of what looked like walking marshmallows blocked her advance. They held out their arms, and all manner of fluffy white goo shot out. Kara used her lance to vault over the stream of nastiness. Then she dropped to a crouch, whirled the lance, and took the legs out from under the spongy enemies. They flounced onto their backs and wriggled like overturned turtles.

Kara was up and running in an instant. She scrambled out of a melee involving several of her obsidian knights and . . . what? Had she just seen armored frogs wielding light sabers?

Kara turned her attention to a rampart that seemed to switch-back repeatedly down to an inner bailey. It looked as likely a spot as any to find one of the Dreamtreaders, so she bounded down the first ramp. She turned corner after corner, loping along without opposition until, near the bottom of the final rampart, she had to slide onto her back to avoid some kind of thorny branch that swept for her head.

No. It was a gigantic, bristling black spider. A soldier in spiked armor rode upon its back. His ominous red visor covered his eyes, and Kara was instantly reminded of the red-capped fellow who had knocked her previous soldier for a loop.

This time, Kara was ready. Her lance low and menacing, she charged the spider and made as if she were going to shove the lance into the creature's fanged mouth. Instead, she jammed it into a crevice in the cobbled stone. Kara used her momentum to vault up out of the way of the charging creature and plant both of her booted feet into the chest of the spiked warrior.

The impact knocked Kara's enemy clean from his saddle, but when he struck the ground, he shattered like a glass bulb. Kara landed in the shards and spun around to contend with the spider. Kara despised spiders, and this was enormous. It couldn't be an accident. "This is Rigby's doing," she muttered through her knight's mouth.

That was when Kara lost her sense of combat. The spider was wearing sunglasses. She almost laughed, but the creature began to rock on its hinged limbs. Back and forth, it swayed hypnotically. Without warning, it raised its huge abdomen. There was a face . . . a hideous, clownish face . . . staring back at her.

Kara screamed. That just startled her all the more because it was a deep man's voice. By then, it was all over. Something shot forth from the spider's jaws, and Kara's soldier went completely numb.

"This is more difficult than I expected," Kara said, back in her own skin once more. She didn't turn to Nick and Bezeal. There was no need to show them how frazzled she'd become. "They have . . . *decent* defenses."

"Any sign of the Dreamtreaders?" Nick asked.

"Not yet," she replied. "They're letting their minions be their first line of defense. I'm going back in."

Once more, Kara closed her eyes and tugged on a thread leading to the consciousness of a different soldier. This one was already down in the courtyard where the battle was raging in full. Spiders and armored frogs dueled her obsidian knights in every crevice and corner. The little red-capped people were wreaking havoc by sneaking past soldiers already occupied with an opponent and then biting them.

Somehow, her soldiers were going down too quickly. Kara checked her mental inventory, rapidly counting the threads. In less than an hour, she had lost more than six hundred warriors. Something had to change.

Kara flashed back into her soldier in the courtyard and sped through the fighting. She kicked a red cap and sent him flying, and then used the momentum to roll underneath a reaching scarecrow. She charged down a corridor, saw the shadow of a lurking spider, knelt, and took aim with some kind of twin-barreled rifle. Kara heard the spider's hiss as she pulled the trigger. The weapon discharged two glowing spheres, one green and one purple, that swirled around each other until they reached their target. Right in front of the creature's hideous face, the spheres collided. There was a flash of brilliant white light, and, when Kara got her night vision back, nothing was left of the spider but a blotchy, quivering shadow.

"Ooh. I like this weapon," Kara whispered, and then she continued through the passage.

She emerged in a very quiet section of the fortress that was open to the sky above. The snow was falling heavily now. Big, feathery flakes, whirling and swirling—the wind drove the flakes in a spiral around the base of the tower in the center of the yard. Beyond that, near the opposite wall, a stairway rose and disappeared into a very familiar building.

"There it is," Kara hissed. "Rigby's house." She drew a second weapon, the revolver, and raced across the yard.

A deep growl came from her right. Kara turned and found three of her soldiers waiting, but something was wrong with them. They were meandering about, taking exaggerated steps, and stumbling often. They looked dizzy or worse, and, when Kara drew near to them, she saw each knight had his or her helm open. The look on their faces was nothing short of idiotic. Googly eyes, crooked smiles, lopsided eyebrows—the works.

"What do you think you are doing?" Kara demanded. She was half tempted to fire on them, but her thoughts flew from her mind at the sound of the growl. It was closer. In fact, it was directly behind her.

Kara was firing her weapon as she turned, but that wasn't fast enough. She came face-to-face with the largest, furriest Siberian husky she'd ever seen. The thing licked her face, and the whole world turned . . . funny. Kara couldn't think straight.

"What am I doing?" she asked, suddenly marveling at the snow. Some part of her mind registered she had a job to do, but there was really no reason to do anything serious, was there?

FORTY-FOUR

THEATER OF WAR

"HEY, BEZEAL," NICK SAID. "WHAT'S GOING ON WITH Kara? She doesn't look right."

Bezeal glanced up to find Kara swaying where she stood, her expression comically absurd. The merchant's pinprick eyes went flat for a moment. Then, he rolled up one sleeve and reached for Kara's hand. The moment his mottled green flesh touched Kara's knuckle, she snapped from the stupor.

"What's going on?" she demanded. "We should have breached their fortress by now."

"They messed you up a fair bit," Nick said. "You should have seen—"

"Silence!" Kara hissed. "The Dreamtreaders aren't using lethal force. They are stunning our troops . . . and some other thing. It's like laughing gas, only worse."

"Ahhhh," Bezeal muttered. "Of violence and death, they've had their fill. Pity for them, they miss out on the thrill. Advantage to us, for they are afraid to kill."

"That's *it*," Kara said. "It's time. We go in strong. Nick, find Archer, Rigby, or Doc Scoville—it doesn't matter which one—and take them out. But if you find Kaylie, notify me immediately."

"And how should I do that?" Nick asked. "Shoot up a flare?"

"If need be." Kara waved him off dismissively and took to the air. She flew over the battlefield, gazing down at the strange combatants fighting on every inch of the suburban neighborhood street. She let them fight, for she was searching.

Kara soared over the parapets and scanned the walls. Those horrifying, giant, clown spiders leaped and spat at her, but she easily dodged or swatted them into jelly with a slash of her will.

"Enough of this," Kara cried, and from a sturdy hook she pulled the whip. Vorcaust's Tongue of Fire lashed out into the night. She gave it a violent jerk, snapping it in an earsplitting crack. As if a mighty switch had been thrown, all of Kara's obsidian knights—wherever they were on the battlefield—kindled with molten light. Their power surged, and they tore into the Dreamtreader-made hosts. Their weapons, now angry orange lances, cut through giant scarecrows by the handfuls. Spiders were left in quivering heaps.

Nick added to the carnage. The Dreamtreader flew to the top of the double wall and unleashed his chain. First, he whirled it overhead to build momentum until it was nothing but a tornado of metal. As he allowed it to drop to chest level, the chain took out piles of silver knights and their husky steeds. A giant armored frog landed next to Nick, dodged a chain swipe, and then let him have it with a powerful double-legged kick. Nick careened wildly over the edge of the wall, but used his Dreamtreader will to keep from falling. With superhuman speed, he chucked five boomerangs.

"Away, me beauties!" he shouted, watching them fly.

Each found its mark. The offending frog fell unconscious from the walls. Two ninjas were flattened along the parapet. One of the giant scarecrows attempted to catch a boomerang and lost its straw hand at the wrist. The last boomerang turned its head into nothing but a dust cloud.

A triumphant trumpet blast echoed across the battlefield, followed by a deep, rolling drum. Nick leaped up, climbing the altitude until he could get a better look around. At last he saw them: Archer, Kaylie, Rigby, and Doc Scoville, soaring out of the central keep and coming fast.

Even with his skills, Nick was no match for those four on his own. Not knowing what else to do, he willed a stout, black pistol into his hands and fired a violent, phosphorescent flare into the snowy night sky.

From her tower perch not far from Nick's position, Kara looked up and saw the flare. The blue-white flare arose high above Scoville Manor and like a comet curled in a hook-shaped arc.

"It's about time!" Kara shouted, her voice high and intense. "The Dreamtreaders, at last."

She leaped from the tower and flew cautiously toward the flare. She wasn't afraid of any of them—the Dreamtreaders or Rigby and his uncle—but she didn't want to blunder into a trap set by all four of them either. *There!* She saw them, all four speeding in her direction, but in that moment, they split up. Two swung eastward, and two continued toward Kara.

Which ones? she wondered.

Kara didn't need to wonder for long, for one of the oncoming enemies landed in the courtyard in the midst of a dozen or more of her obsidian knights. The lone warrior stomped his foot, triggering a blinding flash that sent the knights cartwheeling away.

Archer, Kara thought.

She halted in midair to watch the second enemy approach. Whoever it was fired a thick stream of something that looked like ribbons and confetti down onto a group of obsidian knights racing up the inner ramparts. For one minute, the warriors brandished their lance weapons and seemed to have a free run at the inner gatehouse. The next, they were all trapped in a giant moon bounce.

A moon bounce? It was difficult for Kara to wrap her brain around what she saw. But sure enough, her soldiers were bouncing around within an inflatable square cage. And whatever it was made out of, her troops couldn't even blast their way out.

Kaylie, she thought. *It has to be.* That was the best news she'd had all day.

First, Kara raced toward Archer. She'd planned this attack a hundred times in her mind, down to the finest detail, and she felt certain it would work. Step one was to distract Archer so she could face Kaylie alone, but she'd have to act fast. Kaylie was still trifling with a threesome of obsidian knights and she'd probably dispatch them soon enough. As Kara dropped to the ground behind Archer, she willed her appearance to change. By the time he had turned around, she was ready.

"Why hello, Dreamtreader Keaton," she said, twirling so her blood-red dress rippled. "Kind of chilly out here. I much prefer my gardens."

Archer stood very still, blinking stupidly.

"What's the matter, Archer?" she asked. "Cat got your tongue? What a shame. Last time you visited Lady Kasia, you were ever so much better company."

"Lady Kasia?" Archer muttered.

"There," she said, "you do remember me. I'm flattered. I wonder if you remember my friend here."

With a flexing of her will, she left Lady Kasia's form and stood next to it. This time, Kara wore the Wind Maiden's spectral gown. "Hurry, Archer Keaton," she said, feigning fear. "Come to me. I need your help!"

Archer spun to face her, and that's when Kara took her leave. She stepped out of the Wind Maiden, garbed herself in black, and took to the air. She left Archer to figure out what to do with Lady Kasia and the Wind Maiden as she sped toward the high tower where Kaylie was battling obsidian knights.

Kara gained altitude and readied her will to change form again, this time to Kaylie's mother. Kara hated to play on the girl's sympathies in such a way, but it had to be done to capture such a powerful Dreamtreader. Kara would appear as Mrs. Keaton, throw Kaylie off balance, and draw near to her. She would tell Kaylie how much she had missed her and would approach Kaylie for an embrace. But the moment Kaylie lifted her arms, Kara would slap a triple-hardened pair of cobalt manacles on her wrists. And that would be that. She—

Something grabbed Kara's ankle with a jolting force. *Archer.* Somehow, he'd seen through her ruse. Kara turned and without thinking unleashed a third of her entire will. She hadn't meant to throw so much at him at once, but, in her shock, surprise, and fear, she had simply reacted. Her will took the form of a semi-transparent fist, and it struck Archer's chest dead center.

The Dreamtreader's eyes went wide at the impact, wide and still. Kara knew immediately what she had done. She watched his motionless body fall away, that horrid expressionless face obscured by the snow, but still . . . there. It seemed like an eternity, watching him plummet. When he finally hit the courtyard, a sledgehammer of regret struck Kara in the gut.

What have I done? The thought blazed in crimson through her consciousness, but anger subdued it. *This is, after all, what you came to do.* And for a moment, she couldn't tell if the voice in her mind was her own . . . or Bezeal's.

A reckless blur flashed past Kara and descended onto the courtyard. Kara dropped from the air and spiraled down. She landed softly on the snowy turf and found Kaylie kneeling by Archer's ruined form.

"No, no!" Kaylie cried out. "Archer, wake up! You have to wake up! Please, Archer!"

Kara approached silently, keeping her path behind Kaylie. She was just a few steps away.

"You can't die," Kaylie sobbed. "You're not supposed to die. You promised."

Kara was right behind the girl now. She was ready. Kara whispered, "Kaylie . . ."

Kaylie spun around, her face a mix of anguish and fury. "You!" she accused, and she thrust out her hands—

But no power of will came forth. In a breathless second, Kara clamped the cobalt manacles onto Kaylie's wrists. "I am sorry, Kaylie," Kara said. "But it's for your own good."

Kaylie said nothing in return. She went absolutely blank-faced and mute. *Shock,* Kara thought. *Poor thing.*

Kara flexed her will, lifting herself and Kaylie into the air.

"Hoooroooo!" came a cry from above, as Nick Bushman floated down to meet Kara.

"Rigby and Doctor Scoville?" Kara asked.

"Dead as a Tasmanian tiger," Nick replied. "Color me gobsmacked, but I thought they'd put up more of a fight."

Kara shrugged. "They were overwhelmed," she said, "and . . . they were afraid to kill. I imagine they used a great deal of their mental will to immobilize our forces, rather than taking them out entirely."

"Ah," Nick replied, "that was a mistake, fair Dinkum." His eyes narrowed. "You managed to capture the girl. What happened to Archer?"

Kara shook her head slowly. "He's down below."

Nick hovered to his left. He squinted, and then his eyes widened. "Dooley! You fair ruined him, didn't ya?"

"It couldn't be helped," Kara replied, looking away. "It's what we came here to do. Now, come on, we've still work to do tonight."

"We just gonna leave the bodies?" Nick asked.

"The Harlequin Veil will hide them," Kara said. "And in Archer's father's mind anyway, his whole family will be united and happy for the rest of their days."

Nick nodded slowly and shrugged. Then, he flew off toward Bezeal and their portal back to the Dream Tower.

Kara glanced at her captive Kaylie. The girl was still limp and expressionless. Kara took one last look at Archer Keaton. *He'd been a friend once. And he'd been a formidable enemy. It is a shame that*—Kara froze, staring down at the body.

No, she thought, her mind fraying at the edges. *No, it's not possible.*

FORTY-FIVE

ANCHOR PROTOCOL

KARA GAPED DOWN AT ARCHER KEATON'S PRONE FORM. At first, she thought it had been a trick of the falling snow. But slowly, as she descended closer and closer to the body, the details came into sharper focus. Archer's body seemed to be decaying . . . decaying at an alarming rate. But the way his flesh peeled away—something was very wrong.

The swirling wind threw waves of snow in every direction. Its currents swept over Archer's body, taking layers away at a time. Layers of ash.

Kara turned just in time to see Kaylie's form crumbling. The cobalt shackles no longer had anything of substance to which to cling and fell away. Kaylie's form flew away in an ashen whirl, and then was gone.

"No!" Kara cried out.

"What is it, mistress?" Nick called back.

"Shut up, you worthless thing!" Kara screamed. "We've been had! This . . . this is all a diversion."

"Diversion from what?"

"I don't know," she whispered. She was more focused on the preternatural silence that had descended onto the battlefield. Snow had a way of muffling sound, but it wasn't that. She began to race around the fortress, but, no matter where she looked, the scenes were all the same: her soldiers, all the enemy soldiers as well, lay still. The spiders and marshmallow warriors and all of the Dreamtreaders' forces were actively dissolving to ash. Her soldiers lost their obsidian armor.

They were plain human beings once more, disoriented and shivering in the snow.

"No," Kara whispered, "no, no, no, no, no, no! I can feel it. I can feel my power draining!"

"What?"

"They're reversing the Rift!" Kara spat. "I don't know how, but they're turning it back. I can feel it."

Nick asked, "What do we do?"

"We've got to get back to the Dream Tower!" Kara said. "We've got to stop them!"

"Keep it up!" Doc Scoville commanded over the com link. "Remember, your creation must be large enough to reach the EM levels noted. Eleven teslas . . . no more, no less."

"Got it, Doc!" Archer yelled over the whipping wind. He and Kaylie stood in the midst of Prairie Creek Redwood Park in Northern California. The colossal trees were swaying, especially the new ones.

"How many more?" Kaylie cried out from approximately sixty yards away.

"We're at nine teslas!" he yelled back. "We're going to need a bunch!"

"Got it!" Kaylie turned back to the forest and summoned up her will. Not ten feet away, the turf erupted as a towering sequoia thrust up out of the ground and surged skyward. While that one reached its full, mature height of 375 feet, Kaylie turned, hovered away, and created a new one.

"That's perfect!" Archer yelled. "We're almost there!"

"It's getting harder!" Kaylie cried out. "Can you feel it?"

Archer frowned. *Getting harder?* With all the momentum generated by the surging EM waves, it should be getting easier.

Archer turned to his side of the new forest, called up some will, and created a massive Sierra redwood. This time, it hurt. "What . . . was that?" Archer muttered. He hit his com link. "Doctor Scoville, come in!"

"Here, Archer," came the doctor's static-filled voice. "What is it?"

"We're getting some pushback or something," Archer explained. "It's getting harder to create things this big."

The com link was silent.

"Doctor Scoville?"

"I was afraid of that," came the reply, so low it was almost inaudible over the wind. "As we push back the Rift, as we restore the normal EM balance, we're beginning to lose the extra power it granted us."

"'ow far, Uncle?" Rigby cried out into his com link. He stood on the massive left shoulder of Christ the Redeemer, the statue of Jesus that overlooked Rio de Janeiro from the top of Corcovado Mountain. While Archer and Kaylie were pushing EM waves from the east to the west in California, Rigby and his uncle were pushing from west to east from Rio. If Doc Scoville's calculations were correct and their efforts strong enough, they might just be able to push the waves back into their natural location. Rigby clicked his com link again. "Uncle Scovy, 'ow . . . much . . . more?"

"Not much," Doc Scoville replied. "One more statue should do it. My calculations make it approximately eighty feet tall with a mass of 635 metric tons."

"I'll get it." Rigby thought for several moments. *What'll it be this time?* He had already created monumental statues of the British Brawler, a favorite comic hero from his past, as well as Sherlock Holmes, Winston Churchill, and King Arthur. *Who now?* Then, he blinked. "Of course!"

Rigby poured will into this invention and focused down Corcovado's slope. He built a tall figure, standing upon a hexagonal pedestal. Slowly, it took shape and grew, layer upon layer. Rigby kept one eye on his digital display. Up the statue went, nearly eighty feet. A few more details, and he was finished. But the digital display showed the statue still short a few metric tons.

"I know." Rigby gave the statue a pair of laboratory goggles. He tapped his com link and said, "What do you think, Uncle?"

Doc Scoville looked down the slope at a colossal statue of . . . himself.

"Nephew," he muttered self-consciously into the com link, "I hardly think I'm deserving of a statue, especially among such company as these!"

"Nonsense, Uncle," Rigby said. "You're already a giant in the scientific community—even if they never recognized you as such."

"You're too kind."

"Well, then?" Rigby asked.

Doc Scoville checked and rechecked his instruments. The small displays were strapped all the way up his arm like large wristwatches. "We're there! We've done it! So long as the statues and the Keatons' trees hold their integrity, the earth's EM fields should continue to push back to their original pre-Rift state."

"Can I go, then?" Rigby asked.

"Are you sure about this?" Doc Scoville asked. "Haven't we already had enough of this?"

"You promised me," Rigby growled. "Look, I 'aven't much time. Kara's bound to 'ave discovered our doubles by now."

"Go, then," Doc Scoville said quietly. "Just go, but be careful. Kara's not to be trusted. She's fooled us all before . . . including me."

"Point well taken," Rigby said. "I love you, Uncle Scovy. Good-bye."

Doc Scoville sighed and shook his head. His nephew's plan was madness, sheer madness. He smiled grimly and thought, *I guess it runs in the family.*

FORTY-SIX
FRAYING EDGES

WITH FREDERICK LOOKING ON, KARA STORMED BACK and forth behind the engineers in the Dream Tower's Research and Development lab. "Where . . . are . . . they?" she demanded.

"What's the matter, mistress?" Nick asked. "The Dreamtreaders beating you again?"

Kara threw her will at Nick, lifting him off his feet and pinning him in the corner between the wall and ceiling. "You! Be silent!" she hissed. "Your treatment may be wearing off, but you'll do as I say."

Nick winced but managed a defiant grin. "And what do you say?"

"I say, hang around!" She flexed her will once more and threw a chain net that hemmed Nick in like a metal spidersweb. There was no hungry arachnid in this web, but the chain links were made of heavily magnetized cobalt.

Kara spun back to Frederick and the engineers. "Well? Where are they?"

Frederick leaned over the monitors. "Hold on," he said. "There's a ton of active EM out there right now. It's making it hard to track them."

"And where is Bezeal?" Kara growled. "He was supposed to be back here already."

Frederick said, "Your guess is as good as mine."

Kara slammed down the tower-wide intercom. "I want a platoon of guards around the communication station!" she demanded. "The Harlequin Veil must stay operational at all costs!"

Crouching down behind a wall of rack mounted network gear in the heart of the Dream Tower's communication station, Amy and Razz heard Kara's announcement. "Good thing we're already in here," Amy whispered. She tried to sound enthusiastic, but, truth be told, she was exhausted. As she'd waited for Razz to neutralize the local alarms and open a window, Amy had hovered in the air for far too long. She breathed heavily and repeated, "Glad we're in here. Yep."

"Yup," Razz said. "Just one problem."

"What's that?"

"Getting out."

Amy peered between two network racks, saw the armed guards just outside, and said, "Yep."

Rigby stood on the roof atop the Dream Tower and rolled his eyes at the ostentatious view. "Only Kara," he muttered.

The portal he'd used to travel from Rio to Baltimore vanished with an electric click. "'andy things, these," he muttered, but then he slid to a seat against the air-conditioning condenser. "Exhausting, though."

Rigby had not felt the will-sapped exhaustion like this when he and his uncle had traveled through the portal to Rio. But as the Rift slowly reversed, his extra mental will diminished more and more. He waited as long as he could, trying to restore his energy, but, after a few minutes, he couldn't delay any longer.

A little unsteadily, he stood and went to the roof access door. It was locked tight with all manner of digital equipment and sensors. Rigby shrugged. He didn't need the door . . . when he could make his own. He stepped around to the concrete wall directly opposite the door, mustered a little will, and carved out a rectangle. He gently deposited the stone in a snowdrift as quietly as he could, and then entered the door.

Rigby slipped down the stairs and paused at the bottom door. He knew what awaited him on the other side. In a flash, he ripped open the door, thrust both hands out at his sides, and took down the startled guards. Then he raced up the hallway to find Kara's penthouse. Rigby thought certain his target was somewhere in Kara's private living space. *After all,* he thought, *Kara would want to keep the Shadow Key close.*

"We've got a lock," Frederick crowed. "Northern California."

Kara rushed to the monitors. "Look at that signature," she said, pointing to the escalating numbers by one of the tracking dots. "That's bound to be Kaylie, and this would no doubt be Archer."

"What are they doing in the redwoods?" Frederick asked.

Kara shook her head. She understood at last. "They've figured out the magnetic connection to the Rift," she said. "They're reversing it." Then she looked at the series of clocks on the wall and raised her voice. "I've got to stop them. All we need is a few hours. Wait, what about Doc Scoville and Rigby?"

Frederick slapped one of the engineers on the side of the head. "Well, pull them up."

The engineer's fingers flew over the keys, and the display showed the globe divided into magnetic sectors. "Not in the States, sir," the engineer said. "Wait, I've got something in South America. Here it is. It's—"

"Rio de Janeiro," Frederick said. "But it's just one of them."

"Which one?" Kara demanded. "Doc Scoville or Rigby?"

"I can't tell," Frederick said. "Which one is stronger?"

"Doc Scoville used to be," Kara said. "But, now, I don't know. There must be another signal somewhere. Find it."

"You heard the lady," Frederick said to the engineer.

The man continued to scroll through the magnetic sectors. "It . . . it's not here," he said frantically. "I've looked through every sector—twice—and there's nothing else putting out the kind of EM we should expect to see."

Kara growled, "Look a third time!"

The engineer wiped sweat from his brow. "It won't do any good," he muttered. "It's not hard to see. There's just nothing else—wait."

"What is it?" Kara asked.

"The Dream Tower is emanating more EM than usual," the engineer said.

"How much more?" asked Kara.

"More than a tesla."

Kara scowled. "One of them is here," she rasped. "Where in the tower?"

A few clicks later, the engineer said, "This can't be right. It shows the strong EM signal . . . it shows it below Research and Development, but there's nothing down there."

Kara turned to Frederick. "Find Bezeal," she said. "Meet me Beneath. I know which one it is, and I know why he's here."

Twirling the Shadow Key in his fingers, Rigby sat in Kara's throne and smiled triumphantly. "Bit off more than you could chew," he said quietly so that his voice would not echo. He flexed some will and caused the Inner Sanctum to rise up out of the floor.

The cavern Kara called Beneath had changed a great deal. It'd been hollowed out, and there were armories and barracks. It had clearly been her staging ground for the failed invasion of Scoville

Manor. When the Sanctum completed its ascension, Rigby leaped out of the seat and jogged down the steps from the platform.

With a wave of his hand, light shone forth from the Sanctum's keyhole. Rigby approached. Six steps away, his com link began to chatter.

"Come in," the voice said. "Some . . . gone wrong. Rigby . . . you there?"

Of all the moments. He was tempted to shut off the link, but thought better of it. "This is Rigby," he spoke quietly. "Now's really not a good—"

"Rigby," came a different voice on the com link. "Why aren't . . . in Rio? You've . . . get back!"

"Who is this?" Rigby demanded. "Keaton?"

"It's Archer. Your uncle . . . help. Why aren't you . . ."

A cold chill sliced down Rigby's spine. He tapped hard on the tiny touch screen, trying to channel the unit's strength into his uncle's wavelength. "Uncle?" he called. "Uncle Scovy, are you there?"

There was a burst of static so loud it echoed in the chamber. Rigby looked about nervously but saw nothing. "Blasted storm . . . and calling you," the com link squawked. ". . . terrible is happening, Rigby! You've . . . to get back."

"What?" Rigby asked, the cold chill branching off in a hundred icy rivulets. "What's happening?"

"Statues losing integrity and . . . apart," the voice said. "Causing . . . tromagnetic storm."

Rigby looked up at the glowing keyhole. "I'm coming, Uncle," he said. "I'll be right there."

"No, you won't," Kara said, stepping from the shadows to Rigby's left.

Rigby spun but didn't unleash his will. Instead, he sidestepped toward the Inner Sanctum. "Kara," he hissed. "I don't 'ave time for you. I'm afraid I must be going."

"I'd like to see you try."

"Oh, don't worry, love," Rigby said, pushing the Shadow Key into the keyhole. "I'll leave you some company." He turned the key, and it gave a satisfying click.

But that was all.

Kara smirked. Then, she laughed. She almost fell on the floor she was laughing so hard. "Did you really think I'd leave the real Shadow Key where you could find it?"

Rigby gaped at the key. "But 'ow . . ."

"I knew you'd come back for it," she said. "From the beginning, all you really wanted was to rule the Dream. Fusing it with the Waking World was always my idea."

"It was Bezeal's idea," he growled. "Not yours."

"Rigby!" Doc Scoville screamed from the com link. ". . . intensifying! Come now!"

There came an agonized, howling scream, and then the link broke.

"No!" Rigby exclaimed, slapping at the com link. "Reestablish! Reestablish!"

"Pity," Kara said, stepping closer. "He certainly sounds like he needs your help."

"You witch!" Rigby growled. He strode toward her, but she threw him back with a staggering amount of will. Rigby slid on his back almost to the opposite wall of the cavern. He rolled and got to a knee. "'ow?" he asked groggily. "'ow . . . can you still . . . 'ave so much power?"

"That, my dear Rigby, is the best secret of all," Kara said, reaching into her jacket. When she removed her hand, she held the real Shadow Key. "But why not tell you? You'll be dead anyway. It's the Masters Bindings. I've finished them now, Rigby. And do you know what happens after you finish them? You get to consume them, absorb them—they become part of you and feed you so much power. Oh, I almost wish you could taste that power."

"You fool!" Rigby snarled. "They were made for 'igher beings than us. You don't consume them. They consume you!"

Kara knocked away the false Shadow Key, inserted the real one, and gave it a turn. The heavy slab door began to slide open.

"We waits," came a slithering voice.

"Are we free?"

"Fleshling took care of Kara, did he?"

"No," Kara thundered. "He most certainly did not. I am still your master, and Rigby? Well, he's made you promises he just can't keep. A bad habit of his."

Rigby called up as much of his will as he dared and created a portal in the shadows. He had to escape, had to get back to his uncle.

"No, no," Kara said with a haughty sigh. "You won't be going anywhere just yet." She made a pinching motion with her hand, and the portal vanished. "And now, Rigby, I have other things to do, so I'll leave you to your party. You thought what the Scath showed you before was scary? You haven't seen anything yet."

She turned to the Inner Sanctum and the writhing shadows within. "Rigby is all yours. Do with him as you wish, so long as in the end he really is dead this time."

A hissing erupted from the Sanctum as a shadowy mass of shrieking, screaming darkness engulfed Rigby Thames.

FORTY-SEVEN
ONE DAY

"ARCHER, WHAT CAN WE DO?" KAYLIE ASKED, CLUTCHING her brother, trying to keep her face hidden from the storm.

"I don't know," Archer said. He stared up into the swaying trees. Foliage ripped from branches crisscrossed in all directions. Creaking and snapping sounds grew louder and closer. "It wasn't supposed to go like this."

"Why did Rigby do it?" Kaylie asked. "Why did he leave Uncle Scovy?"

"I don't know that either," Archer replied.

"No, Archer, look!" she pointed over the treetops. "Old Jack!"

Archer saw the Dreamtreader clock. It was a faint, shimmering silhouette. He could scarcely read the numbers, but the position of the hand . . . pointed to one. "What?" Archer yelled. "How can there be just a day left?" Then, he looked more closely. The clock's hand seemed to be moving. Slowly, almost imperceptibly, but it was moving . . . as if the hours were simply draining away. "What's going on?"

A strange, violet light fell over them. Kaylie gasped. Archer watched as the sky churned with sideways funnel clouds and streaks of red lightning. A sharp roar came from behind. Instinctively, Archer grabbed Kaylie, used his will to put a buffer behind them, and raced a hundred yards across the forest floor. He turned to see a mighty tree that had fallen in their wake. His will-infused buffer had snapped it in half; several hundred feet of the tree lay at an angle wedged between two other trunks.

"One thing's certain," Archer said. "We can't stay here for long."

"We have to, Archer," Kaylie urged. "We're the only things holding up the trees we created."

"And it's draining us," Archer countered.

"If we leave, the Rift will collapse back," Kaylie said. "Uncle Scovy will get killed."

Archer cupped her chin in his hand. "I'm sorry. You're right. We'll stay as long as we can, but you have to tell me when your will is getting too low to build a portal. Promise me?"

Kaylie nodded slowly.

Just then, a streak of violet lightning struck no more than a hundred yards away. Archer blinked. The forest floor had begun to burn where the lightning had hit. Another blast even closer made Archer and Kaylie jump.

"Archer!"

Lightning struck again. It was only fifty feet away. They felt the powerful thunder-crash vibrate through them. "It's like it's walking toward us!" he yelled. "Forget this!" He grabbed Kaylie again and leaped . . . just as a feverishly bright bolt crashed down through the treetops.

"Warning!" the computer's voice rang out. "Warning: The Harlequin Veil is shutting down. Full shutdown in fifteen seconds."

"Frederick!" Kara yelled. "How could you let this happen? I was gone only a few minutes!"

"Me?" Frederick replied indignantly. "What? Am I supposed to be working guard duty as well as holding your hand?"

Kara was in his face in an instant. "How dare you! I'll reduce you to smoldering ashes—" She saw something then behind Frederick's sunglasses. It was like a glint or spark of light in his eyes.

"I'm . . . I'm sorry I snapped," Kara said, warily stepping backward. The engineers at the consoles ran from their stations.

"It's okay," Frederick said. "We're all stressed out to the hilt here. Let's calm it way down and address the problem. I'll maintain things down here while you get the Veil up and running again."

"No," Kara said.

"No?"

"The Veil can be repaired in due time," she said. "But I need to make sure. I need to stop them."

"Who?" Frederick barked. "The Dreamtreaders? They're done already. Archer and Kaylie can't generate enough EM by themselves. By the sound of things, Doc Scoville is done. And you took care of Rigby. Right? You did finish him off this time?"

"Of course," Kara snarled. "But I won't let you talk me into underestimating the Dreamtreaders like you did the last time. For all we know, Kaylie could have enough will to do it. We have to make sure."

Frederick took a menacing step forward. "Don't."

"Who do you think you are?" Kara spat. "You'll do as I say—not the other way around. I own this company."

The voice that came from Frederick's mouth then was not Frederick. It was not human. It was a garbled, wet, hateful rumble that said, "But I own you."

Streaks of frozen lightning ran up Kara's forearms and down her neck, but she wasn't going to let this stop her. She'd worked too hard, spent too much time, and sacrificed too much just to let it all go now. She had to be sure. She stretched out her arm and pointed at Nick, still chain-webbed into the corner by the ceiling. The chain web fell with Nick, only half-awake, in it. Kara added length to the net so it became a kind of chain-link bag. She opened a portal in the middle of the computer consoles, used will-infused strength to grab up Nick, and stepped toward her escape.

"Don't go!" Frederick roared.

"I must!" she shouted back, one foot over the portal threshold.

"I command you!"

Kara felt something like a stranglehold around her neck. When she looked up, Frederick was gone. In his place stood Bezeal, his eyes as red as fire. "You!" she hissed. "You . . . all this . . . time."

The invisible rope continued to tighten on her neck, but Kara put both arms around the cobalt chain bag, and then fell backward into the portal.

The portal had severed Bezeal's hold on Kara. She navigated the meandering tunnel of distance, time, and place. Her watch finally indicated the proper coordinates, and Kara descended into the forest, riding a streak of crimson lightning until she hit the ground. She found herself in a narrow clearing in the midst of the tallest trees she had ever seen. Not twenty feet away, stood Archer and Kaylie, their hands down by their sides like gunslingers.

Kara smiled wryly at the thought. *Little Kaylie with pigtails . . . a gunslinger.*

"Kara?" Archer blurted. "How . . . how did you?"

"Really, Archer?" Kara quipped. "You two give off enough EM that my sensors could find you anywhere on this planet."

"She's got Nick!" Kaylie squeaked.

"Yes," Kara said, "I have Nick." She lifted up the chain cage with Nick inside. She held up her free hand, and razor-sharp lances of steel grew out of her fingertips. "I have him, and I'm going to kill him unless you quench your will."

"What?"

"Shut it down, Keaton!" Kara screamed. "Stop trying to undo everything I've worked so hard for. This is my world!"

"We can't," Archer shouted. "Don't you see that we can't? We're Dreamtreaders, and this is our world to protect."

"All I'm asking is that you call back your will for fifteen minutes," Kara hissed. "That's all the time left . . . all the time I need."

"Kara, please!" Archer shouted. "It doesn't have to go like this."

"You've forced my hand!"

"No," Archer said. "Someone else did."

"What?" Kara growled.

"You know what I'm talking about," Archer said. "Deep down, you know these plans haven't really been yours."

Kara swayed a moment, seemed to master herself, and then said, "Of course these are my plans. I steer my own ship."

"I'm sorry, Kara," Archer said. "But we can't stop. We have to repair the Rift . . . we have to try."

"Then Nick must die," Kara said, slowly moving her sword fingers toward Nick within the chains. He was awake and wriggling like a madman, but he couldn't escape.

"No!" Kaylie cried. "Kara, you touch him, and I'll—"

"You'll what?" Kara laughed.

Kaylie tore free from Archer's grasp. Actually, she didn't tear free. She vibrated, became a blur, and then, suddenly, she stood halfway between Archer and Kara.

"I'll tell you what I'll do," Kaylie said. "I'll use it all."

Kara stammered, "W-what?"

Kaylie scrunched her nose and glowered. "I'll use all my will in one shot."

Kara's eyes widened. "But you . . . you'd die."

"So what?" Kaylie said. "So would you."

Kara's blade-hand froze, but she remained defiant. She glared hard at Kaylie, and, to Archer's utter amazement, Kaylie—God bless her—gave the stare right back.

Wait, Archer thought. That itch was at the back of his mind again. This time it was telling him to think. He'd just told Kara that it didn't matter. But it *did* matter. It mattered a lot. It might even be everything.

"Kaylie, Kara, wait!" Archer yelled.

They both looked up, but Kaylie didn't take her eyes off Kara for long.

"Kara, listen to me," Archer said. "Before this is over, I need to know . . . why? Why do you need the whole world?"

Kara half-rolled her eyes. "Really? The answer is simple, Archer. I don't need it. I *want* it."

"That's it? You sound like a spoiled child!"

Kara laughed. "Pathetic," she said. "You're only spoiled if others have to get everything for you. I'm taking everything I want. And what the heart wants, the heart gets."

"It's not your heart that wants it," Archer said.

"That's the second time you've said something like that," Kara growled. "What do you mean?"

"You think this has been your plan all along?" Archer shouted, his eyes growing fierce. "The whole Lucid Dreaming kick, starting in middle school? You really believe you thought of that yourself?"

"What?" Kara blurted. "Of course I did."

"The whole Nightmare Lord plan? The subterranean breaches? The Rift—you really think that was you?"

"Keep talking, Archer," Kara muttered, glancing at her watch. "In five minutes, it won't matter."

"It was Bezeal!" Archer yelled. "Everything. You think it was all your idea, but that's how that little maggot works. He worms his way into your head and whispers his plans. It's what he did to me. It's why

Duncan and Mesmeera died at my hand. And he's been whispering to you for a lot longer."

"You're insane," Kara replied. "Bezeal is a footstool—"

"That's exactly what I called him!" Archer shouted. "And guess where that suggestion came from? From him! He wants us to think he's a little nothing when he's really the puppeteer pulling all our strings."

"Archer's right!" Nick cried out. "That's what his treatment is: whispers. I know. I just experienced it. It's terrible. It gnaws at your will, your hopes, your . . . your dreams."

"No," Kara said, shaking her head. "No, it's not true."

"Think about it, Kara," Archer said, "and think fast! Go back to the first time you had any of those ideas. Was Bezeal there?"

"I . . . no. He couldn't be. I didn't even . . . know him . . . no."

"Kara, I visited your mom," Archer said, his voice both urgent and gentle.

"You what?" Kara cried.

"Amy and I went to see her," Archer went on. "I was trying to find out why you had changed. You were my friend once, but something broke, and I know what it was."

Kara's reply was nothing more than silence.

"Your mother told us," Archer said. "She told us after your dad left . . . that you had an imaginary friend. She told us you'd talk to this invisible person."

"So what?" Kara spat. "Lots of kids have invisible friends. It helps when you're upset."

"What was his name?" Archer demanded.

"What?"

"His name, Kara! What was your imaginary friend's name?"

"Bill!" she shouted. "So what? It doesn't—"

"It wasn't Bill, Kara!" Archer yelled. "It was Bezeal."

Lightning flashed above, and its thunder sounded like a bomb detonating.

Kara dropped Nick. He hit the ground and groaned.

Archer pressed on. "Your mom confirmed it. We didn't suggest it. She told us the name of your friend, your confidant, the one you went to when you were sad or angry—his name was Bezeal. Every one of these devious ideas that entered your mind—that was him."

Kara blinked. The blades disappeared from her fingers. "Every idea?"

"Well," Archer muttered, "maybe not every single one, but . . . most of them. The worst ones."

Kara began to tremble. Slowly, she fell to her knees and covered her face with her hands. But it wasn't out of a sense of defeat.

Archer gasped. He lunged for Kaylie and threw up a will shield . . . one second before Kara unleashed a deafening, banshee-like wail of agony and anger.

That wasn't all. Unseen will flashed out of Kara. Redwood trees began to topple all around the clearing. Archer could barely hold his shield in place. He then realized he wasn't. Kaylie was augmenting the shield now with her own strength.

Branches and whole trunks, driven by hurricane winds, crashed and slammed through the woods, bouncing with great cracks off Kaylie's shield. The leaves and debris made it nearly impossible to see, but slowly the storm ended. Kara looked up. Her eyes were blood-red and crackling with slender crimson sparks. "What . . . what do I need to do?" Kara asked.

FORTY-EIGHT
THE NIGHT OF NEVER-ENDING TEARS

WHEN ARCHER, KAYLIE, AND NICK ENTERED BALTIMORE, the once beautiful city looked as though it had been through a war. It had.

But, Archer thought, *it was a war of people's own making.* Buildings burned out of control, wrecked cars littered the roads, and the Inner Harbor was awash in trash. Waking up to the reality of it all would likely take most people to the brink of madness. Beyond it all, however, was one who needed to answer for his crimes.

"You've got it, right?" Archer asked as they turned the corner on Pratt Street.

Kaylie frowned. "Archer, we rehearsed it a hundred times."

"It's a bonzer plan, mate," Nick said. "We'll give it a burl."

"No," Archer said. "This isn't something we try. We do this, or . . . or the whole world pays."

Each busy with his or her own thoughts, the Dreamtreaders spent the rest of the walk to the Dream Tower in silence. They entered through the revolving doors, and Kaylie happified the guards at the desk and outside the elevator.

They stepped inside, and the elevator doors closed.

"Floor please?" the automated voice asked.

"Communications," Archer said.

The doors opened, and more than a dozen guards trained their assault rifles toward Archer, Kaylie, and Nick. Three seconds later, the rifles fell from their hands, and the guards sat down to suck their thumbs.

"Bonzer!" Nick laughed.

"Promise me, Kaylie," Archer said. "Promise me you'll never happify me."

"It'll cost you," Kaylie said coyly. "Fortunately for you, I'll accept cash, check—actually, I just accept candy."

Archer laughed. "Let's get our friends."

The communications center was awash with muted colors from all the fiber-optics in the tall racks of network hardware. "Razz?" Archer called. "Amy? You guys in here?"

Amy came tearing around a tall battery backup system and tackled Archer with a hug. "I thought you'd lost," she cried. "We've been up here so long. I kept hearing things. It was scary."

Razz tangled in Archer's hair. "Oh, you're back! You're back!" she squeaked with excitement.

Archer felt the blush run hot to his face. "I . . . um, Amy," he said. "Thank you, but, uh . . . can you let go of me?"

Amy laughed, released him, and backed up a step. "I was just happy, is all," she said. "Yep."

Kaylie used a little will to hover up to Archer's height and grab Razz. "C'mere, you little fluffy critter, you!"

"Hey, unhand me!" Razz squealed halfheartedly. "Well, I am rather fluffy."

"Bonzer job here," Nick said. "You cut the Veil."

"I knew you could do it," Archer said.

"But . . . it's gone now, Archer," Amy said. "I can't make things with my mind anymore."

"You're better for it," Archer said. "Be glad."

Nick gestured toward the elevator. "Archer," he said, "we'd better be on our way."

After dropping Amy and Razz at the main floor, Archer told the automated elevator, "Beneath."

"Floor restriction. Initiate recognition protocol or choose another floor."

Archer nodded at Kaylie who placed her will-enhanced palm to the scanning screen. "Protocol Wind Maiden One," she said.

The elevator began its descent, and Archer said, "Figures she'd use that as a password." No one laughed. Not even Archer. When the doors opened in Kara's cavern below, Archer knew they would face their most dangerous enemy of all.

When the doors finally parted, Archer immediately noticed the distant sound of crying, a kind of tremulous sob echoing in the cavern. The Dreamtreader trio charged past the barracks and armories, across the open floor, and halted at the Inner Sanctum.

Kara was there on her knees. Bezeal held the flaming Vorcaust in his green hand. "Give it to me, *now!*" Bezeal hissed. "You failed . . . in everything! The Shadow Key belongs to me."

"I'm telling you," Kara wailed, "I don't have it."

"Of course you do," Bezeal growled. He raised the whip.

"She doesn't have it, *Bezeal!*" Nick yelled.

Archer stepped forward. "We do." He took the key, pushed it in the keyhole, and said, "Scath, get inside, right now."

A flurry of weeping, cursing, hissing shadows fled between the Dreamtreaders, Kara, and Bezeal. They disappeared into the Inner Sanctum, and Archer turned the key. The slab door shut with an echoing boom.

"Saved me a step," Bezeal said. "Thank you, Archer."

"What happened to your rhyme?" Archer asked.

Bezeal hissed in reply. "Hand . . . me . . . the Shadow Key!"

"I don't think so," Archer said.

"Boy, do not trifle with me," the merchant snarled, his voice thick with menace. "The Shadow Key is mine."

"Not from where I'm standing," Archer said, holding up the key and waggling it.

"Insolent child," Bezeal sneered. "Think you're powerful because you unmade the Rift? Pitiful. Your beloved Waking World is ruined."

"Not ruined," Kaylie said. "We've got our anchors back. We won't get fooled again."

"Only a matter of time," Bezeal whispered. "Now, give me the key, or I will slay all four of you . . . where you stand."

"Slay us?" Nick echoed. "Now what a spewing mad thing for you to say. I ought'a punt your sorry rump into the next galaxy, fair Dinkum."

Bezeal's eyes turned blood-red. His voice dropped an octave, and the entire chamber turned suddenly cold. "I will shred you," he whispered. "For the last time, give me the Shadow Key."

"Now, Kaylie!" Archer yelled. "It's our only chance!"

Kaylie threw her hands forward and snapped open the portal to the Dream. Kaylie dove through, followed in a heartbeat by Archer and Nick, but before she could close the portal completely, Bezeal slipped through as well.

Crimson tornadoes slithered down from the turbulent sky, and Old Jack towered high over the Dream landscape. The three Dreamtreaders were waiting when Bezeal appeared.

"Thought you could escape?" he hissed. "Fool, you've ventured into the wrong realm. I will trap you here, and your mortal bodies can rot in the Waking World."

Archer stepped forward. "I didn't think you would follow us," he said. "But I guess I'd better give this to you." He held out the Shadow Key.

Bezeal's Cheshire grin appeared briefly, but vanished, and his eyes grew very small. "You give it . . . freely?" he asked, moving cautiously toward Archer. "Think you that Bezeal will grant you mercy?"

"Just take the key," Archer growled. "And shut up."

Bezeal snatched the Shadow Key from Archer's hand, and then clutched it to his breast. "There will be no mercy," he hissed.

"It's not going to do you any good here," Archer said, crossing his arms. "The Shadow Key, I mean."

"I control the Scath," Bezeal said. "And the Masters Bindings . . . and they are such good bait."

"Well, that's what Archer's talking about," Nick said. "See, you've got no Shadowkeep. Rigby's gone, and Kara won't ever come back. You don't have a Nightmare Lord."

Clutching her Patches doll, Kaylie stepped forward. "You see, Bezeal, we've beaten you. We're Dreamtreaders, and we hold the power here."

Bezeal's eyes turned red. He began to tremble. "Your power is—"

"And," Archer interrupted, "we know who you are."

Speaking once more in that horrible voice, Bezeal said, "If you knew me, you would know there has always been a Nightmare Lord. No. 6 Rue de La Morte was but one Shadowkeep; there have been thousands of others. And I have been there for each and every one of them."

As if a mantle of dark thunderheads had rolled over the landscape, the ambient light of the Dream dimmed, and a faint, red glow surrounded Bezeal. "You call me Bezeal," he said, and his silhouette began to grow, "but I have worn many other names."

"Kaylie, don't look," Archer whispered urgently.

Nick physically turned Kaylie around and ushered her back. Even Archer stepped back.

Taller now than any of the Dreamtreaders, Bezeal was still growing. "Some have called me Belial. To others, I was Beelzebub. I've even been named such a banal moniker as Old Scratch. But would you know my real name, Dreamtreaders? Think you that you could bear to hear it spoken from my lips?"

Archer turned his head, but from his peripheral vision, he saw Bezeal's shape change. The hooded robe was gone. In its place were dark wings, similar to bat wings, but ragged and torn as if from wear. The pinprick eyes had grown to blazing red slashes, and a fiery crown burned in the air above his head. "My name," he said, "spells your doom, and not just for this world but forever. You know me now, don't you? Oh, yes, you know."

A door in the darkness opened, and brilliant white light poured through. Archer, Kaylie, and Nick covered their eyes, but they were not afraid. Now, they were smiling.

Archer saw that Bezeal—or whatever he wanted to call himself—however, had raised a wing to shield his eyes.

"Ah, so that's where you've been hiding all these years!" boomed Master Gabriel, stepping through the door. "I have suspected for centuries, of course, but nothing like a confession to make things certain."

"You!" Bezeal hissed. "You cannot harm me. The time is not yet nigh."

"Oh really?" Master Gabriel asked. He drew his sword, Murkbane, and the blade lit with brilliant white fire. "I am afraid you have that quite wrong. Your greatest suffering is most certainly yet to come. But that does not mean you cannot suffer now as well."

Bezeal held up the Shadow Key and yelled, "Scath, come to your master's aid!"

"I will take that!" Master Gabriel said, snatching the key away. "And Archer, Kaylie, Nick, I think we can dispense with the illusion now."

"On it!" Archer exclaimed. He began to call back his will. Kaylie and Nick did the same, and the Dream Realm peeled away a few strips at a time until nothing surreal remained. They all stood in Archer's backyard, not far from his mother's cherished well.

"Ha, Bezeal," Kaylie said. "You'll think twice before running into any old portal, won't you?"

Bezeal's eyes burned. "You . . . tricked . . . me?"

"Delicious, is it not?" Master Gabriel. "It is a very small token, set against your deceit, Bezeal. But let it ring like a clarion bell that your time in the Dream is over. I know who you really are . . . oh, yes, I know you now, and I know your designs. Such delusions of grandeur! From here on, stay in your appointed place!"

"Maybe I will," Bezeal sneered. "Maybe, I won't. I've deceived the so-called Masters before—even you, Gabriel—I'll deceive you again."

Archer, Kaylie, and Nick came and stood at Master Gabriel's side. "Oh, I am certain you will try," he said. "But know this: you have very little time left. Your Personal Midnight is coming soon. And, personally, I cannot wait."

Bezeal rose to his full height, spread his wings, and glared. His mantle of darkness writhed about his form, and he hissed menacingly.

Master Gabriel brandished his sword, and then lifted the tip beneath Bezeal's throat. "It is time for you to depart," Master Gabriel said, his voice as sharp as his sword.

Bezeal sneered and started to raise a clawed hand. "You do not command me—"

"Perhaps not," Master Gabriel said, "but if you do not want to feel this blade, you will do exactly as I say. Into the well with you."

"What?" Bezeal cried out. "I will not—"

Master Gabriel lowered Murkbane, and the sword flared. "Into the well, now."

Bezeal hissed and began to crawl away, but Master Gabriel countered every errant move and shepherded Bezeal right to the edge of the well. "Go on," he said. "Get going."

Growling like a mongrel, Bezeal clambered over the edge of the well. He hissed once more, and then dropped. There came a splash of water and a bloodcurdling screech. Then . . . silence.

Master Gabriel grinned. "I took the liberty of replacing the water fouled by the Scath with pure water, like the kind your mother drank years ago. I am afraid Bezeal does not find it very refreshing."

"Can we look?" Archer asked.

Master Gabriel nodded. The three Dreamtreaders surrounded the well and stared over the edge into the darkness. They saw Bezeal shrinking back to his hooded form, and he was sinking in the water . . . falling away into the depths. His triumphant grin was long gone. All that remained now was the darkness beneath his hood—darkness and those small eyes, just a faint glimmer. As he drifted down and away, the glimmer became very faint indeed.

FORTY-NINE

Loose Ends

It was nine days after the Rift's repair. When Amy didn't find Archer at his home, she knew just where to look.

"Shame I can't fly, though," she muttered as she ran in the direction of Scoville Manor. That wasn't the only thing that she missed. The enormous castle Kaylie and Rigby had erected was gone now. It was just a big, old regular mansion. Amy rang the doorbell.

Archer and Kaylie answered the door a few moments later. "Amy!" Kaylie cried, leaping to embrace her friend.

Archer grinned. "It's good to see you, Amy. How's your mom holding up?"

Amy pulled away from Kaylie. "She's doing well. Just like most folks, there are a lot of strange memories to tease out. At least the nausea's gone at last."

"C'mon," Kaylie said, taking Amy's hand. "Come see the animals."

As the three took to the basement stairs, Amy asked, "So are you and Kaylie just moving in here now?"

Archer laughed. "No, no," he said. "My dad won't let us, but I've asked Nick and his little brother, Oliver, if they would consider it. It's a long way from Australia, but it would be kind of convenient to have all three Dreamtreaders in the same general area. I'm hoping they'll make the move. Someone's got to take care of all these critters."

The three of them set about feeding, watering, and cleaning up after the zoo's residents. Archer did his circuit with Dr. Who perched on his shoulder just like old times. No one spoke much during the work, but when they reached the bottom of the basement stairs, they paused.

"I kinda wish Uncle Scovy was still here," Kaylie said.

"You mean Doctor Scoville, don't you?" Amy asked.

"That's probably best," Kaylie agreed, staring at the door at the bottom of the stairs. "But he turned good in the end, didn't he? I mean, he gave his life to help get the Rift turned around."

"That's right," Archer said, starting slowly up the stairs. "He did good . . . in the end."

"What about Rigby?" Amy whispered. "Anything yet?"

Archer shook his head. "Kara searched everywhere in the Dream Inc. building before the FBI took her away. She told me there was a pretty serious bloodstain but no body. Odd thing though: Kara said piles of ash were down there. Piles and piles of ash, spread all over but most numerous around the bloodstain. If the Scath took Rigby out, I'm thinking he took a bunch of them with him."

Back upstairs, the trio collapsed into chairs at Rigby's kitchen table. "I'm tired," Kaylie said, the words spoken through her yawn. "I don't know how I'm going to Dreamtread tonight."

"You'll be asleep, silly," Amy said.

"Right, right," Kaylie said. "Good thing."

"Is it bad . . . in the Dream, I mean?" Amy asked.

"We've seen worse," Archer replied with a dry chuckle. "But, yeah, repairing the Rift left the Dream in kind of a semi-shredded state. We've been fixing breaches and weaving up support threads constantly."

"Kind of like here," Amy replied. "I can't even watch the news anymore. Too much sadness. There was so much destruction, Archer. So many people's lives just ruined."

"What did the FBI do with Kara?" Kaylie asked.

"I don't know," Archer replied. "She's admitted to everything, but I hear they're calling it some kind of terrorist attack . . . like Dream Inc. just gassed everyone into some kind of mass delusion."

Kaylie raised her eyebrows. "In the world?"

"Well," Archer said, "is it any more farfetched than Lucid Dreaming? The Rift? Any of it?"

Amy shook her head. "We've all got a lot of healing to do," she said. "Yep."

When Archer and Kaylie came home, Mr. Keaton and Buster had just finished setting the table. They'd eaten a marvelous lasagna dinner in silence, but, as always over the last week and a half, they had exchanged many smiles.

Archer thought his father was doing well, considering the circumstances. The end of the Rift meant the end of his time with his wife. It were almost as if she had died all over again. But he'd gone back to his workshop and started making the wells again. He was even teaching Buster how to do some things in the wood shop. Of course, Buster wanted to make a surfboard first, but he'd have to learn the basics before he got into that.

Archer asked to be excused before dessert was served. As he was leaving the kitchen, he heard his father's voice. "Hey, son, you know those new statues, you know, the new ones near the Jesus statue in Rio?"

"Yeah," Archer said. "What about them?"

"Well, one of them," Mr. Keaton said, "and I know this is going to sound crazy, but they were doing a show on them, and . . . well . . . I could swear one of the statues looked like your friend Rigby's uncle."

"That's not crazy, Dad," Archer said. "I see the resemblance too."

"Funny thing," Mr. Keaton said, "someone's been leaving big bunches of flowers at the foot of that statue. Not as many flowers as the Jesus statue gets, but still. Funny, huh?"

Archer shrugged and headed for the carport door. The winter air was back in full force, and it was going to be a cold night. Archer didn't mind it so much. He went through the backyard gate and tromped down to the wishing well.

He knelt on the frozen ground and put his head against the stone of the well. "Mom, I miss you," he said. "But in a way, I'm grateful I got to see you again . . . even if it wasn't real." Then his words trailed off, and the rest of the conversation took place in his mind in a prayer. *God,* he thought, *please take care of my mother . . . and all those who died during the Rift. And please help us never to lose our anchors . . . ever again.*

Acknowledgments

I, Wayne Thomas Batson, do hereby acknowledge that the following remarkable people invested great love, energy, sacrifice, and kindnesses in ways that I will never be able to repay. *Dreamtreaders,* like all my novels, couldn't have happened without your support and presence in my life. To you, I offer these simple thanks:

Mary Lu Batson: gorgeous wife, best friend, co-dreamer, and life-mate—to you I offer the greatest human thanks. You committed your life to me, a rare thing these days, and extraordinarily precious to me. Navigating life with four teenagers, teaching, and trying to be a writer would be absolutely impossible without your fantastic support.

Daughter Kayla: your passion and initiative and dreams and drive to help others are nothing short of inspiring. Love you, K-doodle!

Son Tommy: you are a tender warrior, my son. I love the joy you find in God's creation, everything from noticing the gold light before dusk or the smell of wood smoke on a chilly evening. You are a constant reminder to me that God's richest blessings are never-ending.

Son Bryce: you are the quiet strength, my son. I love the way you become a student of what inspires you, learning every facet and detail, and then *explode* into action. You are committed to excellence. May God use you to do great things.

Daughter Rachel: upon you, God has also placed His creative touch. You are a teacher and a storyteller, a singer and songwriter. I am thankful for the bubbly life you inject into every day. You have a heart full of love to give, and I'm grateful to shepherd you . . . for a little while.

Mom & Dad Batson: I don't know how else to thank you. You gave up 45^{+} years of your life to directly or indirectly help me be a better son, friend, man, employee, writer, and husband. Thank you!

Mom & Dad Dovel: you gave me your daughter and much love besides. Thank you!

Leslie, Jeff, Brian, Edward, Andy, Diana, your spouses, significant others, families, and friends: thank you for creating a landscape of adventure. It is no small thing to be able to raise a sword with such as you.

Doug & Chris, Dave & Heather, Chris H. & Dawn, Dan & Tracey, Warren & Marilyn, Alex & Noelle, Alaina, Cameron & Jasmine Strauss, Bud, Candy, Angie, Danely, Lisa, and all the SotB Crew, and all friends past and present: I can't thank you enough for the camaraderie and adventures. May there be many, many more.

Folly Quarter Dreamers: Erin, Kirsten, Julie, Regina, Barb, Sherrie, Dreia, Lindsay, Susan—you are one amazing group of teachers! Verily, to you I cry out in a loud voice: Deer!

Students Present and Past: you have no idea what precious blessings you are to me and the world. Pip-pip Cheerio!

Sir Gregg of Wooding: agent and friend. Thanks for being among the first to believe in my stories. It is an honor to know you, my friend.

Steele Filipek: well met, Sirrah! Seriously, you are an amazing editor. Thanks for chipping away the chaff so *Dreamtreaders* could emerge.

Thomas Nelson / HarperCollins: you opened the door for me back in 2004. Thank you for the long and incredible ride.

Christopher Hopper: the disciples told Jesus, "We have left all to follow you. What shall we have?" The Lord replied, "Truly I tell you, no one who has left home or wife or brothers or sisters or parents or children for the sake of the kingdom of God will fail to receive many times as much in this age, and in the age to come eternal life." God is true to His word. He linked us in friendship, and I'm grateful. How many O-dark-thirty writing sessions have we shared? How many laughs? Thanks for your friendship, bro. Through airships, flatulent barrister gnomes, spiders, and much more—it has been an honor to ride together. Right™.

The fantastic staff of G.L. Shacks, Glory Days, O'Lordan's, Rams Head, and other haunts for putting up with me writing there at all times of day . . . or night. Special thanks to Oscar's in Eldersburg. Ralph, you are Da Man!

Thank you to Prog Metal Zone for introducing me to tons of progressive metal bands that both fuel and inspire my writing. Jeff Stevens, Proprietor/Publisher Progmetalzone, always has a great new selection of epic music, music that is the perfect accompaniment to an epic story.

ESTEEMED DREAMTREADERS 3 CELEBRANTS:

Alex Hartsfield
Brenna Alyssa Mahn
Jessica Kost
Noah Cutting
Jake Buller
Michelle Audrey Black
Dillon Lewis
Sarah Pratt
Kara Swanson
Melanie Reynolds
Seaneen Scott Sullinger
Petra Hurley
Julia Garcia
Bethany Ebert
Julie Dick
Nathanael Rebiger

WRITING CHALLENGE WINNERS' NAMES:

Emily Mann
Elizabeth Eiowing Dresdow
Lissi Michelle
Morgan Babbage
Davis Moore
Petra Hurley
Javier Luna
Maria Kercher
Clinton McDonald
Elizabeth J. Hornberger
Brianna Jean Taeuber
LoriAnn Weldon
Mikayla Warfield
Sarah Spradlin
Heather Titus

PATREON PATRONS:

Ama Lane
Josiah Mann
Shane Kent
The Starr Family
Michael Harper
Sam Jenne
Christopher Abbott
Christopher Hopper
Laure Hittle
Elizabeth Hornberger
Bryce Spitzer
Eric Guglielmo
Christian Humbert
Chris Harvey
Stephen Larson
Erin Primrose
Brionna Wheaton
Matt Toews
David Larson
Abigail Geiger
Kaylin Calvert
Ruth Geiger

MEMBERS OF THE MASTERS BINDINGS, AKA THE DREAMTREADER RESEARCH CADRE:

Anthony Beasley
Hannah Falk
Lisa Romano
Ethan Nunn
Tiki C.